James Handscombe

The Apprentice

being the story of an orphan child's journey
into manhood

ISBN 978-1-84753-075-2

James Handscombe works full time as a teacher in South-east London - a situation in which he feels magic powers would come in useful. He would like to acknowledge his debt to all those who helped bring this book into being. Deserving of particular mention are Louisa who has been incredibly tolerant of the demands of Riff-Raff and his confederates to be taken seriously and his daughters, Frankie and Zoë without whose naps this tome would never have been assembled. The characters could never have come to life without the collective insanity of Ben, Malc, Matt and Mike who is also responsible for the first draft of the Law of the Covenant.

All errors, inaccuracies and anachronisms are, of course, his own.

Exodus 13v2

The First Year

"Each Mage shall be free to take an Apprentice as he wishes although no Mage may take more than ONE Apprentice. The Apprentice shall be taught the secrets of Magic for that is his purpose and shall be considered property of his Master who shall take responsibility for all his Actions until he become a full Mage of the Covenant."

From the Law of the Covenant of The Castle of The Lovers

From my resting place on this rock the castle is a low dark smudge. As I get closer it will crystallise into its component buildings: the tall round keep, the almost cubic new building, the high wooden palisade with its thicker gatehouse and the collection of huts in the courtyard. Behind me the sun is setting between the storm clouds and the Fire Hills below but over the castle night has come. Night is the proper time for this fortress I call home for it is named "El Castillo de los Amantes", "The Castle of the Lovers" and when do lovers come to each other but under the cover of darkness?

The storm clouds are rapidly moving away behind me leaving the sky a riot of scarlet and orange; they have done their work. Water still drips through my sparse hair and down my nose. My smock is rain-soaked and dark and as I walk back I will be accompanied by the squelch of feet in my boots. My errand has, however, been successful and I can reach into a leather pouch around my waist and extract thirteen flint pebbles. They are nothing to look at, a mere handful of rock but each one is charged with a peg of chaim, a piece of pure magic. When I take these to my master he will reward me by teaching me the secrets of fire so that I may one day become a mighty mage like him: the great Thengol Greydog. He has already taught me my letters and a few rudiments of magic but this will be the first great mystery into which I shall be inducted. My mind races as I dream of my future. Now I am but a boy, clumsy, uneducated and crude. I own nothing and even my own body is not truly mine for I am tied to my master until I complete my apprenticeship yet, even now, I can have confidence for I am at least apprentice to the world's greatest wizard. As I labour for him, watch and listen as he performs his great conjury I shall learn, grow and gain power. Soon, too soon maybe, my time will be done and I shall be free, a great wizard myself; free to take my place amongst the great of the Castle of

Lovers; free to make my own magics; free, at last, to do as I will and to press others to do my bidding.

I shiver in anticipation as I finger the pieces of flint and then shiver again, this time from cold as I return the stones to their pouch. I get up off my boulder and squelch my way towards the ford that will lead me across the river and back home. I have come a long way in the last four months and yet I have come to feel safe in this strange new family; the only family I can remember.

I must have been an infant when I was captured from my parents and taken to the lair of a monstrous lizard. The philosopher beast he called himself for he could speak when he chose and considered himself wise and discerning. Others called him the philosopher beast after his strange metabolism which caused him to excrete gold and came to its den seeking their fortune. None found it and for years they were entrapped by his terrible magic. The foul beast would demonstrate his mighty power to any visitor and then offer a game of chance and skill. If the treasure seeker won then he could leave, taking as much gold as he could carry. If, however, he lost then he would be forced to serve the lizard for a year. The philosopher beast invariably won and continued to win for as long as any hapless adventurer answered his challenge of double or quits. Those wise enough to know when they were beaten left after a year or two but there were many who would be forced to remain there, magically preserved, for centuries.

My tasks were to attend to the needs of my master and to cast the dice, draw the cards and shuffle the counters in our games. The games were endless for the philosopher beast never slept and the gambling visitors were sustained by enchantment. Those who had conceded their loss would take over my duties when I crept to my blanket to sleep. There, in the dim light of that terrible dwelling, I dreamed of escape. Even then, trapped by a powerful and malevolent monster I dreamed of freedom and hoped for a happier life. I had seen nothing of the world and had heard only a little from my fellow slaves but I listened attentively to their tales of fields, of boundless plains, of the sea, tales of freedom and I dreamed hopefully and yet without hope for my prison was secure and absolute. Above me seven pillars rose to the roof. Each pillar was formed of twisted and fused bone for the beast had been winning for years and many of his victims had eventually died of weariness or had taken their own lives rather than endure the endless game. Their bodies had been skinned and left outside for the vultures to pick clean. I never saw how the strange tent was originally built but, after my imprisonment, it fell to me to deal with the corpse of an old fool whose spirit had been finally broken. It was a messy task, the removal of the outer covering from this lump of flesh but it taught me a secret that I shall never forget: there is no magic about the human body; we are merely machines of meat, blood and bone. I climbed up to the roof and laid the hide over what seemed to me to be a thin patch. It was then I realised that what I had taken for cloth or leather was a patchwork of human skin. When the bones were white and dry the other slaves used them to strengthen the skeleton of the building. Bones were wedged into place or tied with strips of animal hide and, when the beast came to survey the work (for he was meticulous in the upkeep of his lair), he would reach out a scaly claw to a perceived weakness and the bones would melt into each other.

I saw him do very little other magic but I was constantly aware of his malevolent power. Each visitor had to offer a drop of blood before they were allowed to join the game. These drops were kept in a glass column filled with a clear liquid and gave my master power over their original owners. This power was revealed when a brave warrior came from overseas to challenge the beast. My hopes of escape rose as he strode into the hut, a great and famous sword strapped to his side, his muscular frame the finest I'd seen and his confidence almost tangible. I saw a glint in his eye and knew that finally there was someone here with the bravery, decency and strength to best the Philosopher Beast. He accepted the creature's challenge in ringing tones and sat down to play but unfortunately in his preparations he had neglected the study of games of chance and, although it is said that fortune favours the brave, he demonstrated insufficient luck to overcome his deficiency in skill. He demanded a rematch and his spirit was unconquered by three consecutive losses. At this point he realised that he could never win and leapt up, drawing his sword and upsetting our little table. My hopes, dampened by the losses, rose and my heart quickened as he slashed at his reptilian opponent who, finally challenged by a red-blooded opponent, waddled backwards. The warrior struck again but the beast twisted out of the way and waved a claw at the column of blood. There was a soft thump as one of the red drops imploded. The brave warrior turned white, dropped his sword and sagged to the floor like a pile of rags. When we skinned him we found not a single drop of blood in his body. My faith in strength of arms was dinted and I quailed from my master's gestures, fearful of the invisible death that lay hidden inside those claws.

Still, I dreamed of escape but dreamed still without hope. Asleep, I saw myself running from the hut, running down the mountainside, just running. There was never a destination in my dreams, merely a mad flight for miles across the countryside. Eventually, inevitably, I would feel my limbs grow leaden, my heart thump in my chest, my sight darken, my legs crumple and I would awake cold and sweating in the smoky darkness. As I lay awake on my blanket awaiting sleep or recovering from my dreams I would carefully plan my escape. I planned to wait until I was sent out on some errand and then when I was out of sight I would run, run far away. But always I knew that my dreams contained the truth: so long as that drop of blood rested in my master's glass tube my flight would end in failure. I could not imagine how it felt to be magically drained of blood but surely my sight would darken, my legs would crumble and I would not awake. I could not invent a way out of my prison and so, barring a freak gesture of generosity, I would remain enslaved forever.

Dreams are powerful and the intellect still greater and so, at last, in those dark quiet hours between sleep and true waking I constructed a plan that had a chance of success. It would require patience for I had to await a fortuitous circumstance and courage for only bold action could free me but there was a chance that I could make for myself an opportunity. I determined to make that opportunity, to take it and to run with it, to run far away and to keep running until I came to the sea that had in my mind become the image of freedom. So, I waited, refined my plan and dreamed of the boundless ocean.

Finally, my chance came; my master was completely distracted by his opponents, absorbed in a game he stood a chance of losing and I was busy, not at the card table, but at the back of the dwelling cleaning the detritus of life from my master's home. That long awaited moment had come, I felt my heart beat in my throat, tasted blood in my mouth and saw my vision swim. I reached over to my bedding and took out a lump of limestone I'd selected for this purpose many moons ago. I took careful aim and hurled the rock at the fragile glass which held my destiny. There was a great crash and all eyes turned to the corner where, to my horror, shards of limestone lay scattered across the floor. The column of blood was not even scratched. My heart raced as the monster's eye turned upon me. My knees quavered as he lifted his claw but his gesture was merely that I should take a broom and sweep away the stone. When I had cleared up the mess I was sent out to collect thornberries, my master's especial delicacy. I returned at dusk sunburned and bleeding from a thousand scratches but bearing a small basket of dark red fruit. The beast laughed. He saw my spirit break and laughed as he munched each one of those sweet berries. As I drifted into an unsettled sleep, every inch of my skin burned and torn, I heard that dreadful demonic laughter from the gaming table.

I hear it again in my mind as I squelch through the tenant farms that surround our castle. A dog rushes out barking and almost trips me.

"May your claws grow long and blunt," I curse as I kick out at it. It snarls and bares its fangs so I back away, squelching quickly towards the gatehouse.

"Stranger or Lover?" comes the traditional challenge.

"Let me in" I growl, kicking the wooden gates. The small night door is unbarred and opened allowing me into the courtyard from where I take my pebbles, my thirteen pegs of chaim to where my master awaits. Excitement thrills me once again as I walk, squelching unevenly as my right foot dries out, towards the secrets of the magic of fire, the secrets that will make me a great wizard.

The Second Year

"Just as the Year has FOUR Seasons and the Compass FOUR Points; just as all Dead Matter is Governed by FOUR Elements and all Living Matter by FOUR Humours so shall our Covenant of the Castle of the Lovers have FOUR High Mages"
From the Law of the Covenant of The Castle of The Lovers

Rain pours down. Rivulets of water splash off my head, round my ears and run down my chest. Rainwater speeds directly to the nape of my neck and pours down to the small of my back where a small reservoir collects wetly. The cold liquid streams into my eyes, my nose, my mouth. Water fills the atmosphere; I wonder I can find air to breathe there is so much rain. Lightning splits the sky, thunder roars and I run to where a pebble glows white hot. I grab it and put it in my pouch, cursing as my glove steams and scalds my hand. Another flash of light burns red after-images into my eyes and I stagger to where the precious peg of chaim glows on the ground. My fingers burn again and I curse. I curse the sky, I curse the rain, I curse the lightning and most of all I curse my master for sending me.

But I mustn't curse him. No, I mustn't curse the great Thengol Greydog, wise amongst the wise. For he has taught me the secrets of fire: the greatest of the elements. He has taught me to recognise the shapes of the living flame of which lightning is but one. He has shown me great fires, leaping as beacons into the sky; he has shown me fierce flames and has heated iron until it became soft and ran like water; he has shown me small flames, matches and taught me their worth; he has shown me light without fire and flames without heat. From him I have learned my first magic. I have started the great journey that will bring me glory and power. Men shall bow before me; they will cower at the sound of my name. I shall live in a golden palace with a thousand slave women in attendance. Kings shall do me homage for I shall be mighty and magnificent. Fire will bring me power and that is what I crave for in this world only the powerful are truly free. The weak must always do the bidding of the strong and the powerless are forever the slaves of the powerful.

And so this discomfort is as nothing. The chill, the wet, the burnt hand, the cold I shall certainly catch are sacrifices to a worthy end and they are sacrifices in the service of my wonderful master who rescued me from my prison in far off Africa.

I was no longer a child but a boy of eight summers when they came to rescue me. Four they were and foreign. This was not strange; groups of fortune seekers came from across the world to find the treasure of the philosopher beast. What was strange was the way they exuded confidence, power and authority. They strode into the hut and blinked as their eyes adjusted to the light. I watched them as they stood there. The first was tall and lean; dressed in a grey cloak and with fire burning in his eyes. He was the leader, as I thought, and he was to become my master Thengol Greydog, mighty amongst the great. The second was shorter and stout. He wore a travel stained tunic and carried a bag. In his face was a look of cautious enthusiasm as though he was not sure what he would find but expected it to be good. He is the Courtesan: the master of our castle, Señor Phosphortube. The two following bore burdens and weapons. They are unimportant.

The philosopher beast rose and sneered at the visitors, spitting acid which burned through their boots. A line of spines lifted along his back and across his head. He unsheathed his claws and pierced them with his gaze. The threat was clear and unveiled. Watching, I wondered at this, why should my master take such note of such apparently insignificant visitors. He took a step closer and bared his teeth,

"…or perhaps we could come to some arrangement?" he said, ignoring the swords the servants had unsheathed. It was then that Señor Phosphortube showed his weakness; he agreed to take part in the game the beast suggested. They were reluctant to allow their adversary to take a drop of blood which showed that they were not as foolish as they looked but after some discussion they agreed to the terms proposed.

They sat down at the gaming table and played well. They showed intelligence and skill such as I had never seen and the beast was hard pressed to beat them but beat them he did. Immediately he got to his feet and prowled round the hut checking the beams and pillars for damage. This I had never seen before; the philosopher beast was nervous. I knew though that he would be alert to the danger now; the opportunity for beginner's luck to strike had passed.

"You'll never win," I muttered across the table.

"Then we shall leave," countered Señor Phosphotube.

"Not if you value your lives. The blood gives him power over you."

"There are ways of dealing with that connection." This was Señor Greydog talking to his companion.

"I need a distraction."

It was at that moment that I made my decision. I looked at the two purposeful men opposite me. Maybe it was the aura of wisdom they carried, maybe I sensed their power and maybe I was swayed by the close game I had just witnessed. Whatever it was, I realised that there would never be a better opportunity to escape.

"Take me with you," I begged and, seeing a flash of assent in the eyes of Señor Phosphortube, I curled a leg around the gaming table and stood up suddenly. The table was overturned; cards, dice and counters flew across the room. The philosopher beast turned and looked at me, baring his teeth.

"Sorry, master," I grovelled, struggling to lift the table to an upright position. Behind me I heard a muttered chant.

"Sorry, master. An accident, master," I said louder this time hoping that my antics were keeping his attention.

Suddenly there was an explosion. Shards of glass flew across the room and we were covered in blood and clear slime. The two other prisoners, old warriors who had long since given up hope, finally gave up their lives. Without the philosopher beast's magic to sustain them, their old hearts finally stopped. The evil creature turned to the corner where his column of crystal had once stood and let out a cry of anger and rage. I was already on my feet and running for the exit followed by the wizards and their servants. The philosopher beast was powerful and dangerous but he was unable to catch us as we ran away from that horrid dwelling. Finally my dreams had become reality, I was running. My breath came quickly and burned in my lungs, my heart thumped in my chest, sweat stung in my eyes and my legs filled with pain; fear filled me: my dreams had also been my nightmares. I hoped that the destruction of the crystal tube had freed me but feared the reach of the Philosopher Beast's magic. Would I make it? Would I reach the boundless ocean that had loomed so large in my dreams? Would I gain my freedom or was this agonising pain the first sign of the malevolence behind me? I could feel my legs buckling, and feared my sight was fading; even now I could barely see the path in front of me. I feared and yet ran on afraid, stumbling down the hillside, running along that thin path of hope that led to the sea. Finally we were out of sight of the hut and still alive. We could run no longer and hoped we'd come far enough to be safe and so we stopped and made our breathless introductions. It was then that I learned the names of my rescuers and that they were wizards from Spain, a land far off and, to my delight, across the ocean. They offered to take me back to their castle where I could work for them.

"And what would I get from this arrangement?" I asked looking around me at the barren wasteland that represented my new found freedom. I feared to be left alone to make my way through the desert but feared also a second imprisonment. Chanting again, Thengol Greydog, master of the magical arts, plucked something from thin air and handed it to me. I looked at the gem I held in my hand. It was the size of an eyeball and beautifully round. The sunlight glinted off thousands of perfect facets and illuminated its heart with a blue fire. I smiled and put it in my pocket.

"Could I learn to do that?" I asked. Señor Greydog looked at me, his eyes piercing my soul and inquiring into my spirit. He nodded.

"I think I have a new apprentice," he said to Señor Phosphortube.

And I had a new master. Freedom still eludes me for I realised in that moment with the gem in my hand that freedom to be alone and poor is no freedom at all. I am enslaved once again but now I see a clear path to true freedom, the freedom that comes from power, freedom to be great, freedom to work alongside my master. It is to this master I return now bearing my precious treasure. Not this time a mere gem but nine wet pebbles of flint, each one bearing a unit of raw magic. It is not such a good harvest as last year but it will be enough, I think, and when I hand it to my master he will teach me the secrets of the place of creation. There all things wait for the wizard to pull them into existence. It was from there that my master plucked the diamond he handed to me over two years ago and it is from there that I shall pull my first magics. He has promised to teach me my first spell if I learn well enough and then I shall truly be a wizard, a worker of marvels.

My new master is less prescriptive than the old and my time has not been entirely filled by servitude and learning. I have swept and cleaned and fetched and carried and once my chores have been completed I have listened and read and recited and copied but there have often been times when my mind has been too tired for study and my master has stretched his boots before the fire and taken time to relax. Then, we have had time to talk of his great powers and achievements and my desire to be like him has grown and my path to glory has become clearer. He has also indulged my curiosity in other, lesser, matters and in the past year I have learned a little of the history of my safety and shelter, the Castle of Lovers.

I tell the tale less well than my master and may have erred in some of the details for frequently our conversation has been diverted from this story to the greater saga of my master's illustrious life. Still I attempt to set down, as clear as may be, the legend of the founding of The Castle of Lovers.

Many years ago a great and venerable wizard, The Lord Grumio Portent, master of flame and destruction, came to this place seeking a sanctuary from the angry world. He saw in this quiet corner an oasis of calm, a still and silent spot amid the whirling of the storm around him and built a tower of magic by a bend in the meandering river.

For years he lived alone, immune to the clamour of civilisation and hidden from their prying eyes by his magic. The local peasants stayed away from the grim tower and continued their simple lives tilling the soil and tending their flocks. Only those brave young souls whose ardour required a secret place, a hidden tryst, strayed beneath the shadow of the aging fortress and so the castle acquired its name.

One cold spring morning Lord Grumio's solitude was broken by a younger wizard who had fled the city of Barcelona and was pursued by armed men and an angry mob. By chance he found himself in this quiet valley beneath the Fire Hills and saw in the looming shadow of the Castle of Lovers a refuge from the mundane violence behind him. He reached the great door as weariness set into his exhausted legs and the chase began to gain on him. He hammered on the timbers but the wood was infused with the magical power of Grumio Portent and he was unable to gain access. Reluctantly he turned and drew his great broadsword as the soldiers approached. Determined to make the merchant lords of Barcelona regret their attack he loosed a bolt of lightning from his fingertips as he swung his weapon. Two of his assailants were felled in that first moment but more men followed them and the young wizard's strength was finite and already drained by the long chase. He parried their blows, hoarding his magic for the right moment, his back protected by the sturdy door behind him and still they attacked, gradually wearing down his resistance.

The clash of blades and shrieks of the wounded disturbed Lord Grumio's meditations in the tower above and he looked from his window to see the scene below. Mailed soldiers assaulted a lone swordsman and behind them peasants armed with clubs pushed forward and screeched their hatred. His temper boiled, the years of solitude and calm evaporating, dissipated by the appearance of the crass and ignorant. His shelter had been invaded by the very forces he had created it to avoid. As his anger built so he gathered together his mightiest enchantments and hurled from the window a blazing vitriol that destroyed two ranks of the attacking force. Into the moment of pause he leaped, his magic guiding his fall and he stood beside the younger wizard as the assault was renewed. The two comrades fought mightily against their foes; the younger's sword thrust and slashed and into the gaps he flung his thunderbolts; the elder stood without weapon but armed with mighty spells of destruction and none could stand against them. It is said that a few of the mob survived this awesome battle but those that did must have fled before reaching the wizards and none have boasted of such shameful cowardice.

Grumio released the door and the victors turned their backs on the carnage to step inside. Standing then in the hallway, splattered with blood and weary, each recognised in the other a twin soul, a seeker after knowledge and power, a lover of fire and an enemy of the ugly and mundane. In the blood of peasants and merchants was forged a brotherhood of wizardry, an alliance of strength against the weak, of wisdom against the foolish.

Thoughts of my future within this brotherhood flood my mind as I trudge back to the castle. As I wade across the ford I see myself summoning a mighty steed to carry me dry and fresh to my destination. Water streams over my boots as one day gold and jewels will stream from my pockets and buy the finest food and clothes. I look up at the tower ahead of me and think of the mighty citadel I shall build when I am a wizard. I shall build for myself a legend so that the name of Riff-Raff shall me murmured alongside that of Grumio Portent as one who triumphed to build himself the freedom to reject the chains of ignorance and poverty. My reverie is broken by a loud barking and a sudden pain in my calf as the farmer's dog bites through my wet hose.

"May three of your teeth become rotten and drop out" I curse and aim a kick at it as I move hastily to my destination. I hammer on the gate, my dreams of fortune shattered and replaced by a desire to be warm, safe and dry. I hammer on the gate, a modern wizard keen to join the ancient brotherhood, seeking shelter not from the anger of the mundane world but from the damp disapproval of the elements.

"Stranger or Lover?" comes the traditional cry. It is Hawkeye, one of our sentries. Hawkeye he calls himself. Parrothead more like, standing there repeating phrases he has been taught. Hawkeye? Parrothead!

"Let me in, birdbrain!" I snarl.

"Stranger or Lover?" I don't know why my master employs these idiots. When I learn to do spells I shall line them all up and roast them all with a fireball. Each servant who has been impudent and each soldier who has rudely brushed past me will suffer. Until then I make note of their offences and wait. I can be patient when so much awaits me.

"Lover" I say. The night door opens and I walk into the courtyard and up to my master's room.

The Third Year

"Just as the Royal Throne rests on FOUR feet, so our Covenant's Power rests on FOUR Aspects of our Life: our Wealth, our Authority, our Magickal Power and our Knowledge. Accordingly, each Mage of our Covenant shall spend a QUARTER of his time, that is, one Season in Every Year, improving and maintaining these Four Aspects of our Life."

From the Law of the Covenant of The Castle of The Lovers

It's midsummer and to the west the sun is a ball of flame above the Fire Hills. The earth, which has been baked in the heat all day, is now as warm as the sun above and I am sweating heavily as I start to climb. The air is still and humid and the clouds are beginning to gather in the blue sky. Once more I am on my way to make the yearly harvest of chaim for my master, the great Thengol Greydog.

This time, however, I will not be returning to put the precious flints into his mighty hands for he is on a journey. He has gone northwards to seek the wisdom of other magi. There are none so wise as my master but he can generously offer his pearls of intellect and can cunningly garner knowledge from even the meanest magical mind. The castle has been left in the care of the Courtesan, Sparky Phosphortube, and it is to him that I am to report with my harvest at the end of the night.

My studies in the past year have been fruitful and I have learned my first spell. I can now create fire! Not, of course, the great fireballs of my master that rush through the air burning his enemies to cinders but a small flame that sits in the palm of my hand, offers light and heat and is more reliable than even the most cunning tinderbox. Thus I take another step on the road to greatness; each year my understanding of the magical mysteries becomes clearer and my usefulness to my master is increased. As I take another step on the path up the hillside I look forward to the next year. Señor Phosphortube has promised to teach me the magic of the human body when I return with the precious chaim. It is not such a valuable skill as those in which my master excels but it is necessary to my development as a great wizard. It is swifter to burn armies with a vast holocaust of fire but there are occasions when one must tread more slowly and the power to heal and destroy the human body has its uses.

The rain is now starting to fall. Great drops spatter into the dust round my feet, onto my tunic and into my hair. The sun has now dipped below the horizon and the clouds fill the skies above. This quiet opening to the storm that will come is a metaphor for my career as a wizard. Though I now learn scattered morsels of truth and the world makes no recognition of my existence, soon shall I have full knowledge and the whole earth will be flooded with fear and trembling before my might and power. I shall rival even the great Thengol Greydog and princes will bow before me.

These past weeks I have had more time to explore the castle and its lands as Señor Phosphortube is far weaker than my master and allows me time to do as I will. For the first time I have ventured outside the outer walls to where the priest Father Juan lives on a pole. He preaches obedience to his God whom he says will forgive the righteous and destroy the wicked and he lives alone in a rude hut outside the palisade. Every day he studies holy writings and prays for his soul and those of the covenant and every Sunday he preaches to the weak and foolish who come to listen. One week I joined the group of servants, farmers and holy women who flock to his service. He quoted from his holy book and, whilst most of it was mere rambling, I remember one phrase: "Now we see but through a glass darkly, then we shall see face to face". He was speaking of his God but it is truer of my studies. Often the words of magic and the glimpses of power I receive are warped and incomprehensible yet, as I concentrate my mind on what lies beneath and as I develop to full maturity as a wizard I shall see the truth ever more clearly and it will not be Father Juan's God who rewards the faithful and punishes the wicked for I have also begun to see my future more clearly. As a child, suffering in the lair of the Philosopher Beast I dreamed blindly of the ocean and the freedom it represented. Now I understand that my destiny is to be great, to manipulate those around me as tools to amplify my greatness. Freedom limited by mundane law and convention is no freedom at all. I shall be mighty, I shall rule second only to the magnificent Thengol Greydog and it will be a reign of terror and justice for there will be no mercy for those that offend us.

I get ahead of myself and now I must concentrate, for the lightning has begun to strike and I must dash across the hillside grasping the hot flints and thrusting them into my pouch. The rain continues, no longer individual drops marking patterns in the dust but a continuous stream pouring over my face. The water runs round my ears and nose and into my eyes and mouth. I blink and rub my sleeve across my face to clear my vision. Lightning strikes and I must run again to where a single flint lies glowing. The pouring rain quickly quenches its light and I must claim it before it is lost amongst the ordinary pebbles.

Now I am cold and wet through and still the storm shows no sign of abating. I curse the rain and long for the day when even the weather will obey my commands. At least it is summer rain and, though chill, it is not freezing. I was sent on an errand to Lerida, the local town, in cold January to purchase equipment for my great master. My reading is now good enough that he trusts me to deal with the cunning merchants. With me came Lopez, a warrior, to purchase arrows for the archers and to carry our supplies. Of all the soldiers in the castle, Lopez is the largest and the most vicious. He is not educated and, in fact, speaks Spanish very poorly, but it would be a fool who laughed at him for he has a terrible temper and a mace that he can drive through solid wood. As we walked through the mud and freezing rain to the market, his breastplate became wet; indeed we both became soaked through and covered in grime. That night in the inn he kept me awake as he cleaned his armour. He wiped off the mud, dried the mail carefully, then scoured the specks of rust and finally rubbed it fiercely until he was satisfied with his reflection. All the time he muttered under his breath.

"Bollocks rain," he growled. "My armour wet now."

"Bollocks rain," again. "No need for me out in bollocks rain."

"Can't you leave that until the morning Lopez?" I asked.

"No," he replied shortly. "No rust on my armour. Must shiny." I perceived an opportunity to share my education with my comrade and silently resolved to improve Lopez' grasp of his native language.

"Must be shiny, Lopez, must be shiny," I corrected.

"Yes," he said shortly and continued to polish and curse.

The next morning we rose early and made our way to the market just as the stallholders were setting out their wares.

"Less crowds, better deals," explained Lopez.

I gazed at the rows of goods and stared at the simple folk who had come to buy them. Poor and uneducated they might be and yet they still had the freedom to purchase whatever they wanted from the bewildering array of goods before me. I counted my coins and reminded myself that their freedom was limited by the wealth of their pockets. When I become a wizard my freedom will suffer no such bounds. I shall take what I want and offer only in return what generosity urges me to give. I looked again at the stream of humanity that was beginning to fill the square and dreamed of what it will be like when they bow before me.

"Stupid! No time for dreams! Arrows. Supplies." Lopez roughly ended my reverie and strode up to a fletcher where he engaged in some terse bargaining. Finally agreeing on a satisfactory price he carefully bundled the missiles and loaded them onto his back.

"Now you. Purchases," he said and pointed me to where a potter and metalworker had set up next to one another. I saw a collection of dishes that would suit my master's needs and inquired after the price

"Ah, a fine set of pottery but beyond your purse I fear," replied the stallholder.

"I've come to buy equipment for my master, the great Thengol Greydog, and I have plenty of money," I replied indignantly, hefting my purse. The potter raised an eyebrow at the mention of my master's name.

"The great Thengol Greydog will, I'm sure, want only the best and the best costs money. Will your purse stretch to twenty silver florins?"

"Of course," I cried, counting out the money. As the merchant's eyes lit up Lopez' hand closed over my purse.

"Three," he said.

"Three?" the merchant responded, shocked. "Three florins for six fine dishes of such exquisite manufacture? I could knock a couple of florins off for such great warrior but I couldn't go below eighteen." I began to count out eighteen silver coins but Lopez hadn't finished.

"Four," he suggested.

"Four? But that's ridiculous, nowhere could you get such workmanship for under sixteen florins."

"Five."

"I see you're a hard man. I'll offer you a sound bargain. All six dishes for twelve florins."

"Six for six."

"Nine florins and really that's my best offer. Take it or leave it."

"Seven."

"Eight?"

"Done." Lopez released my hands and wordlessly I counted florins back into my purse until only eight were left. I handed these over to the potter and received in exchange the dishes wrapped in rough cloth and padded with straw. I put them carefully into my pack and moved to the next stall where I spotted a pair of iron tongs that would be ideal for manipulating experiments within my master's furnace.

"How much?" I asked, handing the tongs to the merchant.

"For you, sir, eight florins," he replied. I was about to count out the money when I remembered Lopez' cunning tactics.

"Three," I countered.

"Six florins is as low as I can go I'm afraid."

"Done," I cried, gleefully, reaching for the coins. Lopez' arm came across me.

"One," he challenged, gruffly.

"What?" wondered the salesman.

"What?" I asked.

"One," Lopez repeated grimly.

"Who's buying here?" asked the blacksmith.

"Me," replied Lopez. "Iron tongs for one florin."

"Erm, four?" came the bewildered reply.

"No, one." Lopez reached into my purse, extracted a coin, put it into the merchant's open hand, took the tongs under one arm and dragged me away from the stall.

"Rain," he said, pointing at the grey sky above. "Home quickly."

As walked back through the rain and the mud with our purchases I was very proud of myself. My master had entrusted me with a job and I had not only bought the correct equipment but had also obtained a marvellous price by intellect and cunning. Soft, wet, cold drops fell on my shoulders and I saw Lopez looking darkly at the sky. I was about to make a joke but I saw his knuckles were white around the handle of his mace and a vein throbbed busily in his forehead so I kept quiet. When we got home and delivered our supplies he went straight to the room he shares with another soldier and, I imagine, started once more to clean and polish his beloved armour. No doubt he continued his accompaniment of curses.

The lightning has stopped, the rain is beginning to abate and I am slithering over slippery boulders on my way back to the fortress. My boots are old and I lose my footing as I step downwards. I land hard on my backside and grunt as I pull myself to my feet again.

"Bollocks rain," I mutter to myself, grinning as I rub my bruised behind. In my pouch I have a fine harvest of chaim; eleven precious pebbles as payment for my lessons this coming year. Señor Phosphortube will teach me the magic of the human body; I shall learn another spell and maybe I will learn how to protect myself from enemy magics. I wish I was also able to protect myself from enemy dogs; the farmer's hound has tried to bite me again. Fortunately I was not so lost in my contemplations to miss it this year and gave it a sound kick as it bounded up.

"May you become too fat to hunt!" I spit the words out as it growls and slavers at me.

Ahead of me looms the old tower, the great fortress that provided a refuge for Lord Grumio Portent and his young acolyte Juan Misanthrope. The two great magi had much to learn from each other and Grumio saw wisdom in allowing Juan to share his oasis of solitude. The tower was large enough for two and they were able to have their own rooms in which they developed their sorcery, each after his own fashion. They wrote great tomes of magical learning and performed mighty deeds of enchantment so that their fame began to spread through the land.

In those days the lands around the tower were owned by the church and the bishop of Zaragossa was a cruel and harsh landlord. Rents were high and taxes extorted ruthlessly. Farmers found it hard to make a living and young men were tempted to take employment at the enchanted castle despite its reputation. Both wizards found menservants and they employed a cook, a gardener and a man to keep the fires lit and the floors swept. These peasants lived not in the castle itself for fear and superstition kept them from sleeping on enchanted ground. Instead they erected huts, clustered round the tall tower like chicks round a mother hen.

Grumio and Juan were absorbed with their studies and were content to offer shelter to travellers beset by the elements and a world that rejected the unusual and macabre. Thus came the tradition of guests of the castle, not wizards but possessed of unusual and socially unacceptable talents. Some have stayed for a few days but others have settled, enjoying the spirit of tolerance and revelling in the uncertain adventure that associates itself with magical enterprise.

It is to this uncertain adventure that I return as I reach the great wooden gate and hammer on its timbers.

"Stranger or Lover?" comes the challenge

"Lover, you fool," I reply.

"I see you have come through a fierce storm." It is Siero, a fool of a gypsy, who is our sentry tonight. "I see many things."

"You know I've come through a fierce storm; you saw me go out, watched the rain from the shelter of the gatehouse and see me come back drenched to the skin. Now let me in you halfwit." The little door in the gate is unlocked and I push it open.

"I see you are in a great hurry to speak to the Courtesan."
I leave this last idiocy unanswered and take my precious burden into the tower.

The Fourth Year

"The First High Mage shall be the Courtesan, chief Lover, Chairman and Spokesman of the Covenant. The others shall be the THREE Most Senior Mages in the Covenant, excepting the Courtesan. The Most Senior shall be called PATO, the SECOND Most Senior shall be called LATO and the THIRD Most Senior shall be called KATO."

From the Law of the Covenant of The Castle of The Lovers

It is dark. The sun has long since set below the western horizon and the last of its warm purple has left the sky. Above me thick clouds billow and boil blocking out all light from the stars and moon. The darkness is complete except for the small flame that sits on my palm and dances in the light breeze; I'm waiting on the Fire Hills, ready for the storm which, it seems, will never come. The evening looked so promising; thick dark clouds covered the western sky and the heat lay like a blanket across the land. The storm may yet break but as the heat of the day lifts, the clouds will thin and I shall return empty handed. My master will be disappointed and will not teach me the secrets I have been promised. Maybe days will pass before the weather breaks and lightning strikes the Fire Hills, lighting the precious chaim with its burning glow.

My master, the great Thengol Greydog, has returned from his journeys through France and I have returned to the familiarity of his rooms. Whilst on his journeys my master has vanquished many dangerous foes and has written down his great insights in two large, leather bound volumes. On his return journey he was set upon by bandits and, whilst he was able to drive them off with his great mastery of fiery magic, they grabbed hold of his precious books and tore out the title sheets. Now, since my master cunningly disguised his writing, there is nothing to identify these books as his work and it is to be my task for the year to read through them and to write new title pages which can be sewn into their spines.

Whilst he was away, I worked for Señor Phosphortube and learned the secrets of the human frame. I have also learned a new spell which allows me to magically close a wound so that it may heal. The Courtesan's rooms are strange; he spends much of his time in a comfortable chair in front of a fireplace sipping on strong wine. To one side of this soft civilisation is his work space; here there is a long wooden table stained from experimentation. On the walls are human bones and strange diagrams of the body and in a cupboard is a preserved corpse. Sometimes Señor Phosphortube will speak life into the corpse and it will jerkily climb out of its cupboard and stumble over to the fireplace. There it will flop into a second chair and the Courtesan will conduct a conversation with it. After a time he will tire of this pretence, for that is all it is; the corpse has no mind or spirit of its own and merely obeys the commands it is given. Señor Phosphortube's dream is to breathe true life back into a corpse but that is beyond his skills and so he experiments and comforts himself with games and delusions.

"My dear Riff-Raff," he said to me as we sat in the chairs one evening. "We stumble through this world gaining power over our surroundings but still we understand very little of our own, human lives. What is the force that fills a new-born baby and slips from the lips of an old man? Without it the human form is no more than pieces of meat cunningly strung together but with it we are masters of the world, creators of great wonders and awful horrors. It is this mysterious unknown that I study."

"But why?" The question slipped out before I could stop it. The nature of human life was indeed a puzzle and I knew that it had vexed philosophers and theologians for centuries but it seemed a topic unfit for a mage's time. "I mean, it's all very interesting, but what's the point?"

"Come now dear boy, you cannot have been blinded by your studies so far; there is more to the world than can be studied by burning it. Fire is not the only path to greatness. No wizard has ever managed to create human life nor to cheat death; there is a mystery here, we are masters of so much and yet even the most basic understanding of life eludes us. Sometimes I think that Juan is right and our lives are held in the hands of his God and immune to the forces of magic."

"Surely you don't believe that rambling old fool?"

"Juan may be long-winded but he is no fool. He is a wise and good man which is rare enough. It may be that his religion contains some insight into to the secrets I study." A frown of concentration crossed the Courtesan's face as he quoted, "'Yahweh formed man from the dust of the ground and breathed into his nostrils the breath of life and man became a living being.' Just what is this mysterious 'breath of life'?" He peered at me and shrugged, "I don't know. Maybe one day, though, I shall unpick the secret force that lies between our bones and sinews and

25

then perhaps I too shall be able to create life or to truly return it to a dead body. That, young man, is power. That would be fame eternal."

The Courtesan's rooms are cleaned and his decanter refilled by his manservant, M'Benga, who is a stocky man with skin like smooth charcoal. Every evening as the lower curve of the sun touches the western horizon M'Benga brings a steaming glass of spiced wine and a small cake to sustain his master until supper. It's a strange and silent ritual as the manservant pushes the door open and treads softly across the room to place a silver tray at the Courtesan's side. The silent solemnity seems to suit M'Benga who comes from a land far to the south where men have eyes in their bellies and worship spirits of the land. I have often wondered how he came to Spain but his countenance is grim and fearsome and I lack the courage to approach him. He speaks very little and obeys only Sparky Phosphortube. I have not been comfortable working alongside such a strange man as I have served the Courtesan. When he has come to do his chores I have moved away, anxious not to offend by word or deed such an unknowable creature. Señor Phosportube clearly also distrusts his manservant as he tests all his food for poison. After his evening glass of wine is placed at his side he draws a pearl from his pocket and passes it over the steaming liquid whilst murmuring a spell.

"It's a simple incantation and probably a foolish precaution but it may one day save my life," he said in answer to my question. I was fascinated by this degree of foresight, have learned the spell and now carry a pearl of my own with which to detect an assassination attempt.

The Courtesan's studies are intriguing and I have enjoyed the freedom of his light rein but it is good to be back with my master who will teach me the secrets of destruction if this storm ever breaks.

"What is the point of understanding the magic of the human body if all you can do is mend it?" he growled when I told him of my new knowledge. There is no space for sitting and dreaming in his rooms; they are dedicated to his pursuit of greatness. The walls are covered with trophies: beautiful tapestries taken from defeated foes, skulls from creatures he has slain and strange magical reminders of his journeys. Along one wall stands his workbench, the wood blackened and scarred from the experiments it has seen. Above it is a shelf containing a row of books. The first dozen contain my master's notes on his work and his insights into magic. The others are works of reference and strange writings of foreign wizards from which my master wrests fragments of knowledge. On the far side of the room is the forge; a fire constantly stoked to great heat and surrounded by thick black tiles of stone. In one corner stand three great jars of water, each as tall as a mule. These are used to control any fire that starts and to prevent it spreading or damaging my master's notes.

A low rumble sounds overhead and I feel a drop of water on my cheek. At last the storm has come. Another growl of thunder sounds and is followed by another, this time louder and sharper. More rain is falling, splashing onto my outstretched palm and extinguishing the little flame. The hills are now pitch black and filled with the thrumming sound of rain on the pebbly ground. I get to my feet and the flints rattle as they rub across each other. Suddenly lighting strikes and I gasp as the flame streaks across my eyes leaving a glowing purple stripe across my vision. I blunder towards where it struck, half blinded and in darkness. The glow of the struck pebble is obscured by the slash cut vertically across my sight but I manage to reach it and to find its heat with my hands before it is extinguished by the rain. I stuff the peg of chaim into my pouch and turn to see where another bolt of lightning strikes. Again I'm blinded by the brightness and stumble across the slippery slopes. Thunder sounds overhead.

With my master away I have had continued freedom to get to know the inhabitants of my strange home. Lopez is not the only warrior employed to protect the fortress and I have watched him training with another mighty soldier. Mongrol is a huge man with arms like tree trunks. He wields a morning star, a great spiked iron ball on a chain, and is skilled with this awkward weapon. As I watched them fight, Lopez struck at Mongrol's chest with his mace but Mongrol twisted out of the way and struck back, sweeping the deadly sphere towards Lopez' shins. Lopez controlled his strike and leapt the swinging morning star before bringing his mace up to parry as Mongrol aimed a punch at his face with the haft of his weapon. Their skills were well matched and they finally halted their duel, each panting from the exertion. I went over to speak to them and Lopez left muttering,

"Dirty armour. Bollocks rusty." I picked up Mongrol's morning star and tried to swing it but could hardly get the ball off the ground.

"Oof, it's heavy." I said handing it to Mongrol who smiled and lifted it easily to his belt.

"It's a good weapon. Helps Mongrol smosh."

"What do you smosh Mongrol?" I asked, intrigued by this simpleton's skill.

"Enemies, monsters," he said, "and faeries." Suddenly he put his hands to his throat and began to gasp as his face turned red. "Not faeries," he said. "Not faeries." He began to breathe more easily and his face returned to its usual colour. As I looked at his throat I saw a dark mark where a silver chain had cut into it. The chain was loose enough now and I asked him what it was.

"Faerie chain," he said. "Mongrol is faeries' prisoner. Mongrol must do as faeries say, mustn't smosh them any more." He looked embarrassed and walked away back to his quarters.

Lopez, Mongrol and the other warriors train hard in case the peace of our home is rudely broken by intemperate and unwise fools who despise our knowledge and power. The Castle of Lovers is not currently threatened by mundane force but the situation has not always been so relaxed. A few summers after Juan Misanthrope fought his way through the angry mob the rains failed and the crops shrivelled in the fields. The old died in the heat and babies cried from thirst. Autumn came and the harvest was made and a poor, thin harvest it was. Farmers looked at their empty stores and pondered a long and hungry winter. When the bishop sent his representatives to collect the taxes they were sent away empty handed; the peasants simply had too little to satisfy the demands of a greedy church.

The bishop was a hard man and saw leniency as weakness. He sent his taxmen back, this time accompanied by armed soldiers and they took what they could by force. The last gleanings of the harvest were carried off and still the churchman wasn't satisfied. He sent the soldiers back to look for other goods to make up the shortfall. The farmers had nothing and so their daughters were dragged screaming from the villages to act as payment. Fathers were brushed aside or beaten as they fought to defend their families and when the soldiers had gone the survivors put aside their prejudices and sought protection from the wizards at the castle. Grumio and Juan saw an advantage in good relations with the peasantry and when the soldiers returned seeking more entertainment, they were met by two heavily armed wizards. The resulting confrontation was brief and one sided and was followed by a march on the bishop's palace. A mob formed behind the two sorcerers and pulled the great building apart. The prisoners were rescued and their guards fled. A fierce conflagration reduced the ruins to burning cinders. As they returned to their villages the peasants were jubilant but Lord Portent saw more clearly; the bishop had escaped and would seek revenge.

The two magi discussed the protection of their sanctuary and Juan undertook to employ a force of warriors as Grumio strengthened the defences with a tall wall and strong gatehouse. The villages were equipped with beacons and kept a watch on the paths from Zaragossa so that when the bishop's force of knights and mercenaries marched on the land they found deserted cottages and empty stores. The peasants fled to safety behind the walls of the covenant and a trial of strength took place at the ford below the old tower.

The warriors of the Castle of Lovers were fewer in number but were protected by fierce enchantments and magical weapons. Alongside them fought Juan Misanthrope with his mighty broadsword and behind them Grumio Portent cast cunning enchantments and caused flashes of flame to distract and confuse their adversaries. The battle was long and hard; the bishop's men were strangely immune to the fiery magic of the wizards, the prayers of the cleric offered a form of defence against unholy sorcery. Still Juan fought on, impelled by an inner flame, his strength undiminished by the combat. Around him, his soldiers began to fall back as they suffered injury and the loss of their comrades.

Slowly the knights pressed across the river and up the slope to the gatehouse. Lord Portent pulled the rearguard back inside the defences as Juan drove the enemy back with a bold charge supported by a stream of crimson flame. The bishop's forces were dismayed and fell back screaming as the fire burned at their faces and blinded their eyes. In the confusion Juan turned and ran with the last of his comrades. The gate closed firmly behind them and the angry knights were met by a hail of crossbow fire as they hurled themselves at the unyielding wood.

The enemy fell back to regroup but soon the defenders found themselves assaulted once more as the bishop's men felled a great tree and charged at the gate with the trunk. The timbers shuddered and creaked under the onslaught. The archers fired downwards but were short of ammunition and Juan and Grumio were tired from their exertions. Every one of the warriors was wounded and the courtyard was filled with terrified farmers and their families. Hope began to fail as the battering ram began to force its way through the crumpling boards of the gate. The wizards got to their feet and gathered themselves for one last defence of their home when they heard a challenge cry out from outside the gatehouse.

They looked out and saw a solitary figure clad in grey standing on the grassy slopes to the side of the castle. The knights were readying themselves for a charge through the broken gates and the men at arms were pulling the tree trunk back to ram it into the creaking timbers one last time. Both groups of men turned to face the new challenge and a single knight turned to deal with the insignificant distraction. He galloped boldly towards his unarmed opponent, sod flying from the hooves of his horse and sun glinting on his sword. As he approached the figure held out his hands and muttered ancient words of incantation. A great ball of orange and vermilion formed in front of him but still the crusader charged, trusting in his blessing for protection from the fiery doom that sped towards him but the bishop's prayers failed in the face of such intense power and a charred skeleton fell from the scorched steed. A second fireball was hurled towards the men at arms at the gate and they fell beneath the heavy tree-trunk, their screams suddenly silenced. A third incantation scattered the knights as they readied their charge, bowling them over like a row of skittles. Two more spells followed and spread fiery doom through the bishop's remaining forces. As the stranger sank to the ground, Juan led his exhausted troops out of the gate once more and slaughtered the stunned enemy. The survivors fled into the countryside and the wizards' men watched them go, too tired to give chase. As they dispersed, Lord Portent called for two of the farmers to help him carry the slumped form of the stranger into the safety and shelter of the old tower. The great Thengol Greydog had arrived.

Mongrol and Lopez follow the traditions set in the days of the Lords Misanthrope and Portent and are ready to defend our home from the forces of the church. I was again watching the two train when another of the servants sidled up to me. I knew this man was called Antonio. He was an odd job man and had always seemed a shifty character, his face constantly twisted to one side or the other, looking sideways through lowered lashes.

"You must come with me, sir," he said. Nobody had called me "sir" before and I was enchanted by his courtesy.

"Where to, Antonio?" I asked.

"Important business, sir," he said and then turned over his shoulder. "Yes, I know we need him. Yes, he's coming."

"Who are you talking to, Antonio?" I inquired, for we were alone.

"Nobody sir, just thinking, sir."

He led me out of the gates and along the road to Lerida. The afternoon was already wearing on and I began to have misgivings.

"Where are we going to, Antonio?" I asked

"To Lerida, sir. Along this road it is, sir," he replied then broke off. "I can tell him that."

"What?"

"Aaargh," he gasped and a spasm crossed his face. "Nothing to worry about, sir, hurry along now."

My skin prickled in goosebumps and I was about to demand that we return but Antonio had quickened his pace and, not wishing to be left alone on the road in the dusk, I followed him.

We reached Lerida shortly after dark and I was beginning to despair. My feet were sore and my mood foul from the pace we had kept but Antonio had suddenly become cheery and led us through the back streets to the church of San Diego. Antonio motioned for me to be quiet and reached into his cloak out of which he pulled a rope. On one end of the line was a steel hook and I watched in amazement as he deftly threw it up to the roof where the hook must have caught on the stonework. He tugged hard on the rope but the hook held.

"You must keep watch, sir; if anybody comes you whistle, sir."

"But Antonio, what are we doing?" I asked

"Very important, sir, you must keep watch." With that I had to be content as he turned and quickly scaled the rope to the ledge on which the hook was caught. In the half light I quickly lost sight of him against the grey stone and I glanced nervously up and down the alleyway. Half of my mind was in a panic; what was I doing? I hadn't even had time to tell Antonio that I can't whistle and I had no idea how I'd explain myself if I was challenged. The other half thrilled at the adventure and wondered what great exploit was being acted out on the rooftop above me. I looked upwards, hoping for a glimpse of whatever was going on but I could see nothing, even the rope had been pulled up. I looked anxiously along the alleyway again and imagined threats in the shadows, priests demanding explanations or footpads with sharp knives. The dark silence around me sucked at my mind, I heard the blood throbbing in my ears and knew it to be the approaching steps of authority. I felt the wind as a hand on my arm and froze, unable to run from the imagined threat. I feared capture and punishment, I feared humiliation and I feared a cage, a prison from which there could be no escape.

I forced the thought from my panicked mind and reminded myself that I was alone in the dark. Another fear began to grow within me as the silence pressed around me and I strained my ears for some sound that would reassure me that Antonio was still above me. None came, I was alone. Had Antonio left me? Was I truly abandoned to make my own way back to the covenant? Would I be welcome? Perhaps Antonio had been commissioned to lead me away, perhaps I was no longer wanted. I stood alone and afraid in the darkness.

Then a soft thud made me turn and I saw that the rope had been dropped over the edge. I looked up and saw Antonio sliding quickly down the side of the church. Under one arm he had a large and bulky item.

"What's that Antonio?" I asked, delight chasing the fears from my blood.

"Weathervane, sir, very valuable sir."

"A weathervane," I struggled to keep my tones low, anger now chasing delight. "We came here to steal a weathervane?"

"Yes, sir, very valuable, sir." he answered.

"What now then Antonio? Are we going to slip into the church and steal a pew?"

"No, sir, silly idea that is sir."

He turned and made his strange, scuttling way back along the alleys to the road. I followed him caught between fury, bewilderment and amusement at the adventure. We made our way back along the dark wood and climbed over the palisade into the fortress.

"Can't use the gate, sir, or we'd have to share our fortune with the guards."

"Fortune?" I grunted as I pulled myself up the rope.

"Yes, sir, of course rightly half of it's yours, sir."

"Eh?"

"Yes, sir, 'cept you can't have half a weathervane sir so I'll keep this one and you can have the next one."

"Next one?" I gasped as I slithered down the rope and landed in a heap. It had been a fine adventure but I didn't feel that night time expeditions to capture weathervanes were appropriate to one who was being trained to greatness. I can't imagine the great Thengol Greydog slithering over the fortress wall with a purloined piece of ironware. One day he will take me with him on a trip and then maybe we'll break into an evil wizard's castle to capture a magical sword. Not a weathervane. Certainly not a weathervane.

The storm has finished and my pouch contains a dozen pegs of chaim. The night is old and, as the sky clears above me, I fancy I can see the first glimmer of dawn to the east. The stars twinkle above me and I splash through a puddle, almost slipping as I hear the great barking of the farmer's dog.

"Gerroff," I cry, aiming a kick at it. "May your paw fester and make you lame."

Above me the gatehouse stands, rain water still dribbling down its sides. I hammer on the door. There is no response so I kick the door hard with my booted foot.

"All right! Stranger or Lover?" comes the sleepy response.

"You'd be dead if I was a stranger, wouldn't you Parrothead?" I growl

"Stranger or Lover?" he asks again.

"Lover, you bleary eyed idiot. Let me in."

The door opens and I step through and make my way up to my master's rooms bearing my ticket to new learning. Soon I shall be a master of the arts of destruction.

The Fifth Year

"For just as the Mages under the Courtesan protect our Covenant from Magickal dangers, so also we need Defence from Mundane attacks. Therefore the Lovers shall have a Protector who shall be known as the CHAPERONE and he shall employ such Warriors as be necessary."

From the Law of the Covenant of The Castle of The Lovers

I look up from my books and gaze towards the sun drenched hills. The afternoon sun is hot and the air is still. I have abandoned the burning heat of Thengol Greydog's rooms for the cool of the council room and I stand in a recess by the western window. I return to the volume before me; it is one of the books my master brought back with him last year. Inside the front cover the title page reads "A journal of Thengol Greydog" carefully penned in my own hand and throughout the book my master's cunningly disguised writing tells of his dangerous adventures. My task for the last few months has been to carefully read the journal so that my master might test my understanding. The book is, of course, written in Latin, the language of scholars, but the monologue is interrupted by frequent comments written in French, a language unknown to me. Wise is my master, Thengol Greydog, to have mastery of a foreign tongue.

Today I am reading of a winter's day when the snow lay thick upon the ground, the thaw had begun and a cold rain fell constantly. My master's tinder box was useless and he stumbled across the hillside searching for shelter from the desperate cold. The height of the day passed unnoticed as the sun was hidden and the light was beginning to fade through the darker shades of grey before he caught sight of a wisp of smoke, brown against the purer grey of the cloud. He quickened his pace, forcing a last burst of energy from his leaden limbs and found that beneath the smoke lay a chimney and beneath that a crude stone house. He hammered on the door and begged shelter from the flinty shepherd who stood behind it. For three days my master rested there in that hut, sharing both food and bed with the shepherd and his flock. The air was foul and thick with smoke from the dull red fire that burnt in the hearth. For three days more my master stayed there, working off his debt to his host by digging the hard soil and binding thatch to the roof. Not once did he use his magic. In my naïvety, I asked his reasons for not creating a great blaze, keeping the rain from his skin or even turning the soil by enchantment. He explained that his aim was to truly understand the country and the magic which runs through the earth and he had no wish to pollute this insight with his own sorcery. I see that I have much to learn and my will hardens as I consider the mountain of knowledge and understanding I must amass. The years spread out before me full of study and obedience; this is a very different future to the one I had imagined when I dreamed of running from the Philosopher Beast but I comfort myself with the thought that at least I've escaped from the monster's lair and remind myself that with knowledge comes power and with power, true freedom. I choose to take this chance to be free of servitude, free of poverty, free of the attentions of fools and so I study, I serve and I learn at the feet of the great, glorious, wise and discerning Thengol Greydog.

Outside the window the sun is beginning to dip and clouds are beginning to form over the Fire Hills. It is midsummer and I must hurry if I am to get to the hills before the lightning strikes. Immersed in my reading, I have forgotten my duties and must face my master's wrath if I miss so much as a peg of chaim illuminated by tonight's storm. I make my best speed out of the castle, ignoring the jeering sentries, and stumble, breathless towards the Fire Hills. My heart thumps against my ribs and I can feel the blood pouring through my veins. My mind tries to force my body into new exertions and my memory strays back to the winter time.

Whilst the days were short and cool I spent most of my hours in my master's rooms learning the secrets of destruction and adding to my repertoire of spells but Thengol Greydog spent one day discussing weighty matters with the Courtesan and I was glad to take the release from my studies and stand in the courtyard with the sun on my face and my back against the wall watching Lopez train with Pedro. Lopez' armour was bright in the weak winter sunlight and Pedro seemed dark in comparison. Dark, that is, except for his gleaming sword for Pedro has met with an angel and carries a holy blade. He is the most blessed of the warriors in our castle and, although many of them are outcasts and not particularly devout, all his comrades seek his blessing before a battle. As I watched, Antonio sidled up to me and whispered,

"Tonight sir, just before sunset, by the ford."

I jumped for I was immersed my own meditations.

"What's that?"

"You must be there tonight. We need your magic"

"Need my magic for what?"

"Quiet sir, we don't want anyone to hear." He paused and looked over his shoulder. "No, we can't do this without him. No. Yes, I'll tell him."

I looked around but again it seemed that Antonio was conversing with himself.

"Sir," he said. "We're on a mission of great importance. Secrecy is vital."

"But Antonio, why, what, who..." I trailed off as he disappeared behind a storehouse, glancing occasionally over his shoulder and muttering.

I had great misgivings after the last "mission" I had been on with Antonio but his admiration of my magic was evident and I felt that the time had come for me to prove myself and a mission of great importance was clearly the correct opportunity. I only worried that this might be another wild goose chase but I was reassured when Mongrol came up to me a few minutes later and said

"Good you are coming with us."

"What?"

"Tonight. Antonio told me. Very important job. Mongrol go smosh"

"What exactly is this important mission?"

"Top secret. Mustn't talk here. Faeries might be listening. Mongrol hates faeries."

"Well, where can we talk?" But I got no answer because Mongrol had turned purple in the face and, clawing at his necklace, was only able to croak

"No, good faeries, not smosh," before he collapsed gasping to the floor.

That afternoon passed slowly as I waited for the sun to sink towards the horizon. Finally I picked up a dark cloak and walked through the gate to wait by the ford. The edge of the sun was just brushing the tops of the Fire Hills, long pink fingers were stretching down the contours leaving more sheltered slopes in grey shadow. I sat down on a rock beside the river and began to wonder what the secret mission could be.

"Not in clear view sir, down here sir." Antonio was crouching in the shallow water beneath the river bank. I looked down at his soaking boots and frowned as the water splashed his backside.

"In clear view of where Antonio?" I asked for there was no-one to be seen. Just then Mongrol stomped down the path from the castle with his morning star swinging from his right hand.

"Let's smosh" he said and Antonio looked questioningly over his shoulder and then nodded.

We splashed across the ford and turned left along the river bank towards Lerida. The shadows of the forest were dark across our path and a mere glimmer of the sun was visible over the dull hillside. Antonio set a fast pace, scurrying forwards then looking all round, nodding and running on. Mongrol marched steadily behind him and I had to break into a run to keep from lagging behind. A couple of miles on Antonio stopped suddenly and stepped behind a tree off the road. Mongrol joined him and, glad of a break, I leaned against the tree breathing heavily.

"What is this mission we're on, Antonio?"

"Through the woods, sir. Very important sir."

"Yes, but what's through the woods?"

He set off once more along a little track just visible in the gloom. Before long it became too dark to see and I bumped into the back of Antonio who had stopped suddenly.

"We need light sir. Magic light."

I took a deep breath, gathered my thoughts and muttered the magical words of incantation. A flame sprang up on my palm and allowed us to see for a few yards all around. Both ahead and behind the path meandered through the densely packed brush and I stepped forwards to lead the way, glad of the opportunity to set the pace. The little flame danced brightly on my hand and I took pleasure in making it grow when the darkness ahead seemed deeper or the path unclear and then allowing it to shrink again as I saw my way. After a couple of miles we came to a thick wooden gate in a strong stone wall.

"Here we are," whispered Antonio muffling a shriek and turning round. "Aargh. Yes, quiet, I know, but I must tell them."

"Mongrol smosh door?"

"No! We must be silent"

Antonio took the grappling hook from beneath his cloak and slung it gently over the wall. It caught with a dull thunk and he climbed swiftly up.

"You next sir."

I looked up at the wall and thought how slender the line appeared. As I hesitated Antonio showed signs of anxiety and signalled to me to hurry up. I turned to Mongrol helplessly. He looked confused for a moment and then held out his hands as a step. I put my foot on his broad palms, grabbed onto the rope and felt myself catapulted upwards. At the top of the wall Antonio grabbed my shoulder and waved at me to extinguish the flame. We sat in the darkness as Mongrol grunted his way up.

"How do we get down the other side Antonio?" I asked as he coiled the rope.

"Jump sir," he said, suiting his actions to his words and landing silently below me. Not wanting Mongrol's delicate help with this task, I balled up my courage and pushed off from the wall. I landed awkwardly and pitched forwards into a bed of rosemary. By the time I'd got to my feet Mongrol had landed beside us and Antonio was ready to set out his plan.

"We go in through the kitchen window and you two keep guard on whilst I search for it."

"Search for what?"

"Can't say sir. Very secret, we must keep silent."

We crept forward through the herb garden and, out of the dark, loomed a whitewashed villa. The kitchen windows were too small for any but Antonio to climb through but he was able to unlatch the door and we crept into the house. Antonio motioned for Mongrol to stand guard and for me to follow him into the corridor. He edged along the wall, peering into each room as he passed. At the far end of the corridor he found a locked door and, putting his finger to his lips he pulled a bent wire from beneath his cloak. I stood there motionless, willing my heart to beat more quietly as he fiddled with the lock, each click magnified in my imagination to a clash of cymbals. Finally he was able to push the door creaking open and I spun round. He waved at me.

"Stay here sir," he whispered.

I stood there on guard alone in the darkness and the minutes crept past. Fears assailed me as they had last year but I was no longer a child to allow myself to be afraid of the dark and so I banished cowardly thoughts and stood boldly. Suddenly the stillness was broken by the bark of a dog and I heard a thump from along the corridor. Where was Antonio? A glimmer of light appeared and then a man emerged carrying a burning torch in his left hand and a crossbow in his right. I froze in the shadows but he turned towards me. As the flickers of light moved towards me my boldness left me and my mind went blank. What should I do? He must see me soon. He has seen me and the crossbow is moving upwards. His finger is over the catch. Suddenly time reverted to its normal speed and I yelped out the words of a spell. A flash of light leapt from my palm and, as he released the catch, the man lifted his hands to cover his eyes. I felt a burning pain in my shoulder and charged towards him, pushing him out of my way with an outstretched palm. He staggered into a wall bellowing obscenities and I ran back into the kitchen and out into the garden. I ploughed straight across a bed of thyme and have no idea how I managed to scale the wall. I must have managed the feat for, from the top of the wall, I heard a bark of dogs and, throwing myself down, ran blindly through the wood.

Back on the road I ran into the broad back of Mongrol.

"Where have you been sir?"

"Where have I been?" I gasped, "I've been standing guard so that you could get whatever it was you needed to get. I've been shot at and assaulted by dogs and what have you two been doing you filthy scoundrels?"

"We thought you'd leave when we'd finished sir. I couldn't find the weather vane, he must have hidden it."

"The weather vane?"

"Yes sir, very powerful, magical weather vane. Very valuable sir." I stood there, sprigs of herbs caught in my hair, breathless and bleeding from where the bolt had scratched my shoulder and all for the sake of a magical weather vane that didn't even exist. Mongrol shrugged.

I trudged home behind Mongrol and Antonio, fuming. I was furious with Antonio for dragging me on a wild goose chase, furious with Mongrol for giving credence to the insane mission and furious with myself for believing either of them. Ahead of me Mongrol seemed completely unaffected by the failure of the mission, it is possible that he wasn't even aware that it had failed and Antonio seemed totally unfazed by the whole affair. I seethed behind them.

When we got back to the castle Antonio suggested that we climb over the palisade to avoid drawing attention to ourselves and, for once, I agreed with his zeal for secrecy. This was one mission I would be happy to see pass off unmarked and unnoticed. I hauled myself up the rope behind him and dropped heavily into a rosemary bush below. Mongrol followed me and had just reached the top when a cry of alarm came from the gatehouse. Mongrol looked up, lost his footing and fell heavily onto a construction of cane and twine supporting a species of climbing plant. There was a clatter and crack of splintering wood as the poles came down beneath him and another cry from the sentries. Antonio was already gone and I judged that the moment had come to disassociate myself from the enterprise. Even Mongrol realised that discretion was the order of the day and skulked quickly into the shadows.

I ran for cover behind the new building and edged my way round to the entrance. Pushing the door quietly open, I slipped inside and bounded up the stairs. Unwilling to disturb my master's work, I wrapped myself in my cloak and curled up to sleep in his doorway. The excitement of the night made me edgy and all my despair had drained from me. I stretched and twisted on the cold stone, imagining the confusion of the sentries outside and waiting for sleep.

I was weighing sulphur for a powder my master had asked me to mix the next morning when Pedro knocked on the door.

"Lord Greydog, your apprentice's presence is requested in the mysterious D-room," he announced grandly. I turned to my master nervously.

"Is it important?" he asked the warrior, grudgingly.

"It is of the most vital importance; a matter of covenant security," came the reply.

"Covenant security?" he echoed. "Well, Riff-Raff, you are summoned. Tidy up and then you may go and do your duty."

Somewhat confused, I followed the taciturn Pedro down the stairs and across the courtyard. When we reached our destination, we found the room already filled. A large and creaking table dominated the room and at the head of the table sat Father Juan, resplendent in a white surplice. On his right were sat Hawkeye, Siero and young Dylan, the gardener. Hawkeye and Siero looked keyed up and excited, Dylan was a mixture of righteous anger and anxious nerves. I was shown to an empty seat on his left next to Mongrol and Antonio. A feeling of dread crept through me. As soon as I was seated, the priest began to pray. I followed the example of those around me and made the sign of the cross as he asked his God to grant him the wisdom to see truth and the strength to pronounce justice. When this display of foolish weakness was complete, he faced the room and addressed his audience of workers, warriors and peasants.

"Love cannot survive in a community riven with dissent and so in times of dispute a judge must rule lest there be anger and feuding. I am judge over the Covenant of the Castle of Lovers. Do you accept my justice?"

"Yes father," came the reply.

"Dylan, what is your complaint?"

40

"Well, father, last night someone smashed up my tomato plants and left a trail of enormous footprints across my garlic. I seek restitution."

"Very good. Antonio, are you responsible for this mess?"

"No father," he lied, twitching violently.

"Did you have reason to go into the herb garden last night?"

"No reason, no father," he repeated and paused, listening. "I said no. Listen, I said no." He stopped suddenly and looked up at the priest.

"Very well. Mongrol, did you go into the herb garden last night?"

"No father," he replied brightly. "It was a special mission."

"What was?"

"The special mission, father,"

"No!" interrupted Antonio and whispered, "it's a secret, remember."

"Oh yes, a secret father, I can't tell you where we went."

"But you did come back to the castle?"

"Yes, father." Mongrol gave a yelp of pain as Antonio elbowed him in the ribs. "What?" he asked turning to his companion.

"Father Juan already knows we came back or how could I have fallen into the herb garden and broken young Dylan's little house?" Juan smiled benevolently and turned to me.

"Riff-Raff, as one of the more highly educated members of the community perhaps you can give me some answers?"

"Maybe, Father Juan," I replied carefully. "It depends on the questions."

"Did you go on some kind of expedition with Mongrol and Antonio last night?"

"Don't tell him," hissed Antonio

"No, you mustn't tell about the secret mission," added Mongrol. I shrugged, it was clear to me that it would be impossible to conceal either our mission or the damage we caused in our return. It only remained to ensure that nobody realised the laughable nature of our enterprise.

"Yes, we did."

"And was this journey authorised by any of the High Mages?"

"No, it wasn't." The Judge looked at me keenly, as though inspecting my soul.

"I see no reason to inquire into your activities whilst on this 'mission'," he continued. "The wizards have sold their souls in the search for power and the less the rest of us know of their activities the freer our consciences can be. Dylan's complaint is directed towards damage to the gardens. Can you shed any light on this matter?"

"Yes, Father Juan. When we came back over the fence, Mongrol slipped and fell into the vines. We may have caused some more damage in running from the sentries."

"Yes, indeed you may." Siero and Hawkeye looked triumphant and Dylan turned expectantly to the priest. "It seems to me, however, that the footprints are far in excess of what might reasonably be caused by three miscreants fleeing from justice and I suspect that much of the damage may have been caused by the sentries themselves in pursuit of the fugitives." He frowned severely and two exultant faces looked suitably chastened.

"I judge that Mongrol and Antonio are guilty of carelessly causing damage to the gardens. Siero and Hawkeye also caused damage to the plants but they were acting under orders from the Council and must be held blameless. Mongrol and Antonio must both pay two florins to Dylan as a recompense and must aid him in his work until the damage is made good. The damage caused by the sentries will be paid for from covenant funds but they must also help to repair the gardens. It is not my role to judge the mages or their apprentices but as an advisor I suggest that Riff-Raff pay four florins to Dylan in order to avoid bad feeling." Father Juan looked up and surveyed the gathering, assessing the reaction to his judgement. Satisfied he crossed himself once more and offered a prayer of thanksgiving before striding calmly from the room. I turned to my companions. Mongrol was sighing heavily.

"Two florins! Think of the beer you could buy with two florins." Antonio was in a state of confusion, taking part in an effusive debate with his inner demons.

"Yes, but... Well, ... No, but... I said that... No..." I turned from the two conspirators to the gardener and saw the wisdom of the priest's judgement. He looked calm and content once more.

Wisdom or not, I had no intention of paying the four florins suggested by Father Juan but I found myself snubbed by the cooks and ignored by the warriors. It was an unpleasant inconvenience until the great Thengol Greydog assigned me a mission to obtain some thyme from the herb garden. I dared not face Dylan and feared I would be unable to identify the correct plant without his assistance. Grudgingly, I took four silver coins from my savings and took them with me to the gardener. It was the most expensive handful of vegetable matter I've ever heard of.

I grimace at the thought and looking up at the clouds take heart; I'll beat the storm to the Fire Hills and collect the chaim. I will avoid my master's anger and the great Thengol Greydog will teach me the secrets of the earthen element. Stone, iron and gold will all do my bidding. I breathe air into by straining lungs and push on up the hillside.

The Sixth Year

"The Wealth and Power of the Covenant of the Castle of the Lovers shall be divided as specified by the Council of the High Mages and by this means shall the CHAIM of the Covenant and its other riches be assigned to the Mages."
From the Law of the Covenant of The Castle of The Lovers

*T*he Courtesan has a new pet, my master has had a vision and I have fallen in love. So much has happened since I last sat on this rock in the Fire Hills with the purple sunset behind me and the Castle of Lovers in front. Love, lovely, loving lovers. The very word sounds soft and warm like the bosom of my beloved. Down in the valley I imagine her walking through the courtyard to her work in the kitchen. Looking straight ahead, no eyes for right or left (except, perhaps a glance up towards the west, towards me). Around her ankles barks Beppo and she aims a kick.

I smile at the thought. Beppo is Señor Phosphortube's dog. Apparently he grew tired of conversing with an animated corpse and now prefers an enchanted carpet. Beppo was a stray on whom the Courtesan took pity; he took him into his rooms and, after a few months, began to concoct a wizardry that eventually gave Beppo the power of speech. Other changes have also taken place although, unfortunately, not to his odour. Beppo smells like an old rug that has been soaked in urine and then stored in a damp cellar for some years. He thinks himself lovable, yapping happily around your ankles as you go about your business, causing you to trip and then bowing to the applauding sentries. How I long to make contact with a well-aimed kick; sadly some of the Courtesan's magic has rubbed off and any attempted violence invariably results in a prodigious leap on Beppo's part and a scratched face on mine. The injury would not be so bad were it not for the proximity of Beppo to my nose during the manoeuvre. His most irritating habit is to sit in a sunny spot in the courtyard and to give a running commentary.

"Mongrol and Lopez are practising once more and it seems that Lopez is getting the upper hand. Mongrol swings his morning star viciously but Lopez steps out of the way and it seems that Mongrol is tiring. Sparks fly from the rooms of Thengol Greydog as an explosion signifies the ruin of another experiment. The flap of sandals against flagstone can be heard in the courtyard and Señor Greydog's apprentice rushes out of the building on an urgent errand. He is running so quickly that his sandal has become loose and he trips over it and falls at the feet of Conchita who looks at him with disdain."

Conchita is beautiful. Her skin is smooth and soft, her hair long and straight and her round bosom strains the fabric of her apron. She also cooks. It is Conchita whom I love. After humiliating myself in her eyes I dared not approach her so I sought advice from an experienced man of the world.

"Lopez," I said. "You're an experienced man of the world."

"Yes."

"How can I win the love of a beautiful woman?"

"Beautiful woman like shiny armour. Here, bollocks rusty," he said pointing at a duller patch on his gleaming breastplate. "Women distracting. Better not."

"But Lopez, I can't think of anything but her. When I shut my eyes I see her; when I go to sleep I imagine her voice. I dream of her Lopez, what can I do?" In reply I was handed a cloth and Lopez's helmet. It doesn't do to annoy Lopez so I rubbed away at the helmet until sweat dripped from my face and fire burned along my arm. Finally he seemed satisfied.

"Better now?" he asked. I nodded and gratefully took my leave.

The wizards of the Castle of Lovers have gone animal mad. A new magus called Darius has joined us and one day he asked me to join him on a trek into the hills to collect some rare herbs. As we walked, he talked constantly. He explained that mankind's greatest desire has always been to join the birds and fly. He pointed out a song thrush swooping beneath the eaves of the forest and we watched as it landed on the branch of a willow tree, looked about and then took off once more. The light caught on its wings as it swooped and dived for nothing but the pleasure of flight. Finally it flew further into the forest and we lost sight of it in the shadows.

"There it goes, a tiny creature, no bigger than your fist but experiencing a joy at which mankind can only wonder." As we left the woodland behind us and climbed up into the hills he talked about the different kinds of flight; songbirds flit, hawks soar, gulls dive and kestrels hover. He spoke about flightless birds of legend who, cursed by the gods, are unable to leave the ground and, earthbound, flap their wings in vain. He told me of the greatest temptation faced by Christ when he was taken

45

to the top of the tallest building and offered the chance to fly down in safety.

"Imagine climbing to the roof of our keep and being given the opportunity to fly down, the air rushing past your ears, and to land with perfect ease on the ground."
For a long while I listened in silence as the climb was steep and the pauses in my companion's monologue few. Finally we reached a plateau and Darius paused to admire the view.

"Will the herbs we gather today give you the ability of flight?" I asked. He laughed long and freely. Clutching his sides and with tears streaming down his cheeks he answered me in one word.

"Watch!"

He turned to face the precipice, bent his knees, took a deep breath and jumped. Before he was truly airborne his legs shortened, his arms thickened and his head shrunk. Where, seconds ago, had been a tall, angular Spaniard was now an eagle which turned its head once towards me before flapping its great wings and accelerating into the sky. He flew upwards, circling; no longer needing to flap, he rode the currents of hot air. I watched him soar high above a ravine until suddenly he pulled in his wings and dropped towards the grassy hillside. It seems that he had spied a rabbit munching contentedly in the warm sunshine and seconds later had the rodent in his talons. I saw him land briefly and then fly back towards me. As he neared the spot where I stood his body dropped, his wings pulled in and he landed human once more.

"I have no need for herbs, boy," he said. I marvelled at his exploits and felt it inappropriate to mention the splashes of blood that flecked his face.

I spoke to the great Thengol Greydog about what I had seen and my master nodded.

"Very impressive," he said. "But, I think you will find that your friend Darius is nothing but a one trick pony. He is so delighted by the sound of wind rushing by his ears that he is deaf to the call of magical power and will therefore amount to nothing. Fireballs to cut swathes through an army, spells to rend human flesh, this is what magic can offer you. Don't be distracted by pleasant pastimes boy, pursue power."

Our new magus Darius is a bird of prey, Señor Phosphortube has taken in the fiend Beppo, the Lady Adriel has no animal but is mad even so and my master Thengol Greydog has had a vision. He has seen that it does the reputation of the Castle of Lovers no good to have a yapping dog as a familiar; respect is commanded by a more awesome creature. In his vision, which he has generously shared, he saw a monster prowling our courtyard, speaking gently to the lovers and watching strangers for signs of duplicity. Like a giant cat, it crept around our palisade, its whiskers twitching for signs of danger and the mark of magic upon its coat. Legend says that such creatures can be found across the sea in the land of Africa and the great Thengol Greydog, fearing no danger, has determined to seek out the monster that has troubled his dreams. I am to go with him and will learn from him the secrets of the animal kingdom as we track down the dread beast. I shall return with honour and glory and I will win the fair Conchita's heart even though she now looks on my with disgust rather than love.

I was both unwilling and unable to take Lopez's advice and so cast around looking for a more romantic soul from which to beg advice. My eye rested on Romario. Romario is a great musician; his songs have brought tears to the eyes of statues; he has won the stony hearts of ancient magistrats; if anyone in this Castle of Lovers could help me win my love it would be him. I found him sitting by a window strumming his lute and trying to fit words to a ballad.

"Romario, I'm in love," I told him. He nodded.

"It is the essence of humanity. The only greater muse is love unrequited." I was about to explode into vociferous explanation when he continued, "I see your beloved indeed fails to return your affection. Well, my friend, you have my envy."

"I need your help Romario."

"To win a fair maiden's heart?" he asked, brightening. I nodded.

"Against uncounted obstacles?" I nodded again thinking of my limp and unappealing visage.

"And to rescue her from the thrall of an evil sorcerer?" Well, that was putting it a bit harsh; Señor Phosphortube is not exactly evil. I nodded anyway, keen to gain the aid of one skilled in the arts of love.

"We must start immediately. Take up your lute." I had no lute and told him so.

"Then you must borrow one, I shall fetch my spare."

For weeks I practised the lute, my fingers stumbling over the unfamiliar strings whilst Romario winced at my errors and composed a serenade for me. Eventually my desire overcame my lack of confidence and I told Romario that I was ready to play for Conchita.

"But that will ruin everything." I looked at him, amazed. "Either she will fall in love as you play and your love will no longer be unrequited or she will turn from you and your last hope will be dashed. You must not play for her; stay and practise some more."

I was not to be dissuaded and insisted that Romario teach me the serenade.

A few days later I was ready to woo my beloved in song and I took my lute to the kitchen window after sunset. Slowly and stumblingly I picked my way through the tune singing

"I'll tell you a tale of a love so pure,
Of a youth whose heart was true.
A maiden both fair of face and lithe of limb
And of quite unquestioned virtue.
These lovers met beneath the shade,
Of a strange and twisted keep:
Its story is long and ancient as the hills,
That are home to the farmer's sheep.
His background was dark and nobody knew,
From which land he originally hailed;
Her family was mean, no noble she..."

Conchita's face appeared at the window and I looked up. Without a word she pulled a cleaver from her apron and flung it at me severing the strings and cracking the neck of the lute.

"Piss off!" she said, turning back to her baking.

The next day I returned the lute to Romario and took myself back to my books. The cleaver I keep beneath my blanket as a token of my beloved.

My problem is that she sees me as a nobody, a child amongst men, a dolt with skin like wet clay. When I return from Africa with tales of adventure and heroism and with a deeper knowledge of the dark secrets of enchantment, she will fall for me. How could she resist?

As the last rays of the sun gently caress the round tower below I imagine what might lie before me across the sea. My master would not ask me to join him if my skills were not needed. Perhaps I will help him track the monster to its lair; perhaps I will be called upon to risk my life in this quest. I fantasise also over the rewards that might come to me. Surely such a creature will have a mighty hoard of gold and gems; maybe it will be defending a magical sword. I see myself as a mighty warrior, golden helmet glinting in the sunlight as I stride manfully into the courtyard of the Castle of Lovers. I brush off Hawkeye's protestations and challenge Lopez to combat. His skill at arms is no match for my magic sword and I soon disarm him. Beppo's sarcastic commentary dries up as he realises the extent of my powers. From the hallway, Conchita has been watching me and, as Lopez yields to my brilliance, she rushes from the shadows and falls into my arms. She pushes her soft cheek against mine and whispers in my ear.

I shiver. The night has grown dark and my reverie has kept me seated for too long. I get to my feet rubbing my numb backside and set off down the hillside. The last glow in the west is long since faded and I must take care to avoid a twisted ankle. The cold air has blown my fancies away; I have not returned from Africa and Conchita still despises me. But, and oh, my love, what a but, my master has had a vision and I am to travel to foreign lands. I kick out at the barking guard dog as I pass the farm.

"Drop dead." I call out cheerfully and run across the ford to the gatehouse. I hammer the rhythm of my ballad against the wooden gate.

"Stranger or lover?" comes the challenge and this time I am happy to reply.

"Lover!" Oh, lover, love, lovely beloved. Will you come to me Conchita, will my dreams come true? My master has had a vision and to Africa I sail.

The Seventh Year

*"All Covenant Decisions shall be Established by a Vote after the Athenian fashion.
Each High Mage shall have a number of Votes to Cast, according to his Station. The
Number of Kato's Votes shall be ONE, the Number of All Shapes, for Kato is the
Junior High Mage, full of Potential, his Limits undetermined."*

From the Law of the Covenant of The Castle of The Lovers

From my resting place on this rock I look across the valley and try
to make sense of the distant shapes below me. The sun is dipping
on the western horizon but still warms my back with its strong
rays. Above me the sky is clear; not a single cloud disturbs the shades of
blue. The palest, faintest tint shines above and behind me, close to the
retiring sun. As my gaze crosses the dome above it darkens slowly,
imperceptibly but inevitably until on the horizon ahead night is near and
the colour dark and rich as velvet.

The shapes in the valley below are grazing camels and strange
rock formations. These are not the Fire Hills and I have not yet made my
triumphant return to Spain. It is possible that I never shall; our trip has
taken far longer than originally planned and many miles still separate us
from a seaport from which we could return to the safety of the Castle of
Lovers.

We set out with great hopes and light packs, my master and I hiking
down river towards the coast. By night we camped in olive groves,
staring up at the familiar sky above. Sounds in the dark seemed loud and
frightening for I was still young and accustomed to a roof over my head.
We met no dangers on that country ramble to the great port of
Barcelona. The sun was warm on our backs and the breeze cool on our
backs as it followed us down the river valley. We had high hopes and full
bellies; life seemed good.

Our path became a track that became a road and joined the
highway leading to our destination. Here we saw many travellers; traders
leading mules brushed against merchants with horses and carts full of
valuable goods. Groups of labourers seeking work in the city were
brushed aside by a warrior on horseback. I gazed around marvelling at
the people around me great and small and I pondered the fact that none
matched up to my master in power or nobility; the mighty Thengol

Greydog arrived on foot clad in a grey cloak but bearing greater worth in his fingertips than all the nobles in the land combined.

We arrived at the city and passed through narrow streets between shabby houses and stalls. As we approached the centre, the buildings became grander; stone took over from wood and tiles from thatch. Soon we were strolling between stone buildings the size of our keep, their paintwork glinting in the sun. The stinking mud of the streets had dried up and been replaced by stone flags; dirty water running in channels down both sides of the roadway. I marvelled at one great residence; its doors were flanked by tall, carved pillars painted in blue and gold and above them a coat of arms had been polished until it shone. One day I would live in a palace grander and more magnificent than even this; the great Thengol Greydog might be contented to share a shabby castle with lesser wizards but my grandeur would be brighter, harder and clearer; people would look on my dwelling and know my power.

We continued past the great buildings, official residences and palaces and on to a dingier area. The streets returned to their earlier consistency of sunbaked mud running with the effluent of the great city. A small pack of dogs snapped at our heels and chased each other between the passing traffic. I caught a whiff of the sea, a fresh salty thread through the thick stench of the city. As we walked, the scent got stronger and the hot, sweaty smell became mixed with fish. I began to notice that some of the people in the street were no longer Spanish; foreigners with strange voices stumbled along drunk on rum and freedom, Arab traders dressed in bizarre robes passed us by and I saw one man with skin like pitch with thick, rubbery lips and black, soulless eyes. The noise of the street became gradually louder and punctuated by shouts, creaks and the hollow thunk of heavy goods unloaded onto a wooden jetty. Finally I caught sight of the sea; I was blinded by a brilliant flash of white, the sun reflecting off the calm water. I was caught up in the excitement of the moment and began to run. My master's hand on my shoulder and a stern look reminded me of my place and the gravity of my master's role. Still my heart beat quickly in my chest. This was only the second time I'd seen the sea and it still held a fascination for me as the symbol of hope that had sustained me when I was enslaved to the Philosopher Beast.

We strode masterfully out from between the warehouses, across the waterfront and onto a jetty where a boat lay waiting. My master leapt onto its deck, pointed out to sea and proclaimed his destination:

"To Africa!" A burly fisherman pulled himself out of a hatch behind my master, grabbed him round the waist and hurled him into the oily water.

"Get off my boat you lunatic. We're going fishing."

"Punish him master," I cried, leaping from one foot to the other as the great Thengol Greydog pulled himself dripping from the water and lay coughing on the dock.

"Blast him, burn him, slay him master," I shouted at the bedraggled wizard before me. "Show him what happens to those who mess with the great Thengol Greydog!"

I contemplated the following events as I crouched, miserably seasick behind a crate roped to the deck that night. My stomach churned and I held tight to the rail as I spewed into the dark waves that slammed against the side of the boat below. The sea no longer represented freedom but a new form of imprisonment; I couldn't escape my own belly and it had betrayed me, chaining me to the edge of the vessel, unable even to stand. Pale wisps of cloud raced across the black sky obscuring the stars. My mind lurched from my present misery to the embarrassment that filled me as my master walked away from the laughter of the fishermen. No scorching fireball sped across the dock to turn the boat into a flaming ruin; no burst of magic left my master's fingertips to destroy the mocking peasant.

"Best not to make a scene," was all that he said to me as we scuttled away from the scene of our humiliation.

As our frail craft swept along the coast, I pondered the purpose of power. Surely, greatness should protect one from the indignities of life. Truly great men should not suffer like ordinary mortals; humiliation should be a stranger, pain unknown. When I have learned all I can from my master and I become a great wizard in my own right then I shall not bow and scrape; I'll not back down from a challenge. No man shall scorn me and live. Never will I be found scrabbling for a handhold on a wet deck as a wave crashes over me and threatens to sweep me into the nightmarish depths.

For three days we scudded across the voracious waters. By day the sun shone, the sky was a pale blue speckled with fluffy clouds and the sea cool, clear and aquamarine. In the distance I could see a thin line of grey where Spain lay on the horizon. By night this paradise changed. The black sky sucked at my soul, the stars span crazily as the sharp winds tugged at the sails and the sea smashed angrily against the timbers. I lay sleepless and nauseous towards the front of the ship waiting for the sun to rise and offer peace of mind.

On the fourth day the thin line of cloud began to fill and to spread insidiously across the western sky. The near edge was pale and shone like Lopez' breastplate but behind that the brightness faded quickly and the bright steel became dull and grey. As the day progressed, the light paled and the wind picked up. The ropes and beams strained and creaked as we sped southwards along the edge of the cloud. Soon the sun was obscured and the clouds boiled ominously overhead. A first few drops of rain fell, large and heavy they splashed across the white deck. The wind dropped completely and the sails flapped empty. A streak of lightning flashed across the sky; a boom of thunder followed immediately and the rain began in earnest. No longer was it a matter of a handful of individual drops splashing darkly on my smock but a downpour soaking me instantly. Water flooded over me, filling my eyes and ears, running into my mouth and making me splutter as it splashed into my nose. I stared up at the sky and then lurched as the ship dropped from under me. A great gust of wind had caught the sails and deck had tilted sharply. I felt myself falling out of control, my arms flailing helplessly as I tried to regain my balance. Beneath me I saw only the inky depths of the sea and I remember clearly a flash of lightning reflected in the darkness below. I fell, my hands grasping for a line or rail to save me. Fortunately, the wind switched direction, the boat heeled over towards the other side and the rising edge caught me under the shoulder as I fell. My feet scrabbled for purchase, my loose hand waved in futility at the waves and, had the boat tipped back once more, I should have been dumped unceremoniously. The wind held for a few seconds, my fingers found a crack between two planks and I hauled myself upwards before the gale changed once more and I found myself clinging to the deck with both hands as my legs trailed in the water. Gradually I hauled myself back to safety and lay, clinging onto the mast and gasping air into my lungs.

The little boat was tossed about in the water as the lightning flashed overhead and the thunder roared. Wave after wave swept over the length of the boat as the sailors tugged at ropes, changed the sails and hauled on the rudder. A chain of men was formed to bail water from below the decks and I found myself standing in darkness with the sea up to my knees lifting wooden buckets over my head. Above and behind me I heard a familiar voice,

"Do you know who I am?"

"You are a passenger which, right now, means you are a nobody and if this ship sinks then you'll be a drowned nobody. I, on the other hand, am the captain and have no intention of allowing the ship to sink and so you will do as I say and bail." Another indignity from which greatness could not protect Thengol Greydog.

The storm blew and I bailed through the night and morning found us both exhausted. As I climbed back onto the deck, I saw the early morning light glinting off a gently rippled sea, mocking us for the terrors of the night. The sails had been blown away and only a few rags remained to catch the light breeze. The captain was steering for a small bay in the coastline ahead and the broken vessel inched its way towards shelter. Listening to the conversations around me I learned that this was, indeed, Africa and, although this wasn't the port of arrival for which we had planned, we had made it to our destination. As soon as we stepped from the boat onto dry land we hoisted our packs, turned our backs on our shipmates and strode forwards to follow a dream.

As the morning wore onwards the heat grew oppressive and our path steeper as we picked our way up a rocky hillside. We siesta'd in the shade of a steep cliff and I slept soundly, secure and comfortable on a bed of rocks in a strange land. That night we lit a fire and my master revealed that his dream offered him no further guidance. The creature he knew he must find was somewhere in this vast land but he had no way of knowing where.

"We need a guide," he told me. We camped under the stars; it was my first night under African skies and my fears returned. Strange beasts lurked just beyond the flickering circle of light defined by our campfire and I heard their claws striking against rock, their long and scaly tails thrashing through the rough grass and, most awful of all, the howls they made when they devoured their prey.

Somehow I survived it through that night, jumping at every sound, my eyes peeled to catch sight of the dreadful monsters I could hear. When morning came I was exhausted but my master insisted that we press on and we hiked into the growing heat of the day. As the sun shrank, hardened and brightened from its soft dawn glow we reached the top of the range of hills and were able to look back towards the bright glimmer of the sea and forwards across a bleak, rock-strewn waste. A little later, as we were beginning to look for some shade in which to siesta, we saw a group of buildings and changed our course to walk towards them. As we approached, we saw that they were not the small, white huts we'd taken them to be but tents. A man swathed in white cloth stood guard and drew a long, curved sword as we approached.

"I am Thengol Greydog from the Castle of Lovers and I have had a dream which has brought me far across the ocean's briny depths. I seek your aid in finding and capturing the creature of my dream," my master announced grandly in Latin. The guard replied in a strange, musical voice which was, unfortunately, completely unintelligible.

"I did not come here to gibber but to find a guide."

"Maybe they don't speak Latin, master," I suggested.

"How do they expect to communicate with the great and educated men of Europe then?" he asked, outraged.

The stranger put his head on one side and listened to our conversation. When we had finished, he asked

"Spanish?"

"Of course we are Spanish. How many Castles of Lovers do you think there are?" The stranger beckoned to us to follow him and led us, sword still in his hand, to

one of the tents. He motioned to us to wait and stepped inside. Through the felt walls we heard a discussion taking place and I found myself entranced by the melodious voices and began to recognise the sound and shape of a language which must be similar to the one my parents spoke to me so many years ago. When the conversation had come to a conclusion, the guard emerged once more and ushered us into the tent in front of him. Inside, an old man with a strong black moustache sat cross legged on a floor of animal hides and richly decorated rugs. He waved to us,

"Sit," he said in Spanish, "and drink tea." From a bronze pot he poured a steaming infusion into two cups and motioned to us to take them. I sipped the dark brown liquid; it was bittersweet and refreshing.

"I am Abu al-Jamal and I rule here," he told us. "What is your business in these lands?"

"I am Thengol Greydog and I have come to find a creature I have seen in a dream. Like a giant cat it stalks across Africa and upon its coat are the marks of magic."

"And what do you want from me Thengol Greydog?"

"I need a guide, one who will help me track and capture the creature of my vision."

"This is a hard land Thengol Greydog and dreamers die in the desert. Why should one of my family aid you in this quest?"

"I can offer great wealth to those who help me," he replied, muttering an incantation, drawing a gold coin from his purse and handing it to our host who took it solemnly and tested it between his teeth.

"Man cannot eat gold, Thengol Greydog, and gold will not replace any son of mine who follows your vision. There is one, however, who is a guest in our tents and who might be able to help you." Al-Jamal turned to the guard and gave a brief order at which he left the tent and returned a few minutes later with another stranger. Like the others he wore thick, pale robes covering his whole body. His face was gaunt and twisted with a thin, wispy beard and an ugly scar on his right cheek.

After a discussion we were unable to follow he turned to us and, in halting Spanish, said

"Me Wasim. You Fengli Kraydok. You seek vision. Me seek gold. You have?" My master muttered another incantation and held up another gold coin. He flipped it between his fingers before returning it to his pouch.

"I have gold," he said. Wasim's eyes followed the coin greedily then drew his sword, flicked a corner of a rug aside and thrust it into the ground. He held out his hand over the sword and my master took it and shook. We had a guide.

We set off in great spirits; my master would stride ahead, waving his hands and enthusing on the subject of his dream; Wasim followed, nodding and grinning and I brought up the rear, sweating in the heat. After a couple of days of desert, it became clear that Wasim's grasp of Spanish was even poorer than we had thought; he didn't seem able to understand anything we said and was able to tell us very little. The occasional trees disappeared and were replaced by dry grass which, in turn, was replaced by grey sand and rocky outcrops. We travelled by night and rested by day beneath the shade of a light tent. My master continued to try to explain his vision to Wasim who, clearly not understanding a word, smiled and replied in his own language. I lay there dreaming of Conchita and allowing their words to wash over me. As the days passed, I began to realise that I could understand more of Wasim's speech; the occasional word was superseded by the odd phrase and eventually I was able to follow the less flowery of his sentences.

As my comprehension increased, I was entertained by a pair of monologues which intersected and overran my fantasies of Conchita lying waiting for me.

"According to the writings of Ramon the creature is a panther of dazzling speed which evades its enemies by becoming invisible..."

"Of course, when we have passed through the desert, I shall double the price and you will pay me what I desire, old man..."

Her hair is dark and lustrous, a blessing from the gods in recognition of her great beauty or the result of a powerful enchantment.

"On its coat it bears the markings of magic; each sphere of control is represented by a series of dark patches..."

"For then there will be no way back for you..."

Her arms are smooth and strong and they lie folded across her belly.

"No man has ever captured the creature and it lives free and unfettered on the plains..."

"When I return to the tribe I shall have great wealth"

Her belly is soft and round beneath her brown robe and it rises and gently falls as she breathes

"I will have a familiar greater than that of any wizard..."

"I will be no longer Wasim the feckless but Wasim the wealthy..."

I take her in my arms and smooth the fabric across her thighs

"I will have great power..."

"I will have great wealth..."

I will have Conchita.

Our journey continued across the sandy waste and I spent my time walking alongside Wasim asking him about the desert, its plants, animals and weather. I learned of the dangers of the sun and the skills required to find water. In exchange I told him of the hoard of treasure we had hidden when we had reached Africa. I explained to him my master's great wealth and good nature and that he had sworn to provide an honest guide with a third of the gold if his quest was successful. I saw greed glint in his eyes and told him of the beautiful rings and jewels my master had hidden and explained the fanaticism which had led him to seek out this creature. Wasim smiled broadly and quickened our pace as we marched southwards.

Our path led steadily onwards, the rocky outcrops growing more frequent until we were clambering rather than walking and the pace of our progress was slashed. Finally we reached the edge of a cliff where the ground fell quickly away and, after making our way down a steep and vertiginous path fit only for goats, when we reached the bottom we found the ground covered in patches of thick, dry grass. Once more we could walk normally and as we strode through the moonlit night, the patches of grass grew larger and more frequent. The next night we found ourselves walking across a grassy plain interspersed with thickets of thorny trees and, when we camped in the shade the next morning, Wasim announced that we would soon find traces of the creature we sought.

"Its tracks are scorched on the earth and no grass will grow for many seasons..."

"We must find antelope for, where there is game, there will we find panthers..."

Tonight she lies back with her hands flung above her head, a smile of welcome on her face.

"It races faster towards the sun than it flees from it and so we should catch it going west in the morning..."

"Do you know one panther from another? Would a sick lion suffice?"

The movement pulls her dress upward across her soft thighs.

"It is distracted by the call of the cockerel and will ever halt to seek the noisy bird..."

"We must lure it with fresh meat..."

My gaze travels down her arms, over the round swelling of her breasts and across her belly.

That night as we walked across the grassland, my master's eyes were fixed on the ground, seeking the burned tracks of his vision; Wasim kept his eyes on the horizon seeking game and I watched where I walked, keen to stay upright. When the moon set, we rested in the darkness waiting for light to continue our chase and, as the eastern horizon glowed with the coming day, our hopes were rewarded by a great herd of grazing antelope. Wasim picked up his spear and crept off to catch one to use as bait. My master looked confused by this development but, as I tried to justify Wasim's plan, he suddenly broke across my explanation

"Look!"

I peered in the direction of his pointing finger and saw, a hundred yards away, a slight movement in the grey morning light.

"There it is," he said and I saw that it was indeed a panther stalking the herd of antelope Wasim had set off to hunt.

"Drive it towards me and I'll engage it in conversation," my master demanded. "Ramon writes that these creatures will ever stop for debate with a scholar." I looked up for help from Wasim but he was now hidden in the grass.

"Hurry!"

With my heart thumping and the blood thudding in my ears I circled the prowling creature keeping my distance and hoping it couldn't hear me, or else was more interested in antelope than apprentice. When I was in position I looked up and saw the first rays of the sun reflect in its eye. It bared its teeth as it smelt the air and moved into position to catch an antelope. Several things then happened in quick succession; Wasim sprang from his hidden position, the antelope leapt and fled, moving away from me, the panther sprang after them seeking breakfast and I broke cover and chased after the panther. In the pale light I lost sight of it and so did my master for he stood up and peered into the gloom. The creature sprang towards him and in reflex he released a great fireball which missed its nose by inches. It skidded to a halt and twisted to flee as my master let go another sphere of flame, this time passing to the other side of the beast and nearly roasting me. By now I had made up ground and, as the panther crouched in confusion and my master prepared another bolt of fiery death, I hurled myself onto the beast, grabbing its hindquarters and wrestling it to the ground. The air crackled above me and I smelt burning hair as I grappled the twisting feline. Its jaws snapped at my neck and its claws raked my back as the firestorm continued to rage above us. As my strength began to fail and my advantages of surprise and momentum were lost, my grip loosened and its great fore-paw raked across my cheek. I screamed and rolled aside as Wasim arrived, lassoed the creature and dragged it away from me. My master, meanwhile, let go one more blast of igneous magic and fainted.

When he came round it was to a breakfast of grilled antelope and a tethered panther. He looked with joy at the vicious beast and pointed to it

"See the markings of magic on its coat," he cried, showing us the patches of black on its yellow fur, "and see the lines where burning tears coursed across its cheeks as it waited for me." He now looked up at the savannah around him and finally enthused

"And see the burning tracks it has made in the grass. It is just as my vision foretold." I looked up and followed his gaze to see five long black scorches through the dry vegetation. Neither Wasim nor I would deny that the burns had been caused by the panther and the beast seemed in no mood to comment on the accusation.

"I shall call her Cleopatra," my master said as he moved towards the panther. "You are truly a queen amongst the beasts and I offer you a life of royal luxury; will you join us?" he asked. The panther raised her head and growled softly in a manner which might be taken as consent if consent was what was sought.

Six weeks have passed since we captured Cleopatra and I have led her on the end of a rope back across the plains, over the rocks and through the desert while my master attempted conversation and Wasim strode ahead muttering disdain for all things Spanish. Only the promise of great wealth refreshed by judicious conversation by the campfire seems to have kept him with us. We have passed by the village of Abu Al-Jamal and have been climbing through the hills since the heat of the day passed several hours ago. Now we have stopped for a rest and the hills remind me of home. Only two days' journey separates us from the coast and I have survived the adventure so far. My original wounds have healed but have been replaced with other scratches and gashes obtained when Cleopatra has railed against her imprisonment and I have been required to subdue her. Fortunately these occasions have been less frequent recently as my master seems to be truly developing a relationship with this strange and fierce creature. I look back across the valley, struggle to my feet and hope that only fair weather and good fortune separate me from my waiting love.

The Eighth Year

"The Number of Lato's Votes shall be TWO, the Linear Number, for Lato is the Middle High Mage, growing like a young tree, quick and deadly like a Spear. The number of Pato's Votes shall be THREE, the Triangular Number, for Pato is the Senior High Mage and therefore a bit like something Triangular."

From the Law of the Covenant of The Castle of The Lovers

It is midsummer's eve and I am studying in the council room. Thengol Greydog's rooms are too stuffy for study and are, moreover, occupied by a bad-tempered panther. Cleopatra has become a permanent fixture in my master's life and has absorbed his attention to such an extent that I have been left to my own devices in the months since we returned to the Castle of the Lovers. He has been working careful magic to bind her mind to his and to share his arcane abilities with her. As I have watched, my master's temper, which has been ever short, has worsened and the speed of his reflexes have improved. Neither of these developments is an improvement to my mind, especially as Thengol Greydog's instinctive reaction to being awoken is to let off a fireball; a bad temper and fast reactions make an early morning visit to his rooms a dangerous affair. Cleopatra is now devoted to him although, unfortunately, the care and attention she lavishes on him is matched by the hatred she holds for the other inhabitants of the castle and most especially me. To get away from their mutual admiration, I have delved into the subtle arts of control. This magic is not as immediately attractive as creation or as extravagant as destruction but appears to have great potential in the hands of a master. The author of the great tome from which I study speaks of ruling the minds and bodies of men so that their very actions are not their own. Such mastery is, as yet, beyond me and I pore over the great Danielli's work seeking the elusive clue which will make sense of his dense Latin prose. Until then, I am no more able to control the minds of men than is Mongrol who, with Pedro, is lounging against the side of the new building enjoying the last warmth of the sun.

As I look across the courtyard at the two warriors I see the short, bustling figure of a young boy emerge from the door beside them and set off towards the gatehouse. He runs with his head down, carefully avoiding the cracks between the flagstones, oblivious to the workers going about their duties around him. Lopez packs his armour into a chest of straw to be safe against the approaching storm; Romario tunes his lute ready to show off a new ballad and our young gardener, Dylan, is almost knocked flying as he carries an armful of herbs and vegetables towards the kitchens. The young boy is called Braun and in many ways resembles a bear cub; he is short and stout, very furry and has a potentially dangerous sense of fun. He is Darius' new apprentice, rescued in a snowstorm whilst we were away and, as most junior wizard, it is now his responsibility to collect the chaim from the Fire Hills.

Much has changed in the Castle of Lovers since I last collected the chaim two years ago and it came as a shock to me to return to a home I believed fixed and unchanging to find my position usurped. A year ago today I stood on an African hillside reflecting on the difficulties my master had faced in following his dream and looking forward to my triumphant return home. The experience was not quite as I had anticipated.

We were fortunate to have an uneventful trip to the coast and a comparatively easy time buying passage to Spain. Of course, comparatively easy is a relative term when one of the passengers is a fully grown panther. My master was forced to pay well above the going price for our return journey and, devastatingly, to pay in advance. Real gold changed hands in the transaction as Thengol Greydog's magic will not suffice to maintain illusory gold past sunset and we had no desire to deal with a furious captain in mid-ocean. The late summer sun was kind to us and shone warmly. Occasional white clouds scudded across the blue sky but there was never even the threat of a storm.

Although the weather kept fine the journey home was an unending age of pain and distress. The craft sat high in the water and every breath of wind caused her to heel over almost to right angles with the hungry blue waves. Each time this happened, I found myself tumbling leeward. Almost invariably the rail would catch me in the pit of the stomach and I would retch fiercely at the water just inches from my nose. Thengol Greydog fared little better although he took advantage of his status to commandeer a well-protected seat in the bows from which he rarely rose. The task of feeding Cleopatra fell, of course, to me. Twice a day I scrabbled over to where she was tethered to the port rail and passed her the fish which comprised her meal. Rather ungraciously she would leap to the full extent of her rope and try to take my arm to supplement her diet. The sea air was doing nothing for her temper.

When, finally, the awful boat docked in the little port of Tarragona we were glad to step once more onto dry land even though releasing Cleopatra cost me several painful scratches and a deep bite through my boots. My master tipped the captain (this time with magical gold) and we turned our back on the sea. My thoughts sped ahead to our reception back at the castle. There would be feasting and celebration. There would be cheering. There would be wine. And, there would be Conchita. As we walked, I imagined her admiring gaze, her delicate smile and her joyful surrender. Having rehearsed the scene in my mind I started again. This time she put up a show of resistance but I eventually swept her off her feet and into my manly arms. She flung her arms around my neck as I carried her to my bed. As I hobbled northwards, taking care to keep Cleopatra away from my bleeding ankle I played out a multitude of variations on my triumph. Each one, of course, had the same, ecstatic ending.

The weather remained fine and clear as we climbed the coastal ridge and made our way across the plateau above. For four days we hiked and my mind span dizzily as the consideration of Conchita's delightful form made way for a rational evaluation of our trip. The return journey was, on the surface, much like our outward trek; we walked through the same countryside with similar weather. I saw a difference, however, in myself. No longer was I naïve and enthusiastic, out for a ramble with my master, keen to find adventure and fame. Now I was older and I strode purposefully towards my home bearing the spoils of a successful venture. The image was somewhat spoilt by my lame left leg and Cleopatra's tendency to lunge, sending me scurrying sideways but I was sure that Conchita would overlook these deficiencies in an otherwise archetypal tableau.

My mind returns to the books in front of me and the images of sunlit paths along sparkling streams are replaced by lines of curved, Italic script. The book has a complex structure with tales of the great Danielli's exploits interspersed with technical chapters on the magic of control.

"Making the fist of control with the fingers of his right hand the mage summons the fluttering spark from his breast and pours his powerful intellect into his subject."

The great Danielli constantly refers to his "fluttering spark". Sometimes it resides in his breast, sometimes in his temple and occasionally his loins. This last I can comprehend but, in that case, my fluttering spark seems to present me with an unfortunate lack of control. I have studied the diagrams carefully and I believe that I have correctly formed the fist of control but, as yet, I have been unable to release my powerful intellect nor identify my fluttering spark. Maybe the great Danielli speaks in metaphor and I need to unlock his coded script.

"As the mage is a great pine in the forest of the world, so his intellect is a great axe and is guided by the fluttering spark he summons from his belly as fire is called from a piece of flint and catches in the tinder of a mind."

To the side of our path lay a small grove of trees and beyond the trees to the north was a wood. To the north the wood thickened and became a forest and beyond that lay the Castle of Lovers. The road continued westward and so we turned aside and began to stroll amongst the low olive and pine trees. That night we camped in the woodland, a pretty little blaze warming our bodies as we lay gazing at the stars glinting between the branches above. The old trunks around us groaned softly as the wind whispered through the limbs above. The dark surrounded us and seemed more complete than ever once the fire had burned down to a soft glow and sleep began to intrude upon my consciousness. I slept deeply and dreamed richly but incoherently so that when I woke the next morning I had an impression of ancient tales my sleeping self had observed but retained nothing but a sense of age and calm in the forest around.

We had come further than we had thought the night before and what had seemed like a copse on a wooded hillside when we camped was shown in the light of day to be a comparative clearing in a great and ancient forest. We breakfasted enthusiastically and continued northward once more. Our path led between great trunks it would take six men to encircle and above us the tall conifers seemed to reach the sky. The track was soft with pine needles dropped from above over a hundred winters and littered with cones, their petals open and their seeds long since flown. The forest was sheltered from any wind and the dappled sunlight was warm and soft. We hiked onwards and, for the first time since leaving home, my mind was not confused by thoughts of the future, of Conchita and her response on my return or of my life as a great sorcerer. Instead, I revelled in the walk, enjoying the woodland, the ancient trees and the bright white flowers springing from among the decaying brown litter.

Hours passed in silent contentment, even Cleopatra seeming mellowed by the surroundings. Through the trees ahead of us we saw a small hill rising out of the forest and perched at the top, a ruined tower. Drawn by curiosity, we turned towards it and, although we occasionally lost sight of the tower among the trees, bent our footsteps in its direction. As we drew closer we found that our first impression had been misleading and that, far from being a lonely tower, our ruin was that of a great castle with battlements, barbican and portcullis. Finally we emerged from amongst the trees and as we climbed the slope towards it we saw that what we had taken for a ruin in the half light of evening was, in fact, in fine repair and that a flag fluttered from the central keep. Curiosity drove us on, what kind of noble lived in the centre of this deserted forest?

We reached the castle door as the last crescent of sun dipped swiftly over the horizon, a purple shade of dusk chasing the glorious flame from the tips of the trees below us. We knocked loudly and were surprised by the promptness with which the door opened.

"Sirs, welcome and come in. The ball is about to commence." I stared at the slim gentleman standing in front of us dressed in a green and silver livery. Were we expected at this strange court or was there a case of mistaken identity. I stammered, confused.

"Lord Thengol Greydog," my master said, handing his coat to the butler, "and this is my confederate Riff Raff. I trust you will take care of my beast."

"Indeed sirs, now pass this way," he replied, relieving me of my cloak and beckoning to another servant who led a surprisingly docile Cleopatra through a side door.

We were escorted through the great entrance hall towards a set of double doors at the far end and I gazed around, trying to absorb as much of my surroundings as possible. The floor was polished marble of different colours; the stones had been cut to make irregular patterns and the craft was so fine that I could see no join but the sudden change in hue. The walls were of pale birch inlaid with gold in a fascinating intricacy of which I could make nothing. The ceiling above was covered with great flags and banners, deep blue and gold bearing the crest of a silver crown set above the greenwood. Light filled the hall from chandeliers carrying hundreds of tiny candles. We reached the far doors and the butler flung them open and announced,

"The Lord Thengol Greydog and his confederate Riff Raff."

A crowd of faces turned to look at us and I felt terror and shame as I remembered my soiled hiking gear and compared it with the guests now staring at me. Their dress sense ranged from elegant to opulent and passed through untold richness in between. The gentlemen wore hose and doublets of silk and carried fine jewelled swords and the ladies wore gowns of such colour and detail that the dance floor seemed ablaze. I stared around, looking from face to face, struck by the beauty and style of the whole company and regretting my simple and unfavoured appearance.

Then the crowd parted and my attention was drawn to two figures seated at the far end of the ballroom. One was a man, smooth of face but with ancient green eyes that gazed calmly into my soul. His hair was silver and drawn back from his forehead into a long ponytail that was tied at his waist with a blue jewelled band. He wore a suit of blue and gold cut simply but perfectly. On his head he wore a silver crown. I turned to look at his companion and once I looked I neither saw nor thought of aught else. She was truly the most lovely creature ever to have existed. Her face was a perfect oval set about by golden tresses and lit by eyes that sparkled as emeralds. Her gown was of the palest blue and curved protectively over breast and thigh. Her feet were white, perfectly formed and bare and, on her ankle, she wore a golden bangle that chimed when she stirred. My heart beat like a hammer in my chest, I forgot my soiled clothing and untoward appearance, I forgot my wonder at my surroundings, I forgot my master and my quest and, when she beckoned to me with a perfect white hand, I walked helplessly between the lines of dancers and knelt before her.

"Arise, Sir Riff Raff," she said and laughed, a peal of tiny bells that echoed gently around the chamber. I stood and waited. She patted a footstool beside her and I sat, gazing up at her loveliness. She turned to her husband and said,

"I like this one, he amuses me."

He then beckoned to Thengol Greydog who made his haughty way across the ballroom and nodded curtly.

"Milord, milady," he said. There was a long pause as the couple looked first at Thengol, then at each other and then back to the mage in front of them.

"This one is not so amusing." The man nodded his agreement.

"The Comptessa desires entertainment at her ball, have you talents with which to dazzle us?" he asked.

"I am no jester to perform tricks and tell tales at the behest of a petty nobleman and it becomes you ill to suggest such a thing."

66

"Then you shall dance," the Compte decided. My master looked shocked and was about to say that he should do no such thing when the orchestra struck up with a swift jig that was filled with such energy that he couldn't restrain himself and began to tap his feet and hop around, swinging his arms in time with the players. The beautiful Comptessa laughed and clapped her hands.

"Now that is amusing," she cried and tapped out the rhythm on her satin knee. The ball recommenced and I was brought a goblet of wine and sat gazing at the beauty beside me whilst all around people danced and laughed. There was more wine and food of which I remember almost nothing, entranced as I was by the wonder of her voice, her hair, her skin. Throughout the night Thengol Greydog danced, a jig, a reel, a gavotte. He seemed as tireless in his enjoyment of the music as I was in my infatuation. Finally dawn came and the revellers retired, some still dancing and I was led by a young footman to a four poster bed in a large bedroom. I sank down between the soft sheets and slipped swiftly into a deep, dreamless slumber.

The next morning I awoke to find a steaming bowl of hot water on the table beside my bed, soft towels to dry myself and breakfast set out on a table by the window. In a pile on a chair were fine clothes as befitted my position as a guest of the Compte and Comptessa. Immediately I had washed, dressed and finished my second plateful a knock came on the door and a green liveried servant entered.

"Your presence is requested in the council chamber. If you would follow me." Eagerly I walked behind him, taking in the long corridors and mysterious portraits that hung on the walls, so cunningly made that the eyes seemed to follow me as I strode past. We came down a steep and narrow spiral staircase and I found myself back in the ballroom of the previous night. Now, however, I found that the orchestra and the crowd had left and my noble hosts sat at the head of a long table. If anything she was more beautiful than she had been the night before, her hair tied back in a practical style and her glorious figure enhanced by a dark, closely fitting woollen gown. She beckoned to me and I sat in a tall wooden seat on her right.

It seemed that members of the court had the right to petition their Lord on any subject and the day passed with a constant stream of visitors making their requests and being answered. Some left satisfied and pleased with the verdict and some were led away sobbing as the decision had gone against them but all left with a bow or a curtsey and all deposited a silver coin with the doorman as payment for the hearing. I listened only cursorily to the cases that appeared before us, besotted as I was by the beauty on my left. During one of the longer and more tedious affairs which concerned a stolen egg and the vengeance exacted upon the thief, I started to compose a ballad of love which I would dedicate to the Comptessa and sing at the next feast.

I shudder as I remember my foolishness and delve once more into the mysteries before me. I realise now, of course, that we had strayed upon a Faerie court and that I was under the control of a magical spell. This is what has inspired me to study the works of Danielli; if a mere Faerie can take such a powerful hold on a mage's mind then what limits can true magic have? One of the tales in the book is of a visit by the author to a Faerie castle and it seems that he had a similar reception to the one I received. He, however, was well practised in the arts of control and was able to resist the full effects of the enchantment and, gathering his fluttering spark to his powerful intellect made his escape. I shake myself and seek once more for the key to Danielli's code. If only my master would explain the secrets of control to me then I would make great strides in my mastery of magic. Unfortunately Thengol Greydog continues to belittle the magic of control explaining that it is a lesser talent, subservient to creation and destruction.

The second night was marked by another ball and again I sat at the Comptessa's feet, gazing adoringly at her beautiful face. My master had absented himself from the festivities and the entertainment was provided by a squat little man with a bald head and enormous feet who amazed the guests by juggling three, four or five live piglets who squealed as they were flung through the air. The Comptessa found this hilarious and, when the piglets soiled themselves in flight and dung was sprayed across an unfortunate courtier, she cackled loudly.

At dawn the ball ended and I was escorted once again to my chamber where I sank, exhausted, into unconsciousness. The next morning followed the pattern of the one before and I found myself half listening to a stream of complaints and appeals as I considered the beautiful lines of my hostess' ears. I had chanced upon a promising metaphor describing her face as a perfect ideal anointed with shells of purest pearl and was searching for suitable rhymes when a man in a fool's cap came in leading a troop of dancing skeletons. I abandoned my poetry and turned to examine them more closely. The fool was old, with a weathered face and bells on the end of his shoes. Behind him were five dancing figures and I realised that, whilst the first two were clearly skeletons, their white bones clinking against the stone floor, the remaining three were not picked so clean. The third was a decaying corpse with grey, mouldering flesh; the fourth appeared to be on the verge of life and would occasionally blink his eyes open before fluttering back into whatever coma he inhabited and the fifth was my master Thengol Greydog. All five were dancing energetically to an inaudible tune. I stared in horror as Thengol looked to me, his eyes a mute appeal for help and I turned to the Comptessa looking for some kind of release for these unfortunates. Instead of compassion in her eyes I saw a smile spread across her beautiful face and continue to spread until it became a grimace and finally a rictus. What I had thought the most perfect visage was revealed as little more than a grinning skull, skin pulled taut across dry bones with wicked green eyes glinting cruelly from the dark sockets. My stomach turned, I retched and vomited profusely across the polished surface of the table.

The Comptessa screamed and slapped me, her withered hand striking my face like the bound twigs of an ancient broom. The Compte banged on the table and I found myself grabbed by two bronze-armoured guards and hustled out of the room as the fool and his dancers were dismissed from the noble presence. I was rushed down a stone-flagged passage way, tripping and stumbling as my captors ran. My knees were skinned and my shins bruised by the time they flung open a door and hurled me into a bleak, cold cell.

I lay there for some time, shivering and gazing sightlessly at the ceiling. My whole being revolted at the thought of the Comptessa. My imaginings of the last two days seemed horrible to me now, especially the fantasies I'd had of the Compte departing on business and leaving the two of us together. I shuddered and retched at the thought of that dry and brittle skin being lowered tenderly to the silken sheets of a four poster bed, my hands gently sliding the silken gown away from her withered breasts, all the time that ghastly death's head smiling up at me.

Hours passed and the chill of the cell crept through my clothes and filled my limbs. I pulled myself up of the floor and huddled under a coarse woollen blanket on the rough slat that served as a bed. The nature of the court was now clear to me, as was the dire predicament in which my master and I found ourselves. It was clear that the Comptessa held us in her power and seemed unlikely that she would show mercy and allow us to go free. A lifetime of thrall might extend into an eternity if the tale of the skeleton dancers was to be believed. My mind raced over possible means of escape and I explored my cell thoroughly finding only four solid stone walls, a solid, stone-flagged floor and a thick oaken door which was, unfortunately, also solid. I picked at the flagstones, seeking to lift them from the earth below but the skill that had produced the enchanting mosaic in the entrance hall had worked here to prevent any purchase in the gaps between the limestone slabs. I tapped on each stone, hoping to hear a hollow echo or some other sign of weakness but gained only sore knuckles and a whistling in my ears. At last I sank, exhausted, onto the bed and dropped into an uncomfortable and fitful sleep disturbed by dreams of seductive skeletons and a maggot ridden bride.

I spent two days alone in that cold and gloomy cell. My continued searches found no new weakness in my prison and my mind produced no great plan for escape. Despair began to haunt me as I lay, slipping from consciousness into sleep and back again, sensing nothing and dreaming only ill. As the long hours slipped by so my past life drifted away and began to forget my companions, the trip to Africa and even my home at the Castle of Lovers. Once more I became a frightened little boy in the lair of the Philosopher Beast and more than once I awoke with a start, rushing to my feet to return to the card table. As I regressed the sea once more intruded on my dreams, waves playing mischievously across the unending surface of the pale blue ocean. In my mind, the sun glinted on the swell and I breathed deep, my lungs filled with unfettered sea air. This breath of freedom never lasted, however, and the clear skies quickly gave way to black storm clouds and bright lightning. The waves splashed around me and crashed over my head, I grasped at infrequent opportunities to fill my lungs with spray-laden water and slowly, inevitably I felt myself dragged under. The dark seas closed above my head, I struggled hopelessly one last time and gave myself up to the deep. As I released the last bubbles of air from my lungs and began to draw the fatal breath of salt-water I would awake, alive but imprisoned and acutely aware that my only hope for escape was through the door of death.

On the third day, I heard steps in the passageway and a key in the lock. I sat upright as my cell door creaked open and the Comptessa herself entered. Dressed once more in a cornflower gown and with her hair braided with gold and coiled upon her head she was again the image of purest beauty.

"There seems to have been a mistake my Lord Riff-Raff," she murmured, her voice as captivating as her appearance. "If you will return with me to the ball, I will see if we can make amends."

My heart quickened and I swallowed. Discarding my soiled blanket, I stood and stepped towards her. As I did she held out her soft, white hand and smiled at me. Instantly the illusion was broken and I saw her for the grinning skull that she was. I tried to hide my horror but the disgust must have shown in her eyes for she turned away without a word and slammed the door behind her. The hope that had filled me drained away and left me emptier than I had been before her visit.

I sat, dejected, on the bed knowing that my last chance had come and gone. If only I had remembered the illusion then perhaps I could have prepared myself and hidden the horror. If only I had never seen through her beauty I could have spent a lifetime in delightful servitude. I stiffened; delightful it may have been but servitude it certainly was and the future I'd planned for myself as the great Riff-Raff, mighty sorcerer and wealthy lord would not allow me to give myself up to slavery. That future seemed distant and inaccessible as I sat, cold and desolate, in the cell pondering the rest of what seemed likely to be a brief and painful lifetime.

Some time later footsteps came down the passageway and my door was flung open once more. I remembered the butler who had greeted us on our arrival and was immediately awash with memories of life before I met Her.

"The Compte and Comptessa congratulate you on your intellect but deplore your lack of wisdom. They offer you free passage and wish you to leave their lands immediately." I blinked and stuttered. "The alternative is execution. Decide immediately."

"And Thengol?" I asked, unthinking.

"You may take your confederate and your strange creature with you if you leave." I nodded, no words would come to my mouth.

The butler led me out of the cell, along a series of corridors and out into a courtyard where Thengol and Cleopatra awaited me. He was slumped against a wall, his boots worn through and his feet bleeding. She lay at his side wearing some kind of harness fashioned by the faerie children to ride her. I helped my confederate to his feet and half carried him out of the gates and back into the forest. Dusk was falling as we stumbled down the hillside and I turned to see the last rays of the sun illuminate an old ruined tower on the top of a small hillock.

It was a day's hike from the Compte's castle to the Castle of Lovers but it took us three as Thengol was exhausted and his feet badly injured. It was again dusk when we arrived at the gatehouse and answered the familiar challenge. Three sorry looking figures, one limping and being half carried by the second whilst the third skulked behind looking ashamed of herself. As we entered the old tower to return to Thengol's rooms I saw Conchita looking out from the kitchen door smiling proudly. For an instant all my lusts were reawakened for the moment I had dreamed of had finally became a reality. I turned to her, heart beating, legs shaking as my mind struggled to recall the scene I had been rehearsing for months but as I did her smiling face seemed to dissolve into a grinning skull. I shuddered and turned from her. Never again will I be bewitched by a pretty face for I know that the image of the Comptessa will live with me forever.

Night has fallen in the council room and my mind is exhausted from striving to comprehend the great Danielli. I let the book fall closed and promise myself that I will return tomorrow to glean what I can from his convoluted journal. Gazing out of the window, I see Braun returning to the castle. As he negotiates with the sentries, I slip out of the room and run downstairs. I hide myself in the gloom beside the new building and listen to the irregular footsteps approach.

"Hello little Braun." I step out of the shadows and surprise him as he reaches the doorway.

"Oh, it's you, what do you want?"

"Just my peg of chaim," I reply cheerfully.

"What?"

"Each year the eldest apprentice gets one of the pebbles of fire. It's an ancient custom."

"I didn't know."

"Well, it's a good job I told you then. I'm the eldest apprentice so give me the chaim and we'll say no more."

"I think, maybe, I should check with my master." Braun is getting very nervous now.

"Masters are busy people, they wouldn't want to be bothered with a thing like this. We can sort it out ourselves if you just stop wasting my time."

"I'm not sure."

"Look Braun, if you want to disappoint your master and look like a pathetic little fool then you can, but otherwise you'll just give me the

72

wretched pebble." I see him waver and then reach into his pouch. He hands me a piece of flint and, as my hand closes around the magical fragment, I close my eyes. I relish the possibilities afforded me by pure magic and my soul thrills as I take one more step towards becoming a great wizard. Braun looks at me, puzzled, and then turns and steps inside out of the rain.

I stand here, feeling the last drops of the storm fall and enjoying the sensation of power. I can see that Darius' apprentice could be a useful addition to the Castle of Lovers.

The Ninth Year

"After FIFTEEN *Years, the Apprentice shall be ready; for the* SIXTEENTH *year is the year of fulfilment,* SIXTEEN *being* FOUR *times* FOUR, *the Square of the Covenant number. His Master shall set him a challenge and, should he pass it, he will become a Full Mage of the Covenant, no longer Apprentice but* FILIUS, *son of the magic. Any Apprentice who fails his Master's Challenge shall be Slain."*

From the Law of the Covenant of The Castle of The Lovers

Rain pours down. Lightning flashes. Thunder booms. I collect a peg of chaim. Rain continues to pour. Lightning flashes again. Thunder booms once more. I collect more chaim. Rain. Lightning. Thunder. Chaim.

What am I doing on top of the Fire Hills collecting chaim when I should be in the council room studying? Darius and his wretched apprentice who should, by rights, be up here soaking wet have gone on a trip. It is important that they "learn the secrets of the wilds". This is clearly an excuse to avoid a tedious chore and leaves me to do the work of others. It also gave the Lady Adriel an opportunity to remind me of my position within the Covenant. Her rank is Lato, third most senior High Mage after the Courtesan and Thengol Greydog. My rank is apprentice. I am Thengol's property to be dealt with as he chooses. Not even my actions are my own and he must take responsibility for all I do.

Over the last twelve months Thengol has once more been obsessed with Cleopatra and arranged with the Lady Adriel that I should serve her for a year and that she should share with me the secrets of the magic of change. This is a subtle art, lacking to my mind the simplicity of control but offering many opportunities to the mage who masters it. Darius' shapeshifting is a manifestation of this power but a limited one; the true master can change any aspect of anything; the possibilities are endless.

The Lady Adriel is strange; haughty and proud, her deafness seems to add to her grandeur. She is tall and aristocratic with steel grey hair and eyes that burn with fire. It is those eyes that reveal her origins; their flames are green for the Lady Adriel is of faerie blood. Her mother was a human and her father one of the Sidhe, a princeling of some mystical court. She grew up torn between two worlds and, although her magic has carved for her a niche in the world, she retains a sense of lostness; neither one thing nor another, she admits to no allegiance and expects no loyalty.

She quizzed me deeply on my stay in the faerie court for apparently she has had some dealing with the Comptessa. My description of the Comptessa's smile when I saw through the illusion caused her great amusement and she laughed at my discomfort when she asked me to retell the scene. That laugh shone a light on Adriel's split personality; in so many ways she is a human mage, power hungry and calculating, but for a second I saw her faerie side, abandoning herself to laughter at the thought of another's humiliation.

Her workroom also shows this tension; scattered between the instruments of artifice and hand-written parchments there is much taken from nature. Flowers of heartbreaking beauty decorate her desk and her shelves are covered with twisted bones and deformed roots. A mosquito trapped in amber sits as a weight on her desk and the thought of the living insect trapped within the sticky resin causes her much amusement. As I worked for her, cleaning, tidying, holding and fetching I learned that these items were neither an affectation nor mere decoration but an integral part of her magic; in every spell the Lady Adriel casts and in each enchantment she creates a small piece of Faerie twists and inspires.

Rain, lightning, thunder and chaim, my mind wanders as I mechanically collect the precious flints. I think of the small lives of the farmers and herdsmen in the valley below, living under the shelter of our castle and yet understanding so little of what we do. I laugh when I think of the fair that has built up outside the castle gate; hundreds of visitors living in temporary shelters, buying overpriced food and trinkets from dozens of traders and all drawn by the mad priest. So many people so close to true power and yet diverted by a lunatic on a pole.

For as long as anyone can remember, for longer than my apprenticeship, Father Juan Sanchez has been part of our Covenant. He has held mass for the faithful soldiers and servants every Sunday in the mysterious "D" room and has argued passionately with the mages on every detail of his mistaken theology. He views them as heretics doomed to eternity in hell and they view him as a hypocrite, keen to abuse the ignorance of the uneducated. Rather surprisingly then, he is a valued member of our covenant whose honesty and piety are respected by all and who serves as a judge for the local peasants as well as for the mundane members of the covenant.

In the autumn of last year, Father Juan became troubled by his conscience, which, it seems, was telling him that his soul was imperilled by such close association with witches and heretics. Consequently, he began to carry a whip with him and to beat himself regularly. Thus his weak flesh would be reminded of the purity expected of it and his spirit would be purged from all evil taint.

At the festival of the solstice, brandy and seasonal excitement drew him into a detailed defence of the sanctity of Christmas against the twin prongs of Lady Adriel's assertion that Christ was a faerie changeling and the Courtesan's claim that the whole story was an allegory for the discovery of an apprentice. The next morning he was overcome with guilt and remorse and, with the help of Antonio and Lopez, he brought the trunk of a pine tree from the forest and raised it outside the Covenant walls. They stripped the bark off and constructed a small platform at the top. Once this strange device was made secure by six long ropes tied to pegs in the ground, Father Juan climbed to the top carrying his Bible, a bucket and a coil of rope. Since then, he has remained at the top of his pole. Every Sunday morning he reads a mass to those who assemble round the base of this strange pillar. Every morning and evening his bucket does duty to remove waste and to deliver bread and water and every hour he whips himself to retain his purity. The rest of his time is spent in study and meditation.

Word of Father Juan's behaviour soon spread among the local peasants who flocked to see him and to hear his service on Sunday. People started to bring relatives from the next village and one Sunday in February we had a visitor from Barcelona. That was the first drop in a mighty torrent; word has spread across Christendom of the holy man on his pole and folk from every nation have come to worship nearby. Those without friends or family in the district brought tents and soon the ground by the covenant walls became a campsite. Some, more dedicated, devouts settled permanently and have built little huts in which to shelter. Soon Antonio and others saw an opportunity to raise a little cash and stalls have sprung up selling everything from splinters of the true cross to ale. Now the campsite has become a bustling market where farmers come to trade their goods, catch up with the gossip and gaze at the madman on his pole. A series of shelters have even been built that can be rented by the night at a very reasonable price and over it all Father Juan gazes, contemplates, meditates, prays and beats himself for the good of his soul.

The Lady Adriel likes to emphasise her faerie origins whenever the fair is mentioned.

"Humans," she'll spit, "always chasing after the latest fashion, following each other like sheep."

"But surely," I remonstrate, "you can't claim that the Courtesan or Thengol, or even Darius, for that matter, follow the herd. They, at least, have minds of their own."

"What's that?" she shouts, and I repeat myself, "Minds of their own? Well maybe, on some matters, but have you read their beloved constitution?" I look at her, puzzled. "It's in the library. 'The Law of the Covenant of the Castle of Lovers' and never have I seen such a pile of drivel. Don't tell them that, of course. The three of them live by it with their due process and their voting and their councils. So foolish, so human." She spits again.

The Law of the Covenant of the Castle of Lovers was laid down by Grumio the Wise as the community of wizards began to expand. Grumio and Juan had got along without the need for formal rules; Juan had deferred to the more senior wizard and they had avoided interference with each others' work. When Thengol arrived, this delicate balance was upset and the rule of non-interference was made concrete. Other rules followed as the junior wizards abused their responsibilities or infringed each others' rights and the document slowly took on its current form under which all decisions are made by the High Mages in council. Since Sparky Phosphortube joined the Covenant, seeking refuge from persecution as a necromancer, there have been four high mages making the decisions. The actual wizards in charge have changed over time; Grumio eventually died and Juan left after a particularly vehement quarrel with my master; in their place have come Lady Adriel and finally Darius Falconwing.

The Lady Adriel has little need of my services and no desire for my company most of the time and so I've been left to myself for much of the past year. Much of the time has been spent in study, either Danielli whose ideas continue to fascinate and elude or the tome on change through which the Lady Adriel is leading me. It is a copy of a work by Ovid, a Roman scholar, which has been annotated by an unknown wizard. Every page bears his or her spidery scrawl in the margins and the bindings strain under the weight of parchments glued into place across the original Latin poetry; diagrams, descriptions and elucidations direct the reader towards a fuller understanding of this delicate technique. I also spent time reading through the Law of the Covenant of the Castle of Lovers and was fascinated by the detailed rules which ran our community. Adriel was wrong to dismiss it as waste paper; here were structures and ideas which allowed four wizards with conflicting aims and desires to live in harmony, or at least to live together without destroying themselves. Nowhere in it is there a statute entitling the eldest apprentice to extort chaim from his younger colleagues but it is filled with rules that fit together to make an elegant edifice to balance the powers of the different magi.

The lightning has stopped and now I stand here; rain pours across my face, runs in a little stream across my shoulders and collects in the small of my back. I dare not leave until the storm abates and the rain stops; the lightning could strike at any time and I must be on hand to collect the chaim. I think of the visitors to the fair and pity those staying in tents or the poorly constructed shelters; a damp and unpleasant night lies ahead of them. I may be wretched now but warm dry clothes, hot, spiced wine and a blazing fire await me on my return to the castle. These are all courtesy of Conchita who now holds me in some esteem; enough, it seems, to provide me with some basic comforts in return for a small supplement to her wages. My new wealth comes from the fair; it is not only Antonio who has been growing rich these past few months.

On the March equinox I studied through the night, trying to extract some sense from Danielli at a magically charged time when opposing forces are balanced and a tiny effort on the part of a mage can shift the equilibrium in the desired direction. That, at least, was the plan suggested by Danielli's description of the solar cycle. Unfortunately my intellect towered insufficiently to shift any equilibrium and morning found me dejected and restless. I stole some bread and ham from the kitchen and made my way out to the fair. Out here the day was just beginning, travellers crawled stiffly from their sleep into the cold morning air. A fire had been lit and a fisherman was frying his catch for those who could afford it.

"Freshly caught trout! Local delicacy! Beautifully cooked by an expert! Get it whilst it's hot!"

The warm, smoky smell of the fish was tempting but magical coins would get me nothing here; only the most naïve of the traders were unaware of wizards' tricks. I shambled on, mind busy with the magic of control.

"Boy!"

"Hey, Boy!" I turned to see a gangling figure in well-worn travelling clothes.

"Unload my baggage, boy."

I thought about the best response and decided on a cutting retort when I saw that my target had turned his back and stalked away, his long legs suggesting elegance but belied by his clumsy step and crude features. Out of curiosity and a desire to earn enough real money to buy some fried trout I turned to where a pack mule stood tied next to one of the better shelters. I unfastened the harness, my fingers slow at this unfamiliar work and began to carry the heavy packages into the wood and canvas hut. The frame looked remarkably unstable and the roof hardly sufficient to keep off the rain but despite these deficiencies I knew that it was far better than most of the temporary buildings in this little settlement and would have been a considerable cost to my unknown employer.

Each parcel was wrapped in thick felt and tied with twine. Their sizes differed from long rolls the size of a man to squat lumps a foot wide. Their weights were, however, remarkably similar and I guessed that they had been packed to allow one man to load and unload the mule. As I finished the task and leant the last bundle against the pile of baggage the tall man returned.

"And while you're at it, I want the roof repaired; the canvas is far too thin." he was saying to his companion.

"Yes, your honour, this can all be done. Good morning sir." said Antonio, turning to me.

"Now boy, I want the bundles unpacked and then you can help me set up my stall outside." By now, I was fascinated. All the traders I had met so far had been small farmers from towns and villages nearby or local peasants seeking easy pickings. This was clearly a wealthy merchant who had travelled the Orient and the Northern wastes trading with exotic tribes to amass a great fortune.

Just in front of the shelter the merchant had erected a tall booth and, as I unpacked his bundles, was building shelves for his goods. Fine rugs, beautiful ornaments, spices, relics and rare books made up his stock and he displayed it with loving care as, behind us, Antonio worked on the merchant's living quarters. By mid-afternoon the stall was ready and, stepping outside, I saw that great improvements had been made to the little hut behind. The walls had been strengthened and attached more firmly to the ground, the roof had been replaced by a new piece of felt stretched across wooden struts and fastened to the ridge pole stood a brass weather vane.

"Only on loan, you understand sir, but it adds class to the dwelling," Antonio confided in me as he was sent off to hire a bodyguard.

"Now then boy," the merchant said, turning to me, "here are your wages for this morning's work." He gave me a handful of copper, "and I will pay you this silver coin to find out what is the most expensive item that can be bought in this fair." I drew myself up.

"I am not a street urchin to be bought for pennies, I am going to be a great wizard and my name is not 'Boy' but Riff-Raff." Of course, it would have sounded better if I had called myself 'The Great Rifrando' but it takes time to decide upon a new name.

"Well, Riff-Raff, the great wizard to be, I am Paulo and I will not insult you by offering you silver; instead, I will show you the magic of trade if you run my errands." I looked at him suspiciously but curiosity maintained its hold and I agreed.

By the time I had made my way around each of the traders and established that the most expensive item was a small bronze cross said to have been given to Father Juan by the most holy man in Italy, I was exhausted. I relayed the information to Paulo and after agreeing to return at dawn I stumbled, yawning, back through the gatehouse to the covenant and my bed.

I slept soundly and awoke just as the first sunlight crept across the grey hills to the east. Dressing swiftly, I ran across the courtyard and out to the fair, eager to learn what I could of this new magic. Outside Paulo's stall, I met Mongrol standing guard with a fierce look in his eye. I nodded to him as I passed. The interior of the stall had been draped with rich purple materials and this somehow added to the allure of the costly goods. I wondered how the merchant thought he could sell these things to the visitors to the fair. When I asked him Paulo just smiled. I pointed out that he had chosen a poor position for his stall, away from the main centre of the market where the other stalls clustered and jostled to be the first to reach their clients. Paulo smiled again.

"Just wait," he said.

Nobody else entered the stall throughout the whole day and I grew bored; this was not a new magic, it was foolishness. I fidgeted and stamped my feet, flicked the trinkets and rubbed the cloths. Paulo continued to smile. At lunchtime I took my coins and bought myself some fish which I took down to the riverside and ate gazing into the swift flowing water. I was tempted to abandon the market and return to my books but found myself retracing my steps, unwilling to give up without discovering the source of Paulo's confidence.

The afternoon passed as had the morning and sunset came without bringing any custom. We could hear the other stall holders packing up their goods and their profits as darkness came and the pilgrims retired to make the best of their sorry beds. I pulled myself together and rubbed my arms to keep out the cold. A whole day wasted and I had to clean the Lady Adriel's rooms before I could go to bed. Then a customer arrived, a carpenter who sold rosary beads and other trinkets to the pilgrims. He gazed admiringly around the stall and fingered the cloths that hung from the shelves.

"Fine they'd look in my stall," he mused. Paulo smiled.

"Fine my goods would look laid on these in my stall." Paulo smiled again.

"How much for a bolt of this purple?" he asked. Paulo smiled and named a price twice that of the cross I'd found the night before.

"A fine price for fine goods," the carpenter nodded and counted out the coins. Paulo smiled and handed over the material.

Once the carpenter had left, Paulo packed away his wares and Mongrol settled down to sleep across the entrance to the stall. I wandered back to the castle musing on a strange end to a strange day.

I had to work for the Lady Adriel the next morning and it wasn't until noon that I was able to walk through the fair, listening to the calls of the traders and the mutters of the pilgrims as they sat in meditation at the foot of Father Juan's pole or wandered between the shelters looking for inspiration or a cheap meal. I saw the carpenter's stall looking very smart in its purple raiment and surrounded by pilgrims drawn to his woodcraft. Other, less busy, traders looked on enviously and I began to guess that Paulo might see more custom when evening fell. So it proved and, as the days and weeks went by, the fair became increasingly luscious with decoration and frippery dripping from every stall. Pilgrims continued to arrive, traders came from further afield and the trickle of wealth passing our gatehouse became a stream and finally a torrent as wealthy nobles brought their families on pilgrimages to atone for untold sins. Through it all Paulo dominated proceedings, always setting his prices higher than the other traders and never compromising on luxury. Rather than selling to the pilgrims he bought from those who had underestimated the drain on their purses. The goods he obtained in this way were hidden for a day or two, polished and set on the shelves to be sold for a three or four-fold profit.

I learned no magic this spring but was fascinated by the power Paulo commanded with his knowledge of human nature and the value of the trinkets he bought and sold. By keeping my eyes open and being alert to free-spending noblemen or traders with a cash-flow problem I was able to put my education into practice. I hoarded and gambled with my new wealth rather like the Philosopher beast had done in his cave and, following that precedent, I acquired a substantial fortune. I was fascinated by this game and enthralled by the grip that money had over my fellow men. Without summoning any magical power I was able to manipulate them to hand over goods in exchange for cash or coins for my wares. By playing on their fears, desires and needs I was able to get a price that was always in my favour. This kind of control over hearts and minds was like and yet unlike the power described by Danielli and I was entranced.

The Lady Adriel was, of course, dismissive of the fair.

"So human, so futile."

"Faeries do not have fairs then?"

"What's that? Not have fairs? Of course they do, great meetings of folk from across the realm; there are stalls, side-shows and entertainment beyond the wildest dreams of mere humans."

"Then why do you throw scorn on the one outside our gates?"

"There's no need to shout, young man. The difference is that faeries go to fairs to take part, it's all a game; humans take it so seriously; they seem to think that religion or money are important. Faeries know that amusement is the only real reason to do anything." I smiled to myself, "What are you grinning at now?"

"Well, you take such a lofty position and yet you get entangled with human affairs yourself," I replied. "Take the constitution. You complain about due process and votes and meetings and yet you go to every council and vote on how much chaim to allow Thengol this season. You're as caught up with the politics as any of the others."

"Well, it amuses me to see Señor Greydog turn up, expecting to win every vote with his similarity to something triangular, and then lose as Darius and I refuse to fund his wild schemes and the Courtesan stolidly maintains the status quo."

"You're caught up in human politics and couldn't give it up." There was a long pause as she considered her position.

"Well, maybe I am a little entangled but I could easily untangle myself." I looked uncertain. "Look you, I'll not vote in Council for seven years and then you can eat your words."

"Yes, but you must attend the meetings, you could easily disappear into Faerieland for seven years and not even notice time passing," I challenged her.

"Very well, it will be an amusing break."

The rain stops suddenly with a final thunderbolt scorching the ground yards from my feet. I look up in surprise, grab the hot flint and add it to my collection before shaking the water from my hair and starting down the hillside. Next year I'm to continue my work with the Lady Adriel who will teach me the secrets of vegetable matter. I shall learn how flowers are made and how life and death are built into the seasonal cycle. I look down at the castle where my comforts await. What once seemed enormous and dominating now looks small beside the sprawl of the fair and the world beyond my home offers opportunities and adventures that I would not have considered a few short months ago.

In six years I shall complete my apprenticeship and become a full member of the covenant, free to take part in Council meetings and to have my own rooms and maybe take on my own apprentice. Whenever I've considered my future before this is what I'd assumed; a role as the most junior mage in the Covenant of the Castle of the Lovers. Freedom is what I've sought, a life without obligation, an existence without a master. Now, I see an alternative to the futility of attending meetings where I would have no vote and attempting to persuade Thengol Greydog to offer me a handful of chaim. Of course, I will have to complete Thengol's challenge before I become a full mage, but I have confidence I will succeed. My whole life lies beyond that challenge, the whole world lies beyond our gates and there must be many swifter paths to greatness than awaiting gradual promotion at home. As once I plotted to escape the Philosopher Beast now I lie awake at night seeking inspiration to accelerate my rise to greatness. I haven't yet found the burst of inspiration I require but I remain alert to opportunity and now, for the first time, have knowledge and understanding that eludes the High Mages; I know something of how the fair works, of how the greed of others can be put to ones own advantage.

The Tenth Year

"As LOVERS squabble, so shall there be Times of Discord. In case of Disagreement that cannot be Resolved by Due Process then shall one Mage issue a Proper Challenge to another. The Proper Challenge shall then be Resolved according to ANCIENT CUSTOM. At no other time shall one Mage of the Covenant of the Castle of Lovers attack another, nor his Property, his Apprentices or his Wizardry on pain of Banishment."

From the Law of the Covenant of The Castle of The Lovers

𝔐y back aches. My legs ache. Fiery pains burn through my arms. All day I've been cleaning Greydog's rooms and now I'm expected to remove decades of soot and filth from the walls and return them to their original shade of yellow. My knuckles are skinned and dried tracks of blood leak across the back of my hands. Outside it is midsummer and the storm is about to break but that will bring no relief to the heat in here for a fire burns fiercely in the grate. Sweat streams down my face, across my shoulders and pools in the small of my back. My eyes are dazzled and my wits dazed from the light reflecting from the brightly polished mantel. Aye, I've cleaned that an' all and I have a tight red burn on my forearm for my troubles. Last year I would have told Greydog to stuff this waste of time that keeps me from my studies. In fact, last year I did tell Greydog to stuff a waste of time that promised to keep me from my studies.

"I want you to dig a trench," he told me, handing me a shovel.

"A trench, Thengol?" I asked.

"Round the outside of the walls for the zombie dogs to guard," he clarified.

"Zombie dogs, Thengol?" I asked vacantly.

"It's a security issue," he told me. "Come back when you've done and we'll start work on the dogs."

Does he think I am some kind of slave to be ordered around? A menial serf to satisfy his whim? I am a mage and I will be great. The library called to me, books filled with words of the wise, tomes of terrible lore. The Lady Adriel's rooms called to me, a place I could learn subtle magics and develop my talents. The world called to me, demanding that I fulfil my promise and attain greatness; I just didn't see how I was to do that by digging a trench for imaginary zombie dogs.

"Get someone else to dig the trench for you Thengol, I'm busy."
I told him. A look of anger crossed his face, his brows bristled and
scurried towards his nose. I hastened to appease him. "You could ask
Mongrol," I suggested, "or you could dig it yourself."

As I spoke, the face behind Greydog's beard turned paler and his
eyes tightened until they were small black holes in a chalky face.

"Or you could forget about the zombie dogs idea altogether and
we could both get on with something constructive..." I faltered as my
master closed his eyes and began to repeat a phrase to himself. As he
mumbled his colour changed again, blood seeping back into his cheeks,
his temples deepening in shade; gradually the pallor faded away and still
the hue deepened, pink, puce, red, scarlet until even his chin was purple
behind the beard. His eyelids flickered open, his arms reached forwards,
his right hand relaxed and open, his left held up with the palm towards
me. He snarled an incantation and a spark glowed between his hands,
growing as he spoke until he held a great fireball between his palms.

"A quarrelsome apprentice is worse than none," he grunted
pulling his palms towards his body and I saw burning death approaching.

"I'm sorry, great master, I didn't understand. I see now, zombie
dogs, what a fine idea. Security, that's what we need. I was wrong to
question it. What could be more fruitful than digging. Where is that
spade," I gabbled, my eyes fixed on the glowing sphere before me as it
pulsed between those ancient palms. "I'm sorry, great master, forgive
me." I stepped backwards, feeling for the wall and still those eyes looked
at me, black pools reflecting the orange glow. I sidled round the room to
the door, grabbed the spade, turned and fled expecting to feel the searing
pain of magical fire roasting my back. Instead I heard a hollow laugh as
the door slammed behind me.

I ran across the courtyard and through the gate. Not until I was
safely out of sight of the new tower did I stop to catch my breath and
consider the best place to start digging. It all seemed rather irrelevant as
the plan was clearly insane. There are no zombie dogs. Zombie dogs
would be a liability as far as security goes. Why would anyone keep
zombie dogs in a trench. What was I thinking about, there are no zombie
dogs. I began to dig, the anger and terror I felt releasing themselves in
hard labour. Four hours later, I had a small pit that would be great if we
had one, rather small and elderly zombie dog that needed a grave. This
being unlikely on all counts I lifted the shovel onto my shoulder and
knocked on the gatehouse door. A peal of laughter came from behind the
gate and as it opened the feckless sentries giggled,

85

"I see you have been very busy"

"Stranger or Lover?" My temper snapped and I swung the spade round through the air until I held it half an inch from Hawkeye's stupid face.

"What's it to you?" I snarled.

"Oh, yes, Lover," he stammered.

"I see you'd like to come in," said Siero, backing away as I turned towards him. I strode through the courtyard as they grovelled behind me. At least, that's what happened inside my head. In real life my arms are feeble and exhausted and I muttered "Lover" and trudged through the courtyard trying to ignore the laughter behind me.

I sit back on my haunches, rubbing my arms, trying to relieve the burning that fills them. My position is clear; if Greydog tells me to scrub his rooms until they shine then I must scrub. Fortunately he is likely to tire of this enterprise within a couple of days. The trench lies abandoned six feet long and filled with rainwater; it seems that the zombie dogs will be able to guard the castle just as well without a trench. Even allowing for the short attention span, Greydog's chores have been an imposition that has kept me from more interesting work. I have studied diligently in the library and know the writings of the Great Danielli almost by heart. Unfortunately this knowledge has not brought me understanding and it has become clear to me that no amount of study will buy me the secrets of control; I need a tutor. Greydog cannot help me, he so lacks control of himself that it is clear he can teach me nothing of this subtle art. I had hoped that the Lady Adriel might condescend to reveal these secrets to me but when I raised the subject she just laughed and told me that she couldn't teach me without the agreement of my master. Again, my plans are thwarted by that half-wit. The Courtesan and Darius Falconwing are governed by the same restriction and so I returned to my books in despair.

Gazing from the windows of the library one morning I saw Mongrol and Lopez training in the courtyard. My head was spinning from my attempts to decipher a particularly poorly formed script and the warm sunshine drew me outside to watch. Mace and morningstar clashed, feet danced and sweat streamed down the faces of the straining warriors. Finally, by some unspoken agreement they lowered their weapons and stood there blowing.

"Bloody good training today Mongrol."

"Yes, Mongrol nearly had you there. Nearly Smosh through your defences."

"Bollocks through my defences," the two grinned at each other.

"What are you training for Mongrol?" I asked. "Are we likely to be attacked?"

"There's always danger. Always enemies. Always faeries to smosh." The chain round his neck seemed to twitch and Mongrol reached up to try to pull it from his windpipe, "No, not faeries, good faeries, Mongrol loves faeries, never smosh," he cried in a panicked voice.

"Bollocks faeries," grunted Lopez and then turned to glower at a small white cloud passing overhead. "Bollocks rain," he added.

As Mongrol clutched at the silver chain round his neck and as his face faded from the deep purple hue it had assumed, I was struck by a solution to my problem. I did know someone who was a master of control, someone who was not governed by the rules of the Castle of Lovers. Strictly speaking, of course, the Comptessa would be a mistress of control and was not currently well disposed towards me. Still, she had once found me amusing and it was her particular mastery of control that had lit this burning fire of curiosity within me. I turned from the gasping Mongrol and ran up to Adriel's rooms.

"I'll ask the Comptessa to teach me. She can teach me about control," I spluttered, slightly out of breath from the run upstairs.

"Eh? What's that? Make yourself useful boy, hold this." I stood, patiently holding a fir cone as Adriel sighted along a hazel rod.

"Arm up boy. Not that one you fool. That's better," she ordered as she walked slowly around me. "Turn your shoulders slightly. Tilt the cone to the left. No, to my left, not yours you idiot."

Eventually she seemed to be satisfied and, putting the rod down, muttered an incantation under her breath. Nothing happened and I was about to comment on this rather disappointing state of affairs when she twisted her left hand into a gentle curl, leaving her right relaxed, palm upwards. A jet of water sprayed from the fir cone straight into my open mouth. I spluttered and turned, the water shooting up my nose and into my eyes. The Lady Adriel laughed and lowered her hands.

"Put the cone on the side," she ordered. "A very successful experiment, wouldn't you say?"

"Yes, very successful," I said quickly before my curiosity got the better of me and I added "but what does it do?"

"The cone is enchanted to remember half an incantation so that I can speak the words and the spell will remain dormant, apparently doing nothing as you saw, until I release it by forming the correct gestures."

"Very impressive," I nodded, seeing little point in a piece of trivial mischief.

"Clear up the mess then," she ordered, handing me a mop.

As I wiped away the pool of water a chill spread across my skin as the consequences of my decision dawned on me. It was madness to return voluntarily to my prison, insane to go back to the sentence of death that hung over me. Still, inside me a fire burned, I had to learn how to use the magic of control and for that I needed the aid of the faeries. I had no choice.

"Lady Adriel?" I asked, "How could I win the favour of the Comptessa?"

"What's that?"

"How can I win the favour of the Comptessa?"

"Not by bellowing at her, that's for sure. Keep your voice to a civilised level
young man."

"Sorry."

"That's better, now what did you want?"

"To win the favour of the Comptessa so that she will teach me the secrets of the magic of control."

"Hmmm, tricky, very tricky." Adriel pondered, "You could give her a gift."

"What would she like?"

"Something magical, beautiful and valuable," she replied slowly,
"and amusing.
Definitely amusing."

I returned to my studies in the library but found myself distracted, gazing sightlessly through the windows trying to think of a gift to amuse the Comptessa. I tried to imagine what would tickle her sense of humour. Something twisted was in order, no doubt; she had hardly demonstrated a wholesome amusement when I was with her. I had to come up with the right gift or give up on the idea. The prospect of returning to face her wrath was awful but I was driven. I needed her help; I needed to understand the art of control.

I sat and watched the faerie tree in the courtyard, the symbol of peace between the Castle of Lovers and the faerie court. It bent and its branches shook fiercely under a storm that only it could feel. A leaf fluttered off the tree and blew against my face. Absently, I reached a hand up and examined the silvery green surface and the thick veins beneath. As I stroked the leaf, the texture passing through my fingers, an idea began to crystallise in my mind. Just the thing for the Comptessa, but I'd need help. I considered making peace with Greydog and asking his assistance but then shrugged and returned to the Lady Adriel's rooms. After I explained my idea to her she grinned,

"Yes, that would amuse Heloise."

"And can you help me?"

"I'll show you the technique but you'll have to do the work yourself."

"That's fair."

"And assist me in my experiments as payment."

"Alright," I replied reluctantly thinking of the chores I was bound to complete for Greydog. At least if I kept out of his way he might not think up too many new tasks for me to work on.

"First you'll need five pegs of chaim."

"But it's months to midsummer," I protested. Adriel laughed

"You can't steal covenant chaim," she told me, "and anyway fire chaim is no good to you; it has to be linked to the enchantment."

"How am I to get it then?" I asked hopelessly.

"You spend enough time in the library, do some proper research for a change. In the meantime my flowers need watering."

For the next two days, I found myself sharpening stakes to make a fence round the zombie dog trench and it was not until the Sunday that I was able to go to the library. Father Juan has denounced the fair as a haunt of the devil and has come down from his pole in order that he might not give support to such an evil institution. His self-flagellation and fasting continues, however, and he has returned to his habit of reading mass in the mysterious "D" room. Nobody has ever been able to explain this strange appellation to me but Father Juan explains that his God is Lord of all mysteries. His voice resonated through the building and the plainchant made me uneasy as I searched through a pile of Covenant parchments. Maps of the area, sketches of magical sites and descriptions of powerful neighbours mingle with records of covenant meetings. Finally I found a scrap of vellum which seemed to contain the information I required:

"The mage who desires mastery over plants of the earth and seas should hasten to the magical grove by the old shrine as the first frosts of Autumn cause twigs to fall from the ancient willow. These must be collected before the next new moon rises over the hillside or the chaim will return to enrich the soil."

I scrabbled through the maps looking for a reference to the old shrine. Finally I found it crossed out and replaced with the cathedral of Zaragoza. I began to panic. Already the last warmth of summer had gone, the nights were close to freezing and Zaragoza is a week's hike from here. I put the parchments down and ran to the Lady Adriel's rooms. I hammered on the door before remembering that she had gone on a trip searching for herbs. I slumped down onto the floor and racked my brains. I must get that chaim.

I made a decision and got to my feet. Out in the courtyard I found the handyman.

"Psst, Antonio," I whispered, drawing him to one side.

"What is it sir?" he asked softly, looking shiftily from side to side. Stealth comes naturally to Antonio.

"Secret mission Antonio," I replied. "You, me and Mongrol, two week trip, nobody must know." He nodded. "Can you get food and equipment?"

"No problem sir, leave it with me sir," and, as I signalled my approval, he turned and crept away.

Not until sunset did Antonio return with three packs. By then Mongrol and I were ready and waiting. I had asked Mongrol to show me some advanced swordplay in order to provide an excuse for our loitering and Antonio hurried up as I practised my footwork.

"Very nice sir, very nice but we must go now." I sheathed my sword, took up a pack and the three of use walked through the gatehouse where the sentries were changing shift for the night.

"Stranger or Lover?" Siero called.

"Guardian and sentry of both," Hawkeye replied.

"Know you the secrets?"

"Of lovers or friends?"

"I speak of both."

"But of the secrets of lovers can only lovers know."

"And art thou a lover?"

"As I stand before you."

Engrossed in their formulaic banter both sentries ignored our progress out of the courtyard and as we walked through the dusk I heard their voices fading behind us.

"Take you the responsibility of protector of the gate?"

"From strangers will I hold the lovers safe."

"Then come dear lover and let me away."

"Best time for secret journeys sir," Antonio whispered to me.

"What secret journey?" asked Mongrol.

"We're on an important mission Mongrol," I reassured him.

"Oh, that's alright then, just so long as Mongrol knows."

We skirted the Fire Hills to the south and climbed steadily onto a shoulder of land. The waning moon lit the side of small clouds as they scudded across the stars. I shivered.

"Come on, lets find somewhere to make camp."

The next evening found us drying our boots in front of a blazing fire.

"People will see it sir," Antonio had objected.

"Yes Antonio, but nobody here knows us. We're just travellers."

"Travellers on an important mission," Mongrol added, nodding.

"Anyway, we need to get dry or we'll freeze to death. If you hadn't insisted on avoiding the villages we could have used a bridge instead of fording the river."

"Villagers have loose tongues sir, secrecy is vital." I shrugged and huddled closer to the blaze.

Ahead of us, hills rose and for two days we climbed slowly westwards. On the third day we reached the summit and began our descent. Somewhere in the rough land ahead of us nestled the town of Zaragoza and just outside stood the cathedral in whose grounds I hoped to find the chaim I was looking for. The clouds lay thickly above us and the sun's rays slanted through a gap at the horizon, bathing the cliff face behind us in a glorious orange light.

Two more days of pushing our way through rough scrub, scrambling over rock-strewn hillsides and, sheltering by the smallest imaginable campfires, we found the sun setting over the great stone walls of Zaragoza cathedral. Through the last light of dusk we made our way through the terraces of a vineyard and along a cart track towards the graveyard that surrounded the cathedral. The evening stars pricked the sky as we walked through the deepening gloom and the sky was clear and moonless by the time we reached the limestone and slate masonry that surrounds the cathedral lands. It was bitterly cold and the slates glistened with a thin layer of frost. Antonio scaled the wall and slung a rope over for Mongrol and I to climb.

The stones were smooth and icy and it took a boost from Mongrol to lift me over the wall. Safely on the other side I looked round the churchyard, the grassy hillocks lit only by starlight. Closer to the church stood the gravestones, simple slabs and ornate tombs standing side by side for comfort in the cold. Around to the north I saw a dark smudge against the silvery grey of grass and limestone.

"This way," I whispered.

We crept across the open land, three dark shadows moving silently so as not to wake the dead. My hunch was proved correct; the dark smudge resolved into the looming shape of a group of trees and the sound of running water carried through the still night air. We reached the stream and quickly identified an enormous old willow tree, its trunk split by age, leaning on its branches for support.

"What happens now sir?" whispered Antonio.

"I don't know."

Suddenly the silence was broken by a sharp crack and I felt something speed past my face to thud into the ground. Bending down and groping on the ground I found a small branch from the willow tree. If the parchment told the truth then I was holding a peg of chaim in my hand and, for the first time, it was a peg of chaim that truly belonged to me. No longer was I a mere lackey, carrying the goods of my betters or a thief with wealth stolen from weaker men; I was now a man of substance. Another crack, another scramble across the damp grass and I doubled my fortune.

"What's going on sir?"

"Important business Antonio."

Two more cracks in quick succession, one branch found and stowed in my pack. Where was the other one? The sound had come from over to my right and I felt across the floor towards it.

"Ooof!"

"Sorry sir. Mongrol got in the way."

I'd tripped, my foot caught in a knot of grass and Mongrol is a good deal more solidly built than me. I lay there for a few seconds gasping for breath before he helped me to my feet and my lungs were able to return to their vital occupation.

"Help me find the branch," I whispered. "It's round here somewhere."

The three of us felt our way round the tree, bent double like old men, our hands trailing across the ground. Finally I found what we'd been searching for and added it to my collection. Almost simultaneously came another crack and a piece of wood dropped from immediately above me. The sharp twig scratched my face and I grabbed at it blindly. I caught the trailing leaf in one hand and held it up to examine it. Beneath the old willow no light penetrated and I could see nothing. Still holding the branch in one hand I stumbled out from beneath the tree taking care not to slither down the bank into the icy brook. The starlight was dim and I could see nothing to mark this twig as special or distinct from thousands of other similar pieces of wood. As I twisted it round in my hand seeking some confirmation of the parchment's tale, I became aware that the light was slightly better than it had been when we had arrived in the churchyard. Turning round, I saw the moon peeking above the horizon, the faintest sliver of light combining with the stars to improve the visibility. As I stood there the lower edge of the crescent cleared the horizon and I saw the twig in my hands briefly suffused by a pale silver light. The parchment had told the truth and the new moon had ended my hunt for chaim. I had four pegs in my pack and one in my hand; we had reached Zaragoza just in time.

I put the last twig into my pack and Antonio led Mongrol out from under the tree.

"Now let us get down to business sir," he said. "You keep watch round here and Mongrol and I will go over to the Cathedral. He can keep guard whilst I cast a rope around the fancy architecture."

"We're not going to steal the weathervane Antonio, I don't even know if there is one here."

"Yes sir, there is. A very fine one sir, and if you'll just keep guard here we can split the proceeds three ways."

"How on earth do you know about the quality of a weather vane on the top of Zaragoza cathedral Antonio?" I asked. "You never go more than a day's march from the Castle of Lovers."

"Been here before sir," he replied. "Dark business it was, very dark."

"That sounds interesting. Let's hear about it."

"It's a long, debated story of evil deeds and cruel accident."

We sat down in a circle and I held out my hands and spoke an incantation. A small flame flickered between my hands and then leapt onto the grass between us, its blaze casting an eerie glow on the faces of the three companions.

"Years ago it was sir," Antonio began. "Before you joined us and three of us had come here seeking magical stores much as we did today." He continued, glancing up at Mongrol and I, "Lord Greydog and I and the old gardener Dylan crept into the churchyard at the dead of night."

"I wouldn't call Dylan old Antonio, he can't be much older than me."

"Ah yes, young Dylan is Old Mr Dylan's son. We'd come here and while Lord Greydog was searching around by the stream, looking for his magical power, I thought I'd see if there was a weathervane that someone had left lying round. Maybe, if nobody was using it, I could take it back and make my fortune. I don't know what Dylan was doing." He paused, turning and looking over his shoulder. "What? Yes, of course he was sneaking around. Yes, always sneaking." He turned back to us and continued the story. "Dylan was sneaking around and had sneaked up behind me. I was still trying to see where the weathervane was. It's difficult in the dark, I mean, if you have a decent moon or something then you can see them easily but otherwise it can be very tricky. What's that?" He turned quickly and stood staring at a shape that neither Mongrol nor I could see.

"What's up Antonio?" I asked.

"Yes, yes, I'll tell them. No, not that, of course they can't be told that," he paused. "I'd never tell them that."

"Are you alright Antonio?"

"What's that sir? Yes, fine, where was I?" he answered, brightly. "Ah yes, Dylan sneaked up behind me and attacked me. I was caught off guard and he knocked me to the ground. I leapt up and defended myself with my fists and boots. I was terrified that he was going to kill me; those pruning knives look harmless until there's one dancing six inches from your throat. I managed to push him backwards away from me and, twisting on the ball of my foot, kicked out and caught him under the chin. He fell immediately to the ground and lay motionless. Lord Greydog heard the noise and came up, his staff lighting the ground like a torch. He looked at Dylan's body and pronounced him dead. Looking around, he caught sight of a newly dug grave awaiting a coffin. He lifted poor Dylan up and carried him over to the yawning pit. One swing of his arms and he had disposed of the body. Only Dylan wasn't dead, only dazed and the rush of air past his face must have awakened him. He must have seen Lord Greydog's face for he called out a curse as he fell backwards into the grave. I'll not forget the sound as he landed for as long as I live; a crunching cracking noise it was and Dylan never completed his final words. Lord Greydog turned to me and I to him. I said we should confess and face judgement but he swore me to secrecy and we fled into the night. So you see sir," he said, looking up at me, "I never did get to collect my weathervane."

"Nor yet tonight Antonio, we must get back home," I said absently, musing. So Greydog has a murder on his conscience. Interesting.

A flash of lightning reflects off the polished fireplace and lights the stained wood of Greydog's workbench. As I scrub, the water runs thick and black onto the floor below and I am aware that yet another task awaits me before I can attend to my project in the Lady Adriel's rooms and then crawl to my bed. Sleep calls to me, its soft voice murmuring in my ears, my eyelids drifting downwards as my arm moves mechanically across the dark timbers. I must not sleep, I have to complete this labour so that I can return to the enchantment I'm devising for the Comptessa.

I took the twigs of chaim up to Adriel's rooms together with a ripe acorn. This I had chosen carefully from the many forming on the trees in the wood. It was perfect, its flesh smooth and green, the cap tough and dimpled. I placed the branches into a large, terracotta pot, twisting the twigs together to make a support onto which I placed the acorn. We packed good earth from the gardens round the branches and up to the top of the pot before pouring clean rainwater onto the soil. We then began the enchantment, the Lady Adriel showing me the gestures and teaching me the words which cause the magical power of the chaim to seep into the acorn and spark it into growth. Every shower finds me on the roof of the new building collecting rainwater to keep the soil from drying out and every evening I repeat the enchantment. For three days I saw nothing happening but then a small green shoot broke through the brown earth that has grown swiftly into a small tree which I have tended with mundane skill learned from young Dylan as well as through enchantments taught by the powerful mage beside me. There is more to the understanding of plants than mere magic and the Lady Adriel has encouraged me to seek out knowledge wherever it can be found.

Knowing something of his history, I have been intrigued by young Dylan since my return from Zaragoza and have relished this opportunity to get to know him. He was initially rather suspicious and I was glad that I had eventually followed Juan's advice and paid him for the damage we caused to his gardens. His reluctance faded as I helped him hoe and weed, water and prune and, as our friendship grew, I have listened attentively to him telling me the names and natures of the herbs in the garden. Basil and rosemary, sage and mint, thyme, borage, chives and rue all grow in rows. Each one has its place in the kitchen and its role in defeating sickness. I have seen how to protect plants from the sun or the frost, even from too heavy a rainfall and I know how to combat greenfly, blackfly and whitefly, dry root, grey leaf and the weeping brown sores that are the visible signs of a tiny wasp. All this skill I have lavished on my little oak tree and it has grown strongly. Tomorrow, I begin the second phase of my enchantment, the amusement that will delight the Comptessa but now, as the last rumble of thunder echoes off the hills far away and the last drops of rain fall on the Fire Hills, I must mop the stone floors of my master's rooms and then hasten to complete tonight's enchantment before turning, wearily, to my bed.

The Eleventh Year

"The Number of the COURTESAN'S Votes shall be FOUR, the Tetrahedral Number, for the COURTESAN stands over the other High Mages like the apex of a Tetrahedron stands over its base; his is the solidity of the Mountain and the purifying violence of the Flame."

From the Law of the Covenant of The Castle of The Lovers

The air is hot and heavy; no evening breeze comes to lighten the atmosphere. The light of the orange sun reflects off the stone buildings, suffusing them with a salmon glow. The fair has returned and I stroll aimlessly past its stalls and entertainers enjoying the warmth, the atmosphere and most of all the freedom from duties. It has been a long while since my chores have been completed before sundown. Another busy year has passed by and I am another step closer to completing my apprenticeship. I pass Romario, seated on an upturned barrel strumming his lute and I pause to listen to his song.

> "Drummond was a knight so bold,
> As brave as all the knights of old,
> His sword was burnished; his heart was pure,
> He rode upon a milk-white steed.
>
> He rescued damsels in distress,
> And sped across the wilderness.
> Against all evils he brought a cure,
> Of valiant thought or word or deed.
>
> Great was his heart of holy fire,
> Sadly doomed to a fate most dire.
> The lament I sing of sadness tells,
> To us but joy to all his foes.
>
> He fought against a knight most proud,
> And won face bloodied, head unbowed.
> His victim sprang from faerie wells,
> Sometimes evil reaps he who justice sows."

An enchanted tree is a charming gift to give a lady but it is not particularly amusing. This would not normally be a particular difficulty but the Lady Adriel was quite insistent that the Comptessa would want to be amused as well as charmed. Fortunately the Comptessa has quite a simple sense of humour; death, twisted things and ugliness in the midst of beauty are all sources of hilarity. Consequently, I spent last autumn twisting the tree to suit its recipient. Every evening I would make my way to Adriel's rooms and cast an incantation to turn a leaf or a twig to silver before continuing my enchantment of growth. The eventual result was a tiny oak tree more than half silver, its remaining leaves straining to catch the sunlight, its trunk twisted hard against the dead metal. Individually, each part was beautiful; the oak was a perfect specimen and the transformation to silver had crystallised nature's genius. Together, however, it was an ugly creation, the living rejecting the dead, the cold neutralising the warm. Adriel was impressed.

"Heloise will be enchanted," she said.

"But will she forgive me for having seen through her disguise?"

"Maybe, so long as you flatter her," she replied. "Be careful though, it's even harder to be taken in by an illusion you've broken than it is to break one that's captured your imagination."

I waited for three days after the gift was finished, not yet ready to risk my life where countless others had fallen. Returning to the faerie court was foolishness; the Comptessa hated me for seeing her as she was and only her original fondness had saved me from an awful fate. On the other hand, the desire for the magic of control burned in my soul. Yet another year was to pass without this skill being taught for this year I had returned to work for Greydog who was teaching me to use magic to reveal secrets.

"Not that its much use," he said. "There aren't many secrets that can resist a direct hit from a fireball."

It's very dry but I guess there must be something in it if my master thinks it's pointless. The magic of control, however, was what I wanted to learn; I had read Danielli's tome so frequently that I could recite passages by heart and I had scoured the rest of the library for other references to this arcane art. It all made sense; it was so obvious but I still couldn't do it. I needed help and the only one who could help me was the Comptessa. Unfortunately it wasn't clear that she'd want to.

"This victorious battle may be thy tomb,
For I will tell thee of thy doom.

98

Though mortal hurt the faerie took,
He spoke, his voice was crystal clear.

Thou hast slain me and so thou in thy turn,
Shall die, aye thou will burn.
The earth did tremble, the ground it shook,
And Drummond felt his only fear."

Leaving Romario behind to sing to a delighted and growing audience, I wander on. I buy some sticky confection from a swarthy trader to quiet the growling in my stomach and stroll across to where a shallow pit has been dug and surrounded by ropes. Inside the pit stands an enormous Arab. He must be over seven feet tall and has a chest the size of the barrel on which Romario is perching. His limbs bulge with muscle and he roars a challenge to the crowd.

"Come and fight me cowards. I'll match your wager and pay you thrice."

I, like most of the crowd, am not eager to take him up on this generous offer and decide to wait a while to clear my mouth of caramelised nuts and to see if anyone fancies their chances against this one-man army.

I got leave from my master to go into the faerie woods. He was a little churlish about letting me go but didn't put up too much resistance. I think the picture of my skeleton dancing through all eternity appealed to his sense of humour as much as that kind of thing appeals to the Comptessa. I carefully packed the tree into my small pack and set off alone. The rain fell steadily as I left the covenant and trudged southwards towards the forest. The green of summer and the glamour of autumn had long gone and the trees were clad only in drab, brown, tired leaves and their trunks glistened wetly in the weak sunshine. I shivered as a trickle of water penetrated my clothing and ran down my spine like a cold finger; maybe an omen, I thought, and surely not a good one.

I walked quickly to keep from being chilled by the cold water and stopped only for a rather desolate lunch beneath the inadequate shelter of a threadbare tree. Dusk came early beneath the cold shadow of the trees and I used my magic to light a campfire of damp twigs and sodden tinder. The rain had stopped as I curled up by the leaping flames and thought of the soft beds and fine food of the Compte's castle. I had covered most of the journey but had no intention of arriving cold, wet and tired after dark; a much better impression would be made if I arrived fresh and enthusiastic in the morning light. A good impression was vital; as I drifted into uneasy slumber, images of dancing skeletons ran through my thoughts and plagued my dreams. Several times I woke up shivering after a dream in which I was forced to waltz endlessly through all eternity with a rotting corpse in my arms. Each time I would re-light the campfire and then lay back, closing my eyes but finding only fear and old bones in the darkness.

When I awoke the next morning, the sun was shining brightly through the bare branches and my fears of the night were chased away by the light of day. I breakfasted eagerly, washed in a woodland brook and changed into a fine, dry tunic I had stowed in my pack. The water was cold and clear and I leaned forwards to check my reflection in the water. For all my efforts the figure that looked back was still unappealing, skin like wet clay, sparse, dark hair and a tendency to obesity cannot be disguised by the mere application of spring water. I felt a pang of sympathy for the Comptessa and her magical disguise. Fortunately I was not relying on my good looks and charm to carry the day and the beauty of the oak tree in my pack was as warped and twisted as ever.

I stood up, slung my pack onto my shoulders and set off up the shallow hillside on top of which I could see the ruins that marked the faerie castle. As I walked on, I caught glimpses of the buildings from between the trees. Each time I caught sight of them, I expected to see the high battlements and flying flags of the Compte's fortress but as I got closer I was merely able to make out two walls standing out of a rubble of stone and a stunted tower set to one side. Finally, I reached the top of the hill and in the clearing at the summit was quite plainly a ruined keep. It had evidently never been a large building and time and the action of the elements had diminished it further; some time in its past, the tower had been struck by lightning and blackened stones lay around the base.

I looked around in dismay. I was sure that I had reached the right place and that last time I had been here, I had found myself in the faerie court. What had gone wrong, I wondered. After some consideration, I decided that the direction one approached the ruins might make a difference and descended the slope in order to attack the problem from a different angle. Six times I climbed the hill and six times I found myself standing amongst the ruins of a small and decidedly unfaerie keep. After the sixth climb, my legs were aching, my belly rumbling and the bright morning sunshine had turned unseasonably warm and lit the ruins, drying the cold stone. I sat down on a fallen block and ate my lunch. Then, with my back against one of the remaining walls, my legs dangling and the warm sun on my face, I closed my eyes. My sleepless night and the exertions of the morning combined with these small comforts and I fell swiftly into a contented doze.

"Who is it do you think?"

"A vagrant most likely."

"Or a visiting nobleman in disguise."

"Then 'tis some disguise for I see no nobility in his form."

"Hey, you, get up; this is no place for slumber." Strange voices filled my dreams and I struggled to make sense of them.

"Maybe he's dead."

"No, see, he's breathing, his chest rises and falls. Look!" I felt a sharp poke in my ribs and my eyes fluttered open.

"There see." I blinked furiously in as the sunshine broke through my sleep befuddled mind.

"What are you doing here stranger?" I looked up and saw two gentlemen dressed in fine leather jackets and black hose. One had a sharp, angular face with a narrow beard on his chin whilst the other, taller and more heavily built was poking the end of his scabbard into my belly.

"Hey, get off," I cried, standing up and pushing the sword away.

"Again I ask, what are you doing here stranger? Who are you to sleep in the courtyard of his eminence the Compte?" I gazed, astonished, into the eyes of the angular fellow and then glanced around me. Sure enough, the eyes were green and the ruins and treetops had been replaced by a glorious castle and tall stone walls. Even the boulder I had fallen asleep against had transformed into part of a fountain in which a very male stone satyr stood spraying water in a great arc over his head. Behind him the form of a marble maiden lay and caught the stream in her open mouth.

"I think, perhaps, our visitor is a simpleton. Shall we just have him thrown out?"

"Or into the dungeons?"

"Or maybe we should hand him over to the master of revels to provide the court with some entertainment tonight." The court! I came quickly to my senses and turned to my interrogators.

"I have business with La Comptessa, I am here to speak with her."

"Then you would do well to approach the court rather than sleep in the courtyard."

Evidently, this was considered exceedingly witty as the taller fellow turned to his companion and laughed.

"Thank you for your court-esy," I replied and, taking their advice, walked past them to the main door. I knocked and was quickly answered.

"What business brings you to the court?" asked the doorkeeper.

"Business with La Comptessa," I replied.

"And who is it that dresses so plainly when he has business with the lady of the court?" I was tired of being abused by courtiers and flunkies and so replied,

"I dress as plain as I speak and it is not the duty of servants to comment on the attire of their betters."

"I shall tell my lady that such a gentleman is at the door." I was left watching as he turned and strode across the beautiful tiled floor.

I stood, examining the walls where bright gold had been worked into pale birch wood to make the forms of trees, horses, nobles and warriors. It seemed that by following the panels round the sides of the room it would be possible to trace the course of a legend or history of the court. I stared at a scene of a tall, mail-clad fighter standing victorious over the corpse of a serpentine monster; behind him, hidden by trees, a force of waif-like archers stood, their bows bent and arrows ready to loose.

"Le Compte and La Comptessa will see you," the voice held a note of derision but I ignored it as best I could and allowed myself to be led across the room. As we reached the door to the council chamber, I tapped the servant on the shoulder.

"Nice clothes. Original shade of green," I grinned and as he stared at me in disbelief, I stepped past and, after knocking at the double doors, pushed them open and walked in. Ahead of me, I saw a long table and at the far end two figures. I turned to the one on the left.

"My Lord," I said, looking into the knowing green eyes.

"Riff-Raff," he replied. "I believed we had met for the last time." His tone was formal and cool and I shivered.

"I have come to bring my lady a gift," I said, reaching into my pack, "and to ask her a favour." I kept my eyes cast down, unable to look up at the withered form I knew sat next to the Compte. I placed the tree on the table in front of me and stepped backwards. The Compte clicked his fingers and a butler stepped past me, picked up the tree and carried it to the far end of the table. I could feel the pulse beating in my temple and felt a cold trickle of sweat down the sides of my body.

The silence was broken by a peal of laughter and the Comptessa's golden voice,

"The gift amuses me, what is your request?" Focusing on the beautiful tones, willing my mind to be taken in by the illusion, I raised my eyes to look at her. There, seated at the end of the table, clad in a midnight blue robe was a beautiful young woman. My heart beat more rapidly but my thoughts reined it in; I would accept the illusion but not the control over my mind.

"My Lady," I began. "You are both beautiful and noble. You carry great enchantment in your fingertips and rule over the lives of both mortal and faerie. I seek knowledge and beg that you would teach me the secrets of the control you wield. I do not hope to reach the splendour of your abilities but beg that you might grant me the meanest, poorest fraction of your wisdom that I might rise above the rude mortals in whose world I live."

The Comptessa smiled and held out her hand.

"You have mastery over both yourself and the fair words you speak. I will grant your request and, if you have the inner strength, you may learn mastery over others." I bowed, relief flooding through my veins; I had survived the first challenge. "Show Lord Riff-Raff to his room and provide him with robes appropriate to the ball tonight." A sniggering butler opened the door to the council chamber and I strode past him into the hallway.

My attention is dragged back to the ring in front of me as it seems that the enormous Arab has a challenger. Encouraged by Mongrol and Lopez and fortified by an enormous slug of brandy, Pedro steps forward and drops a handful of silver onto the floor of the pit. The giant signals to a small, wizened assistant who carefully counts the silver and stacks it on the edge of the pit. From a bag tied round his waist he counts three more identical piles and beckons Pedro over to check the stakes. He nods his agreement and strips to the waist revealing the hideous scarring on his back; it seems that Greydog's fireballs have a tendency to inaccuracy when Pedro is around. Both combatants dry their hands in the dust and then begin to circle slowly. I feel my heart-rate rising and have to clench my teeth not to join in the cheers; it would be unseemly for me to appear emotionally affected by a merely physical combat.

Pedro steps forwards quickly and, reaching up, places one hand on the Arab's shoulder and one on his hip; he twists his body trying to throw his opponent off balance but the giant moves quickly for one so

103

large and counters the threat with nimble footwork before matching Pedro's hold. Pedro steps back, trying to extricate himself from the grip of the giant who takes this opportunity to rush forwards, trying to push Pedro to the floor. The crowd groans as Pedro appears to stumble and sighs when the ruse is revealed; Pedro twists out of the Arab's grip and spins round behind him. A cheer rises from the crowd, led by Mongrol and Lopez who, it seems, have also been fortifying themselves. Pedro has a grip round his opponent's neck and his forearm is pressing against the giant's windpipe like an iron bar. The Arab reaches up to his throat, grabs Pedro's arm with both hands and bending forwards hurls Pedro to the ground. Only an impressive back-flip saves the Spaniard from being flattened but he lands facing the wrong direction and it is now the giant's turn to grab him from behind. Arms like twin tree-trunks wrap round Pedro's chest and begin to crush him; he starts to struggle for breath and, as his face turns red, his feet are lifted from the ground. I see his lips moving but, instead of an appeal for mercy, I hear the words of the Ave Maria.

"The Lord is with thee and with the fruit of thy womb, Jesus"

He holds his left wrist with his right hand and swings it over his head into the face of the Arab; a crunch, a roar of pain and blood flows from the giant's nose. A moment later, Pedro's booted feet crash the kneecaps of his opponent who stumbles and loosens his grip. Pedro twists free, elbows the giant in the stomach and lets loose a spinning kick. The toe of his boot makes contact with the Arab's left knee which buckles and then bends unnaturally as Pedro grabs him round the neck and pulls. One last bellow of pain and the Arab collapses to the ground as Pedro leaps clear. Red faced and breathless he sweeps the silver into his purse, steps out of the ring and rescues the remains of his brandy from Mongrol's astonished grasp.

"Good fighting Pedro. Mongrol couldn't do better."

"Giant sore many days. Pedro's silver good for much brandy." I watch them weave their way uncertainly into the crowd as the giant is helped to his feet by his elderly assistant.

When evening came on the day of my return to the faerie court, I dressed carefully in blue hose and an enthusiastically yellow jacket before making my way downstairs to the ballroom that evening. As I made my entrance I heard the announcement
"Lord Riff-Raff the badly dressed." I turned and saw the butler I'd made such an impression on earlier. Well, so long as I could stay in the

Comptessa's favour he'd picked a bad enemy; on the other hand, if I fell out of favour he'd have all eternity to make fun of me. I bowed politely, drew myself together and turned back to face the ball at the far end of which sat my host and hostess. The Compte was as cool and elegant as ever and, as I turned to his wife, I was able to maintain a vision of beauty surrounded by a halo of golden hair and dressed in the sheerest of blue silk. As the fabric caressed the curves of her body and as the flickering light fell on it, the colour shifted from the palest shade of summer skies to the cool water of a mountain lake. I bowed low.

"My Lord," I said, "My Lady."

"Call me Heloise," she replied bestowing a radiant smile. I cleared my mind of all
images of grinning skulls and smiled back.

"Heloise," I murmured. She gestured to a seat that had been placed to the side of the two thrones.

For a while, we sat and watched the courtiers dance; silks, velvet, flowers and feathers flashed and shimmered as they moved gracefully in time to the music. I recognised two faces, one angular and one round; they were now dressed more formally and were clearly surprised to see me waving from the Comptessa's side.

"Who are those two?" I asked her.

"The one with the splendid waistcoat is Lord Nepheriel and his large friend is Sir Temperance. Nepheriel is a dreadful liar but extremely charming; Temperance is famed more for his strength than his wit. Neither is particularly trustworthy," she smiled at me.

"Are you thirsty?" she asked. I nodded, my throat was parched and, although I was eager to avoid intoxication and the downfall it would surely bring, I felt I could manage a little wine. The Comptessa held out a hand and a golden goblet rose from a tray carried by a passing servant and floated across the room, swerving between the dancers until it rested on thin air in front of me. I reached out and lifted it to my lips, anxious not to appear too impressed.

"An excellent vintage," I said, smiling, "and an interesting party trick. Will you show me how to do it?"

"Hold the goblet on the palm of your left hand. Now point towards it with your right and feel the weight of it. Gently take more of the weight in your right hand. Gently. Now take your left hand away and the goblet should remain..." she broke off as the goblet failed to remain anywhere and instead fell to the ground. The dancing stopped and all eyes turned to face us; I felt a wave of panic pass from the top of my head to the tips of my toes. The Comptessa laughed,

"Dance," she said, "dance!" The revellers turned back to their partners and, couple by couple, began to move once more. The Comptessa clicked her fingers "Bring Lord Riff-Raff another cup of wine and a small table to set it on." I smiled and relaxed a little.

When the servant had placed a fresh goblet of wine at my side, I tried again to lift it. I held out my right hand and concentrated on feeling its weight. I raised my hand slightly but the goblet stayed obstinately still. After a few minutes the Comptessa reached over and made the slightest of gestures. The cup lifted from the table and shot into the air before falling back and hovering an inch above its starting place; she flicked her fingers and it began to swing back and forth in time to the music.

"The secret of control is to arrange things so that the subject wants to do what you want it to do," she said.

"But the goblet doesn't want to do anything," I replied, "except fall to the ground."

"It doesn't want to fall, it thinks it has to. I give it freedom to reject the call to fall."

"But it doesn't have freedom, it's completely under your control."

"I know that and you know that," she replied, "but I don't think the cup knows that. Get into the mind of your subject and you can always find a handle."

I spent the next hour trying to get into the mind of the goblet, ultimately deciding that it didn't have one. I twisted it round to check that it had no handle either then stood up, drained the goblet, bowed to the Compte and offered my arm to the Comptessa.

"I give up, shall we dance?" She smiled and took my arm. Despite my clumsy limbs, I've always been able to follow a dance and I soon mastered the more basic steps. The Comptessa, it seems, rarely dances and so wasn't disappointed by my rather limited prowess. She laughed in my arms as we span round the dance floor, the throng parting to allow us to progress. Too soon the musicians put down their instruments and the dancing stopped. I escorted her back to the throne, bowed deeply and, trying to disguise my laboured breathing, turned and left the ball. The evening had been, if not a complete success, then at least a partial one and I had no intention of allowing alcohol or fatigue to break my guard.

The next morning I woke late to find the fine weather of the day before had passed on and had been replaced with thick, grey cloud. Looking round my chamber, I found that fresh linen had been left at the foot of my bed and a fine breakfast of bread and sausage had been left on a table to the side of the room. I changed into one and devoured the other before sitting back on my bed and making a plan for the day.

I spent a couple of hours with my breakfast crockery trying to persuade it that it wanted to float off the table and round the room but without success. I couldn't see how I could understand the mind of an inanimate object, nor could I feel the weight of something that lay three feet from my hand. Cross and befuddled from the concentration I decided to get some fresh air and to stretch my legs. I put on my boots and made my way down the grand staircase. By the door stood two green clad servants one of whom swept across the room and bowed obsequiously.

"Can I be of service Lord Riff-Raff?"

"I'm just going for a stroll."

"Very well my Lord." I walked past him then turned and raised an eyebrow.

"Yes, my Lord?"

"Your colleague," I asked. "What is his name?" The servant looked confused by this interest in the menial classes

"Pierre, my Lord, but it is of no importance."

"Thank you," I nodded curtly. As I walked past the other servant, I stopped.

"Pierre," I said. He stepped forward sulkily.

"I am a very good friend of the Comptessa," I told him.

"Yes, my Lord," he replied.

"And I have been most unimpressed by your service thus far."

"Yes, my Lord."

"I wouldn't want to have to bother Heloise about your lack of courtesy."

"No, my Lord."

"Well then, Pierre, let me tell you how it's going to be. Every time I come down those stairs I want you to be standing at the foot of them bowing and asking if you can be of service and every time I come to this door I want you to answer it, take my coat and to apologise for the delay." There was a long pause. "Do you understand Pierre?"

"Yes, my Lord." I smiled to myself and strode past him to the door where I stopped and waited. A minute passed.

"Pierre."

"Yes, my Lord."

"This door needs opening."

Outside snow had begun to fall, soft, thick flakes that lay crisply on the cold ground. All the perfection of snowfall that is, in the human world, invariably marred by mud and slush was there; the snow lay like frosting on the battlements and drifted in the hair of the passing faeries. The air was chill but not too cold and I strode through the courtyard and made my way to where a gate opened onto a street of houses. Groups of children were playing, throwing snowballs and rolling in the drifts which were beginning to form against the buildings. Small clusters of adults stood and talked; snow gathered on the ladies' hats and on the jackets of the gentlemen. Everyone was enjoying the weather and I watched and strolled happily until hunger drew me back to the castle.

I lunched lightly and retired to my room to watch the snowfall over the forest through my window and to practice again the levitation of small objects. The warm room and gentle drift of snow lulled my tired mind and I soon dozed, sitting on the windowsill, my legs tucked up to my chest.

I was awakened by a soft tap on the door and a gentle cough. A servant stood apologetically in the doorway.

"I'm sorry to disturb you, Lord Riff-Raff but the ball is about to begin." I thanked him and changed into a glorious purple jacket infused with silver thread and some tight black hose. My figure is not something of which I am ordinarily proud but in the court of the Compte it seemed that arrogance and glamour took the place of style and good taste. I picked up a silver handled cane, which affection many of the noble faeries were sporting, took a deep breath and set out for the ball.

"Lord Riff-Raff the Unmerciful!"

"Better, Pierre, much better." I murmured as I passed him on my way to the Comptessa's side. "My Lord, Heloise," I bowed. The Compte nodded, the Comptessa smiled.

"What sport would amuse you tonight?" she asked as I sat down.

"I will follow your direction," I answered.

For a while we sat and watched the dancers as servants brought us gold plates laden with tasty morsels and goblets full of delicious wine. Among the dancers, one of the men clearly lacked my resolve to avoid drunkenness. He was young, of dark hair and smooth complexion and was attired in a loose white shirt and black hose even tighter than mine. He danced ever more furiously, sweeping up one lady after another, carrying her spiralling round the dance floor before leaving her dizzy and breathless and moving on. The orchestra spotted him and increased the tempo of the music; gradually the other dancers dropped out and watched him, unable to match the pace and soon he had exhausted all possible partners. He danced alone, feet flashing and arms swinging as he came towards the thrones at our end of the room.

"Will you dance, my lady?" he asked, pausing to bow deeply before recapturing the beat. The Comptessa smiled and I saw she was considering taking a turn around the floor when the young man slipped on a small pool of wine and fell spectacularly, landing on his back. The Comptessa's smile broadened,

"I think not young man. Not until you can control your limbs." She turned slightly towards me and whispered "Watch!"

As the red-faced dancer got to his feet she held out one hand and twisted it from side to side. As she did so his hands and feet jerked upwards in a grotesque parody of dance.

"I'm sorry, my lady, have mercy," he begged as he performed a stately pirouette, panic spreading across his face.

"Maybe," she replied and lowered her hand. "We needn't be limited to bodies," she whispered raising her hand once more and fixing the poor young man with a glare. "Cross the room and kiss the doorman."

A glazed look flashed across his face and then he turned and strode across the dance floor. Nervous laughter rippled round the audience as he put one hand round the unfortunate Pierre's back and raised the other to support his head. Leaning forwards and ignoring the servant's vigorous protests, he pushed his mouth against Pierre's. A shiver of glee ran through me at the sight of Pierre struggling unsuccessfully to free himself from this amorous embrace. Eventually the young man rose for air, turned to the Comptessa, bowed, turned back to Pierre and realised what he had done. Mortification filled him, he turned a shade of red fit to match the most lurid of ball gowns and he shrank back into the crowd, willing the earth to open before him.

"Dance," ordered the Comptessa, "dance!"

I've found a quiet corner of the fair and I'm sitting on a bale of straw enjoying the cool night air. I see the faces of people passing by, some in a hurry, some just strolling, and I wonder about their lives. What needs or desires drive them? Are they happy, contented with their lot or do they strive for a better life? What dirty secrets lie behind their eyes and wake them shivering in the night for fear of discovery? What fears prevent them sleeping? What hopes protect them from despair? Do they realise as they walk, run or saunter that they are passing the Great Riffrando, a wizard of such potence that one day they will bow before him? Their lives lie in his hand, he only has to close it to crush all their desires and add another terror to their remaining hours. He can blot out their hopes with one finger, can destroy their lives with the blink of an eye and he holds their very souls in his palm. For those who stand against him there is only oblivion but for those who remain faithful there will be reward. They will stand before his iron throne and receive recognition and riches but even these will be considered worthless when set against one word of praise spoken by his mighty lips.

It's a pleasant fancy and I smile and stretch my legs out, enjoying the strain of my muscles. The Great Riffrando doesn't exist; Riff-Raff takes his place and the iron throne has transformed back into a bale of straw which I think might have fleas. I get up, scratching, and continue my tour of the fair.

Days passed in the faerie castle and I fell into a routine. Every evening I would attend the ball and sit at the Comptessa's side to learn from her the techniques of control; every morning I would sit in my room and practice what I had learned and every afternoon I would explore a little more of the Compte's lands. The evenings passed in a whirl of gaiety but my mornings were filled with despair as I was no closer to a mastery of control than I had been when I fell asleep amongst the ruins. I couldn't make any progress with the goblet because it clearly had no mind to get inside and so the Comptessa suggested that I go down to the dungeons and practice on one of the inmates.

Returning to those cold stone cells caused me to shudder; once I had believed that I would spend my life here, trapped forever within the walls of a faerie prison. I took a deep breath and reminded myself that I was the honoured guest of the Comptessa but then came out in a cold sweat when I thought about the consequences of losing that status. I had to learn mastery of this art and quickly, before I stopped being amusing. I selected a short, stumpy prisoner who was securely chained to the wall and looked less dangerous than some of the others. When I entered the cell, he growled and I saw that his teeth had all been filed to points, giving his face a most savage appearance. His head was completely bald and his ears gave the impression of having been stuck on. He was dressed in a ragged tunic and, as I got closer, I saw that his limbs were thick and wiry. I took a step backwards but he didn't seem inclined to pull his chains apart so I relaxed a little.

110

I looked him in the eye and focussed my mind on his. At least his desires were clear enough; he wanted his freedom. Unfortunately, this left me in the same position as I had been in with the goblet. I knew what my subject wanted to do but was unable to persuade it to do anything different. I worked until I was cold from sitting still and concentration formed flashes of light that burst across my vision. Then I made a breakthrough as the creature's arm moved just as I had been focussing on it. I quickly lost my control over his body and he went on to scratch himself thoroughly. At least he was scratching himself on an impulse from my mind I thought and tried again. After a further hour of effort I bowed to the inevitable conclusion. The prisoner had wanted to scratch himself and had coincidentally moved at the moment I had focussed my thoughts. I sighed.

My failure disheartened me and the next morning I was unable to bring myself to practice; I just lay on the bed and stared at the gold inlaid wood of the ceiling. It had seemed such a fine idea when I had sat in the Lady Adriel's room. All through the summer as I had worked on the tree I had focussed on persuading the Comptessa to help me. It had never occurred to me that she might be willing but unable. Then a dreadful thought occurred to me; maybe it was a flaw in my mind, in my magic, that prevented me from using the power in this way. Maybe I would be forever like Greydog, a mage with power but no control. I pulled a pillow across my face and closed my eyes.

That afternoon I went for a walk through the woods; the faerie forest grew thick and splendid. The trees were all taller, thicker, more perfect than those found elsewhere. I walked between towering oaks, tall, smooth ash trees and beautifully formed pines. Leaves and needles mingled on the forest floor and whispered as my feet shuffled through them. The sunbeams lit the ground and reflected off the silvery trunks and green foliage. After a while, I grew tired and sat on the trunk of a fallen olive tree. The time was approaching when I would have to take my leave of the faeries whether I had what I came for or not; I had no wish to outstay my welcome. I thought about returning to the Castle of Lovers a failure; I remembered the dull grey of the stone walls, the dim light of the library and the burning heat of Greydog's rooms. A soft wind fluttered through the trees and an unseasonable blossom fluttered through the sweet air, landed briefly on my shoulder and fluttered to the ground. I smiled; blossom had never fallen on me whilst I had been reading the works of Danielli in the library. I recalled my favourite

111

passage and repeated the words, speaking clearly, addressing the trees around me.

"Making the fist of control with the fingers of his right hand the mage summons the fluttering spark from his breast and pours his powerful intellect into his subject."

In answer to my own command, I closed my right fist. I looked down at the fallen blossom, almost hidden amongst the leaf litter and my left hand naturally fell into the shape I used when creating the Comptessa's enchantment; my thumb coiled across the palm, holding the middle finger down, away from the other three. I took a deep breath and looked up to the canopy above. Maybe, I thought, the regimen of the Castle of Lovers was not too terrible; I had begun to tire of the endless balls and the days in which nothing happened. My mind was becoming dull, something that had never happened when I had been studying from Danielli. I smiled and as I did so I caught a tiny movement out of the corner of my eye. I quickly looked down; it seemed that the blossom had twisted on the ground. Perhaps it was a slight wind but a hope grew in my breast, could it be that I had done it? A feeling of exhilaration filled me and I clenched my fist tighter, willing the blossom to shift again and as I felt my desires crystallise, I saw the tiny white flowers lift slowly off the floor and float upwards, twisting in the breeze and brushing my cheek as they passed. I held up my arms and the blossom flew upwards, spiralling through the branches and leaves until it was out of sight. Still I stood there in a pose of triumph until a note of despair shook me. Perhaps it was a fluke, a one off I would be unable to repeat. Perhaps this was a dream or perhaps the blossom was a vision. Beginning to panic, I focussed on a small forked twig, its three leaves just twitching in the wind. I held out my hands to it and roared the incantation, willing it to bend towards me. The power I unleashed was such that the twig bent, broke from its tree and sped towards me, tearing a small gash in my temple. I felt the pain but it was immediately replaced by sheer joy. I had summoned the fluttering spark from my breast and had control over the world around me.

I sped through the forest back to the castle to tell the Comptessa, I had to share my exultation with her; she had patiently demonstrated her powers and finally I had grasped the lesson. I ran, my feet flailing behind me, my arms pumping. Unfortunately my new powers had not granted me greater fitness and I soon decelerated to a slow jog and then, as the forest path began to lead me uphill to the castle, to a walk. The exertion seared my lungs, a trickle of blood was drying on my cheek, fire burned

112

through my legs but sheer excitement forced me onwards. I looked at my hands as I walked, searching them for something new, a visible sign of my new ability. I reached the top of the hill and looked up. I had found my way not to the Compte's castle but to the ruined manor that lay in the same place. I sat down, back against the warm stone, smiling and breathing heavily for a while and then got to my feet and started my journey back home.

I savour the memory of my triumph and look up from my dreaming. It's late and as I walk back to the gatehouse I see a familiar figure.

"Paulo!"

"Ah, Riff-Raff, you've grown."

"I didn't know you were here."

"Are you surprised?" he asked. "But why? I brought the fair back."

"What? How? Why?" I asked rather foolishly.

"It's a good location for a fair, there's local business from the castlefolk and the villagers. Father Juan is good entertainment, they say he's a saint and saints always draw the foolish and encourage them to part with their money. Anyway, I had business in Zaragoza and so I let it be known that I would be doing some secret business up here."

"So how did you get the other traders to come?" I asked.

"They all assumed that I knew about something they didn't and so, in order to pre-empt me, they all changed their schedules and set up their stalls. All I had to do was turn up a couple of days late and take advantage of the situation. They were all so desperate to go one better than me." Paulo smiled. "The secret to controlling money, Riff-Raff, is to find out what people want and then to offer it to them." I grinned back,

"The secret to control of anything," I said, "is to persuade them to want what you're offering."

"You may well be right young Riff-Raff," Paulo replied patting me on the shoulder. "You may well be right."

I wave farewell and knock on the gate.

"Stranger or Lover?"

"Which would you prefer?"

The Twelfth Year

"The COURTESAN is the Chairman of the High Mages. His Votes are not to be used at all times, but sparingly as his wisdom is Precious. The COURTESAN'S Votes are to be counted if the Votes of the other High Mages are Tied, and Otherwise only during the TYRANNY OF THE WIZARD."
From the Law of the Covenant of The Castle of The Lovers

*I*t's Midsummer and the heavy raindrops are beginning to fall on the Fire Hills, soon they will fall here in the courtyard and I hurry back to my Master's rooms bringing a handful of mustard grass from the garden so that we can complete our experiments. I have three more years of apprenticeship to complete and I have realised that these would be unendurable if I continued to struggle under his tyrannical rule. I have served under another master, the Philosopher Beast and was forced to seek the aid of strangers to escape from his tyranny. Thengol is not in the same class as the Philosopher Beast and nor am I a mere child to require assistance and so I have found a better way. I shall not struggle openly but shall ensure that he works to my ends just as I work to further his. Our relationship is mended and once our current enchantment is complete, my master will teach me the secrets of the element of water. My master rather despises this manifestation of magic as it opposes fire, his true love, but an understanding of all the elements is crucial to a thorough mastery of magic as each one affects the others as do the strands in a column of bindweed, each stem spiralled around its brothers.

Understanding of the aqueous world will complete my elemental education as we have worked on air over the last twelve months. Thengol explained that air was the sister element to fire and that just as a breeze can fan a ember, so my knowledge of this magic will encourage my limited knowledge to burst into flames of power. We have worked with winds and breezes, stinks and stenches, mists and storms and I have revelled in my mastery of this subtle, intangible element. Thengol has been impressed with my understanding of the magic of control and has taught me a spell to blow people off their feet by manipulating winds around them.

I reach my master's rooms, shake the rain from my hair and begin to prepare the mustard grass. The green leaves, white stems and tiny black seeds must be separated from one another, a tiresome, fiddly task, and my master is quickly bored and returns to the grate where a copper pot is bubbling with a thick sulphurous mixture. I carefully slice the plants and make three piles of the ingredients as he chants an incantation over the cauldron and hurls a fine dust into the flames making them burn a fierce purple.

My studies with the Comptessa have taught me that my magical powers are limited and so they will always be. Even when I am a full mage and free of my master's rule there may be times when I must accomplish my ends through mundane as well as magical means. Paulo's rule for traders has stuck with me; find out what people want and offer it to them. Thengol desires power and recognition; this year I have worked to provide him with both and my success has bought apparent peace between us. Of this, I am glad; I was in danger of being fried if the open warfare had continued. Thengol is content that I have learned my lesson and am once more his deferent apprentice. By this situation am I satisfied.

Last Autumn Hawkeye announced the arrival of three men from the far side of the Fire Mountains asking to speak to the Lord of the Castle. The Courtesan duly met them in the courtyard where I joined a small crowd eager to hear what these strangers wanted. Wizards are not welcome members of society and we seldom receive visits from strangers; the church is very clear that anyone even speaking to us imperils his soul. Occasionally a traveller will request lodging for the night and we have regular business with the local peasants, but apart from that, we are pretty well ignored by the conventional world.

The farmers had heard something of our magic and had come seeking aid. They stood nervously before the Courtesan; one screwed his toe into the ground like a naughty child whilst the leader stood up straight and kept eye contact, keen to bolster his sense of self-importance. The third stood beside him with his hand on a short cudgel hanging from his waist. His stance was designed to be a threat to any who should attack him or his friends but his position was laughable against the mighty force of magic. Fortunately for them the Courtesan is well disposed to his fellow creatures and listened attentively as they explained their predicament.

It seemed that a monster had been terrorising their village, stealing sheep and poisoning the land. It took a form something like large black dog with scaly wings and a long serpentine tail and flew over the village most evenings. It would swoop down from the hills and circle a couple of times before choosing a suitable victim and diving like a hawk to capture the poor animal. It would then fly off a short distance and devour its prey before returning to its lair. When the farmers examined the ground they found that the crops where the beast landed were dead and blackened, killed by some poison in its skin. One shepherd, bolder than the rest, had lain in wait for the monster, keen to protect his flock; when it had swooped down to grab a sheep, he had leapt from his hiding place and struck it forcefully in the face with his club. It was a crushing blow and the foul horror staggered backwards under its force but the relief was only momentary and it quickly sprang forth, rending the shepherd with a savage slash of its claws. In vain he attempted to parry the blow; his defences were struck down and the talons tore through flesh and clothing. He fell to the ground, awaiting death but the monster turned, grabbed one of the terrified flock and flew off to complete its supper in peace.

The villagers had run to the stricken hero and had found him still alive but in great pain. He had been carried to his cottage where the women had removed his jerkin to tend to his wounds. What they saw filled them with horror. Three red cuts had been made in his chest and around each one the flesh had turned black. They began to clean the wounds but as they watched, they saw the black marks spreading across his chest, slowly at first but then, as the three wounds merged, they reinforced each other and the poison accelerated. The shepherd's breathing grew shallow as the blackness covered his thorax. His face blanched and he let out a short cry as an offshoot spread up the side of his neck. His limbs twitched frantically and the women watched helpless as the discolouration covered his face. His eyes rolled into the back of his head, his boots crashed once against the table and he lay dead.

The village priest said prayers over his body but insisted that the corpse was infected by the creature's evil and so could not be buried on holy ground. The next day the villagers had decided to seek help and had sent this delegation to the Castle of Lovers. In the meantime they were resolved to accept the loss of their flocks rather than the sacrifice of their men. The leader of the group looked up to Señor Phosphortube.

"Please help us." The Courtesan considered him gravely,

"I will have to discuss this with my colleagues," he replied. "In the mean time, M'Benga will attend to your needs." The men went pale when they saw the manservant approach.

"Come," he said, his white teeth showing bright in the dark face. "You must be hungry." Rather nervously, keeping their distance but wishing not to cause offence the three Spaniards followed him into one of the outbuildings.

That afternoon there was a council meeting to discuss what could be done for the villagers. I asked Thengol about it in the evening as I washed stoneware pots in his rooms.

"Not that it's any concern of yours, young apprentice," he began, eager to remind me of my position, "but the Courtesan was, of course keen to help them. He said that we should do our best for these people."

"And what did you say, master?"

"I said that they were no concern of ours, the monster was on the far side of the Fire Hills and was unlikely to attack our lands; there was nothing to be gained by attacking it and so we should charge them for wasting our time and send them away."

"A wise response master." Thengol smiled at this compliment.

"Yes, I thought so. Darius then said that he thought they were lying, no flying creature could be so clearly evil. Sparky sighed and murmured something about flying demons and the genuine distress felt by the supplicants."

"And Lady Adriel?" I asked.

"She said nothing and merely spat when it was suggested that she offer some assistance."

"The Lady Adriel has very little time for ordinary humans." I offered but, seeing that my master was a little touchy about my relationship with Adriel and faeries in general, I swiftly moved on. "So what was the result of the council master?"

"Sparky is too busy with his experiments to go on a journey now and the rest of us don't think the problem merits our time so they will be sent home to deal with the creature themselves."

"A very wise decision master, but maybe the problem might merit my time?" I suggested. "Maybe I could deal with this monster."

"Now why should I let you do that? I need your help here," Thengol replied. "I gave you leave last year. Remember you must complete your apprenticeship with me before you are free to do as you please."

"I remember master. I thought you might want me to do this for you."

"For me? Why would I want that?"

"The creature might guard a valuable treasure that I could collect for you." At this Thengol's eyes lit up, "or maybe its corpse would contain powerful magical ingredients."

117

"Hmm," my master pondered, "I've been thinking about this and maybe you should go on a mission to deal with this monster. It is a suitable task for an apprentice of your level." I smiled and nodded.

"I would need one of the warriors to accompany me for protection master."

"Then you must address the council meeting tomorrow and request permission."

The next morning the disappointed visitors left the Castle of Lovers and began their journey home. M'Benga saw them off.

"Take these provisions for your journey," he said, handing a sack to the leader who grunted his thanks and backed away.

"M'Benga," I asked, walking over to the gatehouse where he stood watching the dispirited travellers trudge away. "Is it true that in your country people have an eye in the middle of their bellies and worship spirits of the earth?" He looked at me gravely.

"Is it true that in your country fire flows from the fingertips and men believe that faeries live in the woods?" he answered, waiting briefly for an answer before returning to his duties inside. I watched his retreating back in confusion; what did he mean by that rather cryptic response?

In the afternoon I spoke at my first council meeting. I had made myself as smart as possible, I wore a clean tunic and my lank hair was slicked back over my temples in imitation of a nobleman I had seen in Barcelona. I looked around the council room; three of the stone walls had been covered by dark wooden panels and only on the outside wall could one see the grey stone of our fortress. In the centre of the room four chairs stood around a heavily polished table. At the far end sat the Courtesan and on the wall behind him hung a painting of the Covenant showing the buildings, fortifications and the people going about their business. On the left side of the table were two seats to be filled by Adriel and Darius; behind them was a painting of the founding Courtesan, an ancient face surrounded by a mane of hair and beard. Below the picture the name of Grumio Portent was proudly inscribed. Thengol's seat was on the right hand side of the table and behind him the window let afternoon sunlight into the room. Immediately to my right in the corner of the room stood the Cupboard of Untold Treasures, a tall storage cabinet kept locked and under guard except when the Council was in session.

As I looked around, the Magi filed in and took their seats; I was left standing. Señor Phosphortube knocked on the table three times.

"This meeting of the Council of the Covenant of the Castle of Lovers is called to order. Present are the Courtesan Sparky Phosphortube, Pato and Chaperone Thengol Greydog, Lato Lady Adriel and Kato Darius Falconwing together with Riff-Raff, Pato's guest and apprentice." The three High Mages nodded gravely. "What business do we have before us today?"

"The defence of the Covenant," replied Thengol.

"Ah yes, Chaperone, what news do you have?"

"I have spoken to the Council about the defensive value of a band of Zombie Dogs and I feel that the time has come to start creating this army," Thengol looked up at the faces opposite him. Darius seemed shocked, Adriel disdainful and the Courtesan listened with mild interest. "In order to achieve this aim I will require twenty pegs of chaim."

"Twenty?" yelled Darius, getting to his feet. "We do not have such riches available. Our resources can surely be spent more wisely. My research..."

"Enough," said Sparky raising a hand. "How many zombie dogs would this enable you to enchant Chaperone?"

"The position is a little unclear but I'm confident that I could make at least five ravenous and deadly zombie dogs from that much chaim. I will know more once I have begun the enchantment but the Covenant defences are a priority of the first order; at the moment we could be overrun by our enemies without any chance of protection."

"We all understand that you take the defence of the Covenant very seriously Lord Greydog. Where would the dogs be kept when the enchantment was completed? You have spoken about a trench?"

"Yes, they would live in a trench around the palisade. This has not yet been completed but I have made good progress with a spell which will quicken the digging of this vital structure."

"Hmm, I have severe misgivings about keeping an army of zombie dogs in the Covenant before we have a proper place for them and so I would not be in favour of this use of the Covenant chaim. Kato, what is your view?"

"This is insane Sparky, zombie dogs are a ridiculous idea and Thengol only wants the chaim for his own purposes anyway."

"Please use the proper titles during council," came back the soft rebuke. "Lato, would you be in favour of this use of resources?" Adriel shook her head. "I'm sorry Chaperone, I don't think we need to go through the charade of a vote do we?" The Courtesan fixed my master with a steely gaze and he shook his head and shrank back into his seat.

"Do Lato or Kato have any business for the council?" Adriel looked bored and turned away; Darius shook his head, and cast a triumphant glance at Thengol.

"I have a request Lord Phosphortube." My voice squeaked as I spoke my first nervous words in Council.

"Yes, Riff-Raff, what is it?"

"I believe that I can help the villagers with their problem; I think I can kill the monster."

"Does your master have any objection to you leaving the Covenant for a few days?" Thengol shook his head. "Then I don't see that there is a problem," Señor Phosphortube said, rubbing his hands together and starting to lift himself out of his seat.

"I would need one of the warriors to accompany me for protection." The Courtesan sat back down.

"Ah," he said. "Chaperone, can we afford the absence of one of our warriors for a few days on such a worthy cause?"

"Well, if we had an army of zombie dogs we could always afford to send our warriors out to guard us when we went on errands. This is the point I have been trying to make, our defences are sorely stretched and we must invest..."

"We are aware of your wishes in this matter Courtesan, the question to hand is whether we can afford for one of our mighty warriors to accompany Riff-Raff as he undertakes this quest." Thengol looked crestfallen.

"I think we can just about manage," he replied.

"Very well, I think we can consider that settled and if there is no further business then we can all return to our work." He gave a quick glance around the table, got to his feet and left.

"Thank you master," I said as we left the room together.

"What makes you so sure we can get something out of this quest?" he asked.

"Monsters always have magic hidden in their corpses master, it's well known," I replied.

"And what makes you think you can defeat this creature?"

"You've taught me well master, how can I fail?"

Thengol seemed content with these replies and I returned to the library and the book I had searched for after listening to the villagers' story. The leather bound volumes entitled "A Journey of Thengol Greydog" are filled mainly with the narrative of a journey through France but this tale is interspersed with magical insights and advice. It's odd that Thengol himself didn't recall this passage:

"When journeying through the ancient hills I heard the rumour of a Kernelwyrm. The Kernelwyrm is a fearsome beast with the body of an enormous black dog, the tail of a serpent and the wings of a dragon. Its fangs will rend the toughest armour and the poison of its claws brings creeping death; pity be to any man wounded by the foul creature. It is afraid only of fire and can be killed only by a steel blade lit by the moon. I was keen to find and kill the beast for its blood is a mighty treasure, doubling the destructive power of any spell. Care must be taken in its storage, however, as impurities can transform the potion into a poison of great speed and potency. Magic is powerless to detect the poison of Kernelwyrm blood and the only safe recourse is to avoid polluting the precious fluid."

I read the passage again, confirmed in my belief that Thengol may have stolen rather than written some of the pages of the books and returned to my master's rooms to pack. I took two clean crystal bottles, scoured inside and out by fire and some of the magical powder I have been making for my master. Inside this grey mixture of saltpetre and charcoal lies the power of flame, distilled from the mind of the mage by incantation and ritual. I wrapped it carefully in a length of linen then placed it inside an oilskin at the bottom of my pack. I turned to leave and then turned, tucked a short dagger into my belt and, thus reassured, went to look for Lopez.

It took us three days to cross the Fire Hills and every morning Lopez would wake up, glower at the heavens and start to clean his armour.

"Bollocks dew," he'd mutter, rubbing furiously as I prepared breakfast. Fortunately, it didn't rain although for the first two days of our journey the skies remained overcast. Lopez walked in silence, occasionally glancing up at the gloomy clouds and quickening his pace; I had trouble keeping up with the big man and found that I had no breath spare for conversation.

On the third morning the clouds parted, the sun came out and we walked across the hillside enjoying the warm October sunshine. We were following a mule track that crosses the Fire Hills just to the north of the castle; the main trade route is further south and runs from Lerida to Zaragoza. The track is not well used and was so overgrown that in a couple of places it was quicker for us to scramble over rocky outcrops than to hack our way through the scrub. We lunched in the shade of a small grove of stunted olive trees, and for the first time since leaving the Castle of Lovers I felt that we should take a siesta rather than walking through the heat of the day. Lopez looked up at the sky.

"Clouds small, white fluffy," he said settling himself against the bole of an ancient tree and, closing his eyes, mumbled "Siesta good." I followed his example and dozed gently as the sun passed its zenith and began its slow decline to the western horizon.

The olive grove may have been enchanted by ancient spirits of divination for I dreamed of the future; I sat upon a royal throne as a long line of nobles queued to bow before me. My clothes were of silk and golden thread and I held in my hand a wooden orb. Kings and princes bowed down before me, addressing me as "Great Rifrando", "Mighty One" or "Master". As the Comptessa curtseyed her obeisance, I saw Conchita standing against a wall gazing at me with adoration in her eyes. Next in the queue to kneel before me was an ancient Arab chieftain who had difficulty getting to his feet. I stepped forwards and offered my hand; as he took it I looked into his face and saw that it was Sparky Phosphortube. Looking down I saw that the wooden orb had turned into a bright steel dagger and that instead of helping him to his feet I had skewered him. As the corpse slid off my blade I looked around the room and saw the Comptessa's face dry and shrivel and then all the other faces in the room gazing at me followed suit. Each of my guests, young or old, male or female was swiftly turned into a grinning skeleton until there was only Conchita still looking human. She walked over to the corpse in front of me and rolled it over. She bent down to close the staring eyes and when she looked up I saw that the flesh had melted from her face and her eyes glowed orange from within her withered skull.

I jerked upright as I awoke. I was sweating and afraid that I had seen my own future. My heart thumped in my chest and my breath came fast and shallow. Even in the warmth of the afternoon I felt chill as the sweat dried on my limbs. I gazed into the middle distance emptying my mind of emotion and applying my intellect to the dream. If this is a vision of the future then my confidence is well placed; I shall be great, all shall bow before me and no power, mundane or magical shall stand above me, not wealth, not arms, nor rank or beauty. I relished the thought and a shiver of anticipation ran through me. The afternoon was wearing on and it was no longer warm to sit still beneath the shade of the olive grove. I woke Lopez and we set off once more, squinting into the lowering sun.

We made good progress down the western slopes and as the orange disc clipped the next line of hills we looked over the tilled fields and wooden buildings of a small farming village.

"What now?" asked Lopez.

"This must be it," I replied, rather disappointed. I'd expected something a little grander than three houses and a collection of barns.

"We here tonight?"

"I don't know. Maybe we could ask for shelter." I pondered, considering our next move. As I hesitated, Lopez grabbed my arm and pointed northwards. There was a brief bleat and I saw a black shape rising from one of the fields, its wings flapping furiously and a struggling sheep caught in its talons. It flew directly away from us for a minute before we saw it settle on the top of a scree slope to devour its prey.

"We after it?"

"Yes, come on," and I broke into a run.

"Us, monster, now?" asked Lopez as we hurtled towards the creature's resting-place.

"Good point," I puffed and stopped suddenly. Lopez's armour clanked as he drew to a standstill beside me; the noise sounded loud in the still evening air and we saw the creature look up from its meal. I could almost see the details of its face and imagined the cruel eyes gazing at me. After a moment it clearly decided that we were not worth interrupting a meal for and returned to the task of separating mutton from bone. Lopez and I stood quite still, watching the fearful beast at its dinner. Eventually there was no more flesh on the corpse and, giving us one last glare, it turned and flew northwards once more.

"A Kernelwyrm," I breathed.

"We after it carefully," instructed Lopez with emphasis.

"Yes, try to see where it goes," I told him. We followed the trail northwards, struggling over the scree and pushing our way through the rough vegetation. As the light grew dim and the bulging yellow moon rose behind us, we found ourselves climbing again across a hillside of rough boulders, rockfalls and cliff faces.

"Which way now?" I asked

"Boff," replied Lopez, shrugging expressively. We made a rather uncomfortable camp between two enormous lumps of limestone and munched our supper of cold meat and hard bread before I left Lopez to keep guard and tried to find sleep on a mattress of hard rock.

We spent the next day exploring the hillside, clambering over, climbing round and squeezing between the boulders which defined it. We found a number of small caves and crevices in the rock but no sign or spoor of the Kernelwyrm.

"We should just wait and watch when it comes out for its dinner," I said as I slumped exhausted to the floor and let the warm rock massage my back. The heat of the day seeped out of the hillside and the warm sunlight slanted across my tired body; my eyes closed drowsily.

"No," grunted Lopez and pointed to where a broad slab projected from the hillside. "Good view there." I nodded my agreement and we inched our way to the edge; turning back we had a good view of the whole hillside above us, the rocks were bathed in orange light and the caves and crevices flung into dark relief. The slope continued upwards away from us and beyond the first summit we saw rows of yet greater hills, lines of golden stone broken by grey shadows and sliding beyond the horizon to the high Pyrenees.

The calm was broken as we saw our quarry emerge from a broad crevice in a cliff face to our left. It stood on the grassy sward for a few moments, looking into the sun, before leaping mightily into the air, its wings beating noisily as it rose above us. We watched it swoop past, its bulk diminishing as it flew southwards until it seemed no larger or more remarkable than a raven.

"Quickly," I said, getting to my feet. We scrambled across the rocks to the clear spot in front of the cliffs. There we saw a cleft in the rock, as broad as a man's shoulders and three times as tall. I paused before the chasm then marched forwards.

"What plan?" asked Lopez, restraining me with a firm hand.

"We must explore its cave," I told him. "I need to know the layout." Lopez looked a little dubious but followed me into the darkness. As his broad form blocked out the last of the sunlight I muttered the incantation to set a small flame fluttering in my palm. The passage climbed steeply up towards the slab of rock that formed the roof. Just before the ceiling and floor met, the ground levelled off and the boulder above cut away so that I was standing in a huge cavern. Behind me Lopez had to stoop to get through the entrance.

"Bollocks damp," he said, rubbing his greaves nervously. He was right, the cavern was damp and, in fact, a pool of liquid had gathered at the lowest point of the floor. I increased the power of my spell and the flame doubled in size, sending its flickering light to the edges of the lair. The walls were covered in black slime, the same substance that filled the pool. Both Lopez and I instinctively drew back from touching the stuff as we trod warily across the sandy floor.

124

"Out?"

"Not yet," I replied, skirting the pool and moving to the back of the cavern where the ceiling was only an inch above my head. It too was coated in the noxious substance and I held up my hand until the top of the flame flickered against the shiny black rock. Where the fire touched it, the stone quickly dried and the slime hardened into a black mud that cracked and fell to the floor leaving a small patch of bare white stone.

"Out now?"

"Not yet." The ground levelled off in front of me and, although I had to bend over, I was able to walk further back into the hillside. I turned round and looked out, past the circle of magical light into the darkness. I saw a gleam of light as the flame reflected off Lopez' steel shin guards and then the gleam became a flicker and I heard the thump of boots against the stone as he came running towards me, almost bent double to get under the overhang.

"Bollocks," he said and I felt a breeze on my face as if a pair of enormous wings had flapped once at the entrance to the cavern.

"Quickly," I decided. "Keep going."

We stumbled forwards, bent over, Lopez desperate not to brush his armour against the sticky ceiling above us. The ground remained smooth and level but the walls on either side began to close in and I heard a snuffling noise behind us. I cancelled the incantation and as we flickered into darkness, I noticed the last light was reflecting not from black slime but white stone. I grabbed Lopez' elbow and we shuffled forwards into the darkness. With one hand on Lopez' arm I felt out with the other and felt my fingertips touch cool rock. We stumbled forwards, following the wall of the cave until Lopez' shoulder clanked against the other wall. I led us on into the narrowing tunnel until the two walls met and I could go no further.

"It's a dead end," I whispered.

"Dead right." We listened for sound of the monster behind us and were rewarded by a worryingly loud scrabbling noise.

"Draw your sword Lopez," I told him, "I'll try to frighten it off, you stab it."

"Too small. No sword," he whispered back. I felt my spirits sink. I was about to be killed due to my own stupidity; simply because I didn't think of setting a guard, we were about to be devoured by the monster. Our remains would lie at the back of this dismal cavern, they would probably never be discovered. I stood up and stepped back against the cave wall; at least I'd go down fighting, being Thengol Greydog's apprentice had its shortcomings but at least I had a firm grasp of offensive fire spells. I took a last gulp of clean, sweet air and realised that the air at the back of this dark and cold cave had no right to be anything other than foul and putrid. I reached up, feeling my way across the wall behind us. My heart raced, once more good fortune had come to my rescue. Thrice in my life I had been trapped with no hope for escape and thrice I had been saved by a quirk of fate. It seemed that I was destined to survive, destined to be free and destined, I hoped, to be great. This was not, however, the time for reverie; fate had smiled upon me but this time it required action on my part. No longer was I a blossom blown in the breeze but a masterful wizard taking a full part in my own destiny.

"Hang on Lopez," I said, "There's a way up here." Feeling for handholds in the rock I was able to lever myself onto a ledge. I reached further up, scrabbling with my fingertips and found a small opening through which I felt a cool breeze.

"Come on Lopez, climb up behind me."

"No, armour too heavy."

"Leave your armour, hurry."

"No, must armour with me." My arm muscles were burning and I gave one great pull, jack-knifing my body into the little space. Unfortunately, the tunnel was too small to turn round and there was only one direction to go. As I inched my way forwards, I fancied that the blackness was becoming lighter. I wriggled onwards until I found myself lying at the mouth of a cave at the edge of a wide ledge in the cliff face. I took deep gulps of fresh air and gazed joyfully at the moonlit hillside spreading out below me. I was not, however, able to stop to enjoy the scene; I had to rescue Lopez. I turned round and crawled back down the passageway.

When my fingers felt space below them rather than hard stone, I grabbed the edge with both hands and pulled myself forwards until my shoulders were free.

"Lopez," I whispered. Seven agonising heartbeats followed before I heard the monosyllabic reply

"Yes." Rejecting flames in favour of the moon that had welcomed me back to the land of life, I summoned a pale beam to light the cavern. Lopez stood a few feet below me.

"Pass me your armour." I hissed, "Quickly," I added as he looked dubious. Thinking of the broad talons and fearsome jaws he unbuckled his breastplate and passed it up. His helmet and sword followed and I tugged them into the hole, awkwardly shuffling backwards. I was unable to maintain the spell and darkness fell again as I heard Lopez haul himself to safety. The breastplate was heavy and clanked against the ground.

"Careful."

"Do you call that gratitude? I came back to save you and your wretched armour."

"Not wretched"

"Alright, I came back to save you and your splendid armour."

"Better." We inched our way along the crevice; I crept backwards tugging the breastplate behind me with the helmet and sword piled upon it, Lopez followed, pushing them in front of him.

"Be careful," I grunted as he shoved the sword against my forehead.

"Sorry."

Eventually we reached the open air and sat with our backs to the cliff, breathing deeply and blinking in the bright moonlight.

"Well that was a successful reconnaissance, I think."

"Good because I reconnaissance not again."

Cleopatra has woken, rises from her spot before the forge and comes across to watch Thengol at work. My relationship with this hell-cat is still icy but she no longer assaults me without reason and I no longer feel the need to aim a kick in her direction whenever I see her approach. Earlier this week, in fact, I was able to feel some solidarity with her as she encountered the Courtesan's pet. Beppo is an affront to Cleopatra. He is short, she is long; he is scruffy, she is elegant; he smells like wet carpet, she is perfectly groomed; he is a dog and she, beneath the spots and fearsome teeth, is fundamentally a cat. The High Mages had had another council meeting and Thengol had once more failed to obtain the supplies of chaim his experiments require. As he stomped across the courtyard to his rooms, Cleopatra, following behind found herself face to face with Beppo. She hissed, he growled and I, passing the other way, stopped to watch the fun. She stepped forwards a pace, her body elongating and her belly almost sliding across the floor. He yapped and sat back on his haunches as she continued her serpentine progress.

Suddenly she sprang forwards and he leaped and met her in mid-air. Cursory blows were exchanged and they fell apart momentarily before beginning the battle proper. Despite his inferiority in size, Beppo was performing well against his opponent; he was knocked sideways by the force of her paws but was protected from real harm by his matted and disgusting coat. Despite my dislike for Cleopatra, I was affronted by the success of this revolting and pathetic creature and found myself supporting her as she twisted, clawed and bit. Blows were landed and exchanged but neither animal was able to gain any advantage and, beside me, I heard Antonio taking bets on the result of the fight.

I believe that he was forced to return the stake money as the battle was prematurely halted by Conchita who heard the fracas, left her kitchen bearing a bucket of water and emptied it over both combatants. Cleopatra yowled, glared at Conchita and slunk off, bedraggled and lacking in dignity. Beppo was washed off his feet and slid halfway across the courtyard from where he shook himself dry and yapped his objection. Antonio was a little more lucid

"But Conchita..." he began.

"What?" she demanded, hands on hips, bosom heaving gently beneath her dress. Hearing no reply, she turned on her heel and swept back to work, her splendid hips swinging as she went.

Lopez refused to do anything the day after our first encounter with the Kernelwyrm but tend to his armour which was slightly scratched and somewhat damp following our escape from the cave. I spent the day in nervous anticipation of the challenge ahead. I checked that the enchanted powder was still dry, carefully packed it back into the oilskin and then rehearsed the detonation spell before returning to check the powder once more. The skies remained clear, the sun inched its way across the sky and we waited for dusk.

Finally the bars of cloud on the western horizon were suffused by golden light and the time had come to make our way to a hiding place close to the mouth of the Kernelwyrm's cave. We lay on our bellies beneath an overhanging rock looking back to the slash of blackness cut into the pale wall of rock. Minutes crept by and I forced myself to breathe evenly, my ribcage filling as I inhaled and then collapsing as I let the air escape from between my teeth. I could feel Lopez' body tensed beside me; presumably he was worried about his armour stacked carefully to the side of our lair.

As I watched the line of shadow, I fancied I saw a patch of deeper darkness and as I peered into the gloom I saw the blackness solidify and the Kernelwyrm stepped out into the light. It stood on the grass, sniffed the evening air and looked slowly from side to side. I felt its gaze, the black pupils staring out from the yellow eyes and saw the saliva drip from its fangs. The gelatinous green liquid hung in the air from the creature's jaw and drifted towards its chest in the faint breeze. Goosebumps swept over my skin and a cold trickle of sweat started at the nape of my neck as it looked towards us; I feared that we had chosen a position too close to the cave and that it would sense our presence. We would be doomed, trapped and unarmed if it chose to check beneath our rock. I held my breath, my muscles frozen into inactivity, blood booming in my ears until it stretched its wings, flapped once and disappeared into the sky to the south.

I exhaled slowly as we lay still, letting the beast fly away. After a couple of minutes we wriggled out of our refuge and I picked up my pack.

"How long until the moon rises Lopez?" I asked.

"Not long, soon after dark."

"And you'll be ready?"

"Yes." Lopez' conversation may lack flexibility but it does have an admirable brevity. Summoning my courage, I turned away from my companion and, flame in hand, strode into the darkness ahead of me.

Once again, I walked down the tunnel to the great cavern and skirted the pool of slime. I lifted the pack off my back and extinguished the flame. From now, I would have to work in the dark as I unpacked the fire-powder. I poured it out, carefully making a line across the sand at the back of the cave just in front of the overhang. When I was satisfied, I stepped high over the strip and walked backwards under the low roof pouring the last of the powder slowly as I went. I lay in the dark, peering towards the exit, trying to identify any glimmerings of light that might reach into the blackness from outside. Now there was nothing to do but wait and hope. I waited. I hoped that the magic of the fire-powder would remain unextinguished by the oppressive blackness. I waited a little longer. I hoped that the Kernelwyrm would flee before my flames rather than freeze in panic until the fires were exhausted. I waited. I hoped that Lopez would remain faithful to his commission and courageous in the face of the angry monster. My waiting was halted as I heard scrabbling and felt a gust of wind blown by the flapping wings. I hoped that it wouldn't detect either me or the fragile line of magic I'd left in the sand. I heard its footsteps on the floor of the cave and felt the gloom as its bulk moved across the cavern. I hoped that the moon would have risen. I waited a little longer to make sure.

Finally I could wait no longer and I held my hands out as my master had taught me. I paused, drawing breath, feeling my heart beat against my ribs and then I bellowed the syllables of flame. The time for hiding and hoping was over. Fire ripped from my palms and split the darkness searing its brightness across my unaccustomed eyeballs. The blaze swept through the cave and lit the fire-powder. For a brief moment I saw the Kernelwyrm, only feet away from me, its eyes pools of blackness cut by scarlet reflections. In that moment, I felt myself small and helpless, unable to defend myself against this dreadful adversary and the flames died in my hands. Then the main line of powder caught fire and the explosion blew me back, my head slammed against the rock above me. Light, fire and heat filled the room, sucking air from all around, roaring in fury, burning cloth, flesh and stone.

I awoke to find blackness, silence and cool sand beneath me. I rose slowly and banged my head, sending a flash of whiteness across my mind and starting a dreadful thumping that filled my skull. I bent forwards and clutched my temple, trying to squeeze the pain away. Darkness covered me once again and I conjured the familiar flame to dance reassuringly on my palm. By its flickering light I could see the Kernelwyrm's cave empty before me and I crept forwards, across the cave and through the tunnel to the exit.

There on the grass I saw Lopez, his sword gory with black blood and his breastplate triply scored where the Kernelwyrm's claws had struck. Between us lay a black corpse, its wings forever stilled, fangs and claws no longer a danger. I opened my pack and found the bottles miraculously intact. Lopez lifted the monster's body and I filled both containers from the chest wound that had ended its life. I looked up at the great warrior and our eyes met; satisfaction at our success and joy at our survival filled us.

"Bollocks armour broken now."

Thengol was somewhat confused when I presented him with a glass bottle stained with gore and filled with black fluid but adopted a pose of great knowledge when I reminded him of the properties of Kernelwyrm blood. I layered my explanations with sycophantic references to his awesome potency and fabulous intellect and he softened remarkably, even calling me "faithful apprentice" and "offshoot of my magic".

I look up at him now and see a look of intense concentration on his face as he scribbles some new insight into the margin of his notes. He looks back and smiles as he reads my thoughts. He returns to his experiment secure in the warmth of my adoration and renewed in his desire to expound his knowledge to such a sincere student. I look away, relieved that our quarrel was over and keen to absorb the knowledge I required to complete my apprenticeship.

The Thirteenth Year

"Should any of the High Mages vacate their responsibility for Any Reason, the COURTESAN shall appoint more junior Mages to fill the roles in Order of Seniority. However, on the Death, Disappearance or BANISHMENT of the COURTESAN shall PATO assume the title, responsibility and privileges of Chief High Mage for, as the Triangle forms the base of the Tetrahedron, so PATO waits below the COURTESAN."

From the Law of the Covenant of The Castle of The Lovers

*R*ain pours down. It washes my hair, soaks my scalp and floods my tunic. As I breathe, my nose fills with water and I sneeze; if I look up, the torrent pours into my eyes and I am blinded. Water covers all surfaces and soaks all garments. Behind me, the palisade wall stands sodden, its base sinking into the sodden ground. Beyond it lie the rain-drenched buildings, rivulets running over their dark stone walls. Inside I believe it is warm and dry but out here I have forgotten what it means to be dry; the pounding, falling, pouring rain has driven the memory of comfort from my brain.

Before me stands a huddled mass of wet fur; nine dogs and one donkey are crammed into a hastily constructed pen and each one is seeking shelter from the storm. The mass of bodies writhes as each animal tries to bury itself beneath the warm pile of fur. I delve into a sack lying at my feet and extract a handful of meat and bone which I hurl into the cage. This act has no effect on the creatures within; the rain is so universal that my presence has not even been noticed. I reach into the sack once more and pull out another piece of flesh.

"Here boys," I call, trying to make myself heard above the downpour. "Dinner!"

Since returning to Thengol's good graces I have been subjected, with ever increasing frequency, to complaints about the Courtesan.

"Can he not see how badly defended the Covenant truly is? Is he blind to the needs of others? The Covenant has supplies of chaim! Why should they not be used as I see fit to benefit the entire Castle? We're called the Castle of Lovers but I truly believe that Sparky Phosphortube hates me. He sits in his council meetings and he abuses his power and he refuses to give me the chaim I need for my experiments. He's not even a

132

true wizard; he can't conjure a fireball large enough to fry a dormouse. He adopts a superior attitude whilst complimenting me on my great breakthroughs. It's as if his magic is better than mine simply because it's unnoticeable. If it's unnoticeable then it isn't doing anything! How can magic that does nothing be better than my magic which pours its destructive power into my enemies? If it's magic to do nothing then that great lump Siero must have the stuff running in his veins. The chaim belongs to me; without it, I am unable to complete my experiments. Sparky has no right to keep it from me. Who said he should be Courtesan anyway? I'm a greater wizard and care more for the well being of the covenant. He's obsessed with the care of the servants and doesn't pay enough attention to the people who truly matter, the mages. This state of affairs cannot be tolerated; I'll see him dead before I allow him to continue to push me around like this."

One day, after listening to a particularly long grievance, I asked him why he didn't put the matter to a vote in council.

"I haven't bothered with that rubbish for years, it's so humiliating. I only get three measly votes and so when Adriel and Darius vote against me, like the faerie-loving animal obsessives that they are, the scores are tied which means that Sparky gets the casting vote. It's a conspiracy, I tell you. I should get a reasonable number of votes and then they wouldn't be able to do this to me." As I listened, my mind recalled a challenge I'd thrown out to Adriel when I was working in her laboratory. I'd made the bet out of amusement at her faerie pretensions and out of exasperation at her dismissal of all things human. It had seemed like a joke at the time but if she was taking her vow seriously then I could see a way to make a profit out of the situation. I thought quickly, preparing a suitable approach.

"I've got to know the Lady Adriel quite well, what with working for her so many years."

"Don't tell me you've joined her side and plan to live with the faeries forever in faerieland where everyone is a faerie and goes around enjoying faerie dancing," he snarled.

"I was just going to say that I might be able to persuade her to abstain from the voting." Thengol looked up sharply.

"Then it would just be Darius voting against me and he only gets one vote because he's useless. I'd win the vote three one and Sparky wouldn't even get a say in the matter. But can you do it?" he asked. I thought for a moment.

"It might cost me," I said, slowly.

"How much?" I thought again.

"I don't know but I'll make you a deal; I'll do whatever service the Lady Adriel requires and provide her with whatever she demands and you pay me one fifth of all the chaim the council votes you."

"So if you don't manage it I'm no worse off?"

"Exactly."

"And if you are successful, I'm better off?" I nodded.

"Riff-Raff," he said smiling. "You have a deal."

I went over to Adriel's rooms immediately. She was a little surprised to see me but was happy enough to accept my offer of help when I explained that Thengol had thrown me out again. I stayed with her long enough for Thengol to believe that he was getting good value for his putative chaim and long enough for me to learn Adriel's delayed action spell. It amuses her greatly to enchant mundane objects around the castle and then to set the spells off with a flick of her fingers; I think I can put the skill to better use.

The dogs emerge from their heap just long enough to snatch the meat from my hands. I look up at the sky; blackness covers the heavens from east to west. I smile at the thought that we hardly need the defences we have when the weather prevents any enemy from marching against us. Zombie dogs seem a little superfluous under the circumstances. Thengol is still in the process of researching the theory of animation of the undead and, until he is able to produce the required enchantment, it has been decided to retain living dogs. These require feeding and, since the servants refuse to have anything to do with the enterprise, this job has been left to me. I fling the last scrap of mutton into the darkness and turn back into the pouring rain.

After a couple of months of peace and quiet with the Lady Adriel, I tired of her inane jokes and returned to Thengol with the glad news that my efforts had proved successful. He pressed me to reveal the cost of the deal but I deflected him with a shudder saying,

"It's better you don't know."

"Well, if you're right and she doesn't vote against me then I'm grateful."

"And you'll keep your bargain?"

"Of course," he replied. "I'm just so glad that I won't be pushed around by that bunch of weaklings any more."

The next council meeting was one week later and Thengol asked me to attend. I think he wanted me on hand if anything went wrong and I was keen to see what would happen and to claim my share of the chaim if the plan was successful. We arrived and took our places as before, Thengol sitting by the window whilst I stood next to the Cupboard of Untold Treasures. Darius and Adriel followed, and sat down opposite my master. The scene was set, the combatants ready; all that was missing was the impartial judge to ensure fair play.

"Good Morning Pato," said Adriel, addressing my master by his formal title.

"Lato, Kato," replied Thengol, nodding to Darius who twitched nervously, got up and stood behind his seat, hands gripping the back of the chair. The Courtesan arrived carrying a stool and, setting it in the corner opposite me sat down. The four of us looked at him in amazement wondering why he had eschewed his seat at the head of the table. Our surprise was compounded when he was followed into the room by a shambling figure that made its way around the table, bumping into Darius, brushing against Adriel and taking the Courtesan's seat. Our visitor was a well-built, adult male of indeterminate age with dark hair and greyish skin. His face was expressionless, his mouth loose and flaccid and he moved jerkily like a puppet on a string. He lifted his shoulders and clumsily put his hands on the table in front of him scrabbling to get a grip on the little wooden hammer. After several attempts in which he was unable to maintain a hold on the gavel, he swept it onto the floor and thumped on the table with his fist.

"Lright," he said, his voice an expressionless mumble. "Shallow re megin?"

"What?" asked Adriel, the first to regain some composure. The figure twitched his mouth, licked his lips and, very carefully, enunciated

"Shall we begin?" Three pairs of eyes were fixed on the strange apparition that had dominated the meeting. Mine had already switched to the Courtesan. I recognised the fist of control and saw his lips move as he mumbled an incantation.

"I thing the vurst ving id the Shaproe."

"What's going on Sparky?" asked Adriel, turning round.

"Ah yes, this is Augustus," he replied brightly. "One of my little experiments. I hope you don't mind him chairing the meeting today. He's quite harmless." We returned to Augustus' limp form. His head hung forwards and his dead stare transfixed the table in front of him.

135

"Where did you get him, it from?" asked Darius, correcting himself hurriedly.

"It's a simple little spell. It could do with some work, obviously; Augustus isn't the perfect physical specimen. Anyway, shall we get back to business? I'll just sit here and Augustus can run things."

"No he can't. This charade is bad enough without meetings being chaired by an animated corpse," replied Adriel.

"Yes, I refuse to take part in this meeting unless you forget about this ridiculous idea." Darius was getting quite angry.

"Very well, if you feel strongly about it." The Courtesan was clearly disappointed that none of the other High Mages shared his interest in dead bodies. He shrugged, keen to avoid confrontation. "Come here Augustus, you can have my seat."

The corpse staggered to its feet and stumbled back across the room, knocking into Darius' chair as he leaped athletically out of the way. Eventually normality was restored except for the corpse in the corner and a twitching muscle in the side of the shape-shifter's face. As his cheek tightened he looked more like a hawk and I feared that the meeting would have to be halted if he made the transformation involuntarily. This didn't happen but I could see that it would not take much to push him over the edge. The Courtesan sat down in his appointed position and began again.

"If everyone is satisfied with the current arrangements I think I can hand over to the Chaperone for a report on the Covenant defences."

"Plans are progressing for a pack of zombie dogs to patrol the perimeter ditch," Thengol began.

"And to dig such a ditch?" interrupted Adriel.

"And, as you say, to dig the perimeter ditch. Great strides have been made but to complete the work I will require twenty pegs of chaim in order to enchant the beasts."

"Must we always have this discussion Thengol?" asked Darius petulantly. "It would be irresponsible for the council to grant you such a large amount of chaim to do something so fundamentally pointless."

"And mad," added Adriel.

"Kato, I must ask you to follow proper procedure during the council meetings. I think that I have made my position clear that until the pits are dug I would be against the creation of a pack of zombie dogs in the Covenant and so do not feel that the grant of chaim is appropriate. Lato?"

"I agree," answered Adriel.

"Kato?"

"Yes, of course I'm against this ridiculous plan."

"So, Lord Chaperone, I'm afraid that we shall again have to refuse your request. Is there any other business concerning the defence of the Covenant?"

"I'd like to put the question to a vote if I may, Courtesan."

"Well, if you must. Pato, how do you vote?"

"In favour." Sparky's eye passed round the table to Darius,

"Kato?"

"Against."

"Lato?" I found myself holding my breath, hoping that Adriel considered the challenge to her faerie nature a greater pressure than the desire to avoid unwanted expenditure.

"I shall not vote on this measure."

"Huh?"

"What?" screeched Darius, turning on her. "You'll let him take chaim from the Cupboard of Untold Treasure on the pretext of forming an army of zombie dogs?"

"I just don't think it's very important."

"Well, unless Lato wishes to change her vote? No? Well then the vote of the council is in favour and the Chaperone is awarded twenty pegs of chaim to be taken from the Cupboard of Untold Treasure to be used in the defence of the Covenant." Darius screamed and leaped across the council table to the window and flung it open. Hauling himself to the sill, his legs shrinking and hair coagulating into feathers, he hurled himself out, gave an angry flap of his wings and soared into the sky.

Adriel, who had been rather tense during the vote, gave a bright peal of laughter, got to her feet left the room. As she reached the door she turned,

"Make sure you enjoy it Thengol," she said. My master opened the cabinet and pulled a bloodied wolf pelt from one of the shelves.

"Twenty pegs of purest animal chaim," he murmured. "Come on Riff-Raff, let's get to work." I lifted the gory skin onto my shoulders and followed him out of the room, leaving the Chaperone alone.

"What was all that about?" he asked.

"Are duwoah," shrugged Augustus.

The pelting rain continues as I pass through the gatehouse muttering dark imprecations against whichever dimwit it is that keeps me waiting whilst he fiddles with the lock. A flash of lightning illuminates the courtyard as I pass the faerie tree. Unusually it seems to be suffering from the same weather as us; its branches are shaken by the wind and water pours off its leaves. In the instant of brightness I see the old tower standing above me, three stories of ancient stone briefly bleached to a chalky white. The windows stare out, blocks of darkness in the receding memory as the after images fade from my eyes. I open the door and make my way up the stairs to my new room; an added bonus of Thengol's abuse of power is that Siero and Hawkeye have lost their top floor chamber and have been rehoused in one of the wooden huts outside. I have a splendid view and accommodation appropriate to my status and they have a leaky roof and straw on the floor.

Having obtained the chaim he wanted and having paid the associated debts, Thengol surprised me by suggesting that we form an expedition to look for dogs. I'd assumed that the zombie dogs plan was a rather weak cover story for one of my master's igneous experiments. On the contrary, it seems that he is quite taken with the idea of resuscitated canines set to guard the castle.

    "There are a number of advantages," he explained, "even over regular dogs. Number one, zombie dogs are particularly terrifying." I had to admit that point. "Number two, zombie dogs don't require feeding." I had not been aware of this but conceded that, if true, it was a sound advantage. "Number three, enemies can't distract zombie dogs with cats or chunks of meat." I'd never heard of enemies using cats to distract guard dogs and said so.

    "Besides," I added. "Maybe they would be distracted by zombie cats?"

    "Yes, but who's going to enchant a fleet of dead cats just to attack our Covenant?"

The flawless audacity of his logic left me without answer.

    Darius had been publicly ridiculing the idea of zombie dogs for several years and so the servants were unwilling to assist us in our quest, especially when it became clear that it was not sanctioned by the Courtesan. Consequently, Thengol and I packed our bags and strode out of the gatehouse one spring morning in search of potential victims of experimentation. Siero stood guard, watching the road.

    "I see you are on a fool's errand," he said as we passed. "I see many things."

"Siero," I snapped, turning round a few yards from him. "Look into my eyes and tell me what you see in your own future." Thengol had also stopped and stood behind me smiling pleasantly.

"I see many things." My master's face hardened, "I, I see a period of quiet reflection on the benefits of discretion?" We turned and set off once more, leaving the inane gypsy giggling quietly behind us.

"We should punish him master," I said.

"You're right, what do you reckon? Should we make the gatehouse fall on his head, turn his guts to lead or just turn him into crackling with a fireball?" I brightened as the images flew through my mind. The list of possible fates reminded me that compared with the majesty of a great wizard the lives of simple warriors are worthless, mere ephemera beside the mighty strength of magic.

"You know what?" I grinned, "I can't be bothered. Let's go get some dogs."

Our first stop was the farm just across the river from the castle. An aged peasant could be seen planting vegetables in the small patch of fertile land by his home.

"Aged peasant," Thengol addressed him. "I seek dogs for special purposes. Do you have such a beast I could purchase?"

"No sir," the man replied in a slow, country burr. "Leastways, I did have one but he passed away he did. Always were a sick one was Bernard. One year his claws just grew and grew until they were too blunt to do anything with and too long for him to walk on. We had to cut them for him every month from then on. The next year, I remember, he had a dreadful sickness in his mouth. He howled night after night until his teeth fell out and gave him relief. Not all of them mind, just three teeth. The funny thing was that they didn't seem rotten or nothing, they just fell out. After that, he got well again. Too well really, he got so fat that he couldn't get after the rats no more and just sat in the sunshine all day. The year after that he hurt his paw and the sickness got into it. He had a limp after that and wasn't much use. Fat and limping Bernard he was for a couple of years. I wouldn't have been bothered with him but my wife had grown accustomed to having him around the place and kept slipping him bits of food. She was in floods when he died that summer. Just dropped dead he did, one moment stumbling across the yard, next flat on his back with his legs in the air. I took it as a bad omen and we both went to mass and did a penance to avert the curse."

"So you don't have a dog?"

"No sir, like I said," began the peasant, restarting his long and sorry history but before he'd finished, Thengol had turned on his heel and we were off.

We made our way up the river to where the village of Marenzos stood a few leagues upstream. The weather was pleasant; warm spring sunshine filtered down through the cool morning air and dried the young leaves, damp from a night-time shower. The river gurgled over its rocky bed, birds twittered in the trees and white clouds soared above the hills. I smiled, Thengol in a good mood could be good company and he was cheered by his recent victory in the council and I was enjoying the expedition; the trip might be nonsense but at least it was unlikely to be dangerous.

We arrived at our destination late in the afternoon and found most of the peasants tending their crops in the fields around the village. We separated, Thengol to go round the fields and I to try the houses. As we parted, I heard my master's voice,

"Aged peasant," he began, "I seek dogs for special purposes."

I felt that I might have more luck with a subtle approach and ran my fingers through my hair trying to produce a smart but innocent appearance. I knocked on a cottage door and was greeted by a boy of about eight or nine. He looked at me suspiciously.

"Yes?" he asked.

"Hello, yes," I replied unconvincingly. "My master has asked me to make enquiries about the purchase of a dog, for the purpose of guarding his property and I wondered if you or your family might be in the possession of such a creature and would be interested in selling, for a fee, said beast to me for the benefit of my master." The boy looked at me curiously.

"What?" he asked.

"Can I buy your dog?"

"No." My monosyllabic acquaintance shut the door firmly and disappeared inside the hovel.

This was more difficult than I had expected; the appearance of a young boy was a blow to my plan which had rather relied on an older woman being charmed by my youthful appearance and air of naivety. More practice was needed. I knocked on the next door and was greeted by a similar small boy. My heart sank.

"Young peasant," I hazarded. "I seek dogs for special purposes."

"What?" What indeed! What was I thinking?

140

"Look," I tried to start again. "My master has sent me out to buy a dog. Do you have one you want to sell?"

"No."

"Right then, thank you," but the door was already shutting and I turned away. This was clearly going to be a long day. I sat down beneath the shade of a tree and planned my next move. I was getting nowhere and I could not bear the thought of meeting Thengol in the evening and have him disappointed or, worse, sympathetic when I hadn't picked up a single dog. My subtleties were wasted on these folk; a more direct approach was required. I concentrated hard and formed the image of a hand bell in my mind. Speaking slowly and carefully, I cast the spell required to bring the instrument into reality. The result was rather misshapen and would vanish at sunset but it released a satisfying clunk when I waved it and would suit my purpose.

I strode through the hamlet, walking along lanes between farms and past houses clanking my bell and shouting,

"Dogs, dogs. We buy dogs. Fine prices, paid in good coin. Dogs, dogs, sell your dogs. Pups too young or hounds decrepit and old in the tooth, we'll buy them all. Dogs, dogs, sell us your dogs."

Finally my humiliating performance bore fruit. A well-built signora approached me.

"Do you buy dogs then?"

"Yes."

"How much for?"

"Well, I'd have to see the dogs first, before I could say," I replied, stalling for time. I had no idea of the value of a dog. Paulo would know, I thought. I followed the woman back to her home where she showed me a litter of mongrel puppies. There were six of the creatures yapping and climbing over each other. I inspected them gravely and thought hard over the lessons that I had learned when working for Paulo. We had traded furs and rugs and ornaments and clothing from all round the world but had never delved into bartering for livestock. Finally it struck me, the first lesson of working for Paulo was that goods are worth what someone is willing to pay for them. I breathed a sigh of relief.

"I'll give you three silver crowns for each one." I saw a gleam of greed spring into the woman's eye. Clearly this was a fortune to her but she was unwilling to accept my first offer.

"Four," she bartered.

"Done," I said counting the coins out of my purse. There was a look of ecstasy in her eyes as she secreted the treasure deep in the recesses of her dress. I then discovered that I had nothing to tie the dogs up with and had to buy six lengths of rope from the woman for a further crown. The woman helped me to harness the animals and then hustled me out of the door, clearly keen that I should leave before I realised the stupidity of the deal and changed my mind. She, of course, had no idea that the coins would go the way of my bell as soon as the sun slipped below the horizon.

Satisfied with my work thus far and not wishing to prolong the humiliation of parading around the village, I returned to the spot where I had agreed to meet Thengol. The puppies ran in circles as we walked and were constantly tying themselves in knots around my ankles. It was with a curious, skipping gait that I progressed out of the village and I was glad to reach my destination, tie the beasts to a tree and sink gratefully into the soft grass. The end of the day was approaching and the sun was already a scarlet semicircle on the horizon; it would not be long before it set and my deceptions would be exposed. I began to feel that the distance separating me from the village was insufficient and to hope that my master would make an appearance in the very near future.

As the segment of fire still above the horizon shrank to nothing I heard a shout and looking up saw Thengol hurtling towards me with three dogs running alongside. Behind him was a small group of angry farmers waving their tools and shouting.

"Riff-Raff, come on. Let's go." My master's voice was hoarse and punctuated by deep, gasping breaths. I got to my feet and hurriedly untied my puppies who had managed to plait their leads together as I had rested. The farmers were in better physical condition than my master and were gradually making ground. Thengol continued to sprint past me.

"Come on Riff-Raff, run for your life." Seeing that this was no idle exaggeration I ran after him, almost dragging the yelping tangle of puppies behind me. My master's first burst of speed was coming to an end and exhaustion was setting into his muscles so I was easily able to overhaul him. Unfortunately, the farmers were also catching up at an alarming rate and were now close enough for us to hear their shouts.

"Thief, scoundrel. Stop."

"They seem angry master," I said, turning. Thengol also turned and drew to a halt. Holding his hands up in the familiar gesture, he spoke the syllables of incantation firmly and clearly between his rasping breaths. A spark of flame sprang up between his palms and grew swiftly into a great ball of fire that shot with unearthly swiftness towards to approaching farmers. It sped through the group, knocking one of the peasants to the ground and scorching two others. The whole band stopped and bent over their fallen comrade whilst keeping a careful watch on the chanting wizard. A look of blind exultation had crept into my master's eye and I saw him preparing another spell. Remembering the desert and not relishing the prospect of carrying an overweight wizard across the countryside whilst leading a team of over-excited canines, I waited until a second fireball had driven the farmers back and then leaped at my master. I wrestled him to the ground as the terrified villagers pulled their wounded friend out of range.

"Create. Fire. Burn. Death. Explode. Incinerate."

"No master, calm down master. You mustn't exhaust yourself." As I forced his hands apart the gleam of exhilaration faded from his eyes. I relaxed and looked up. The dogs whined and cowered from the side of the pathway and, a little further away, the terrified locals backed towards the safety of their village.

"A success, I think master," I said, looking down. "Help me catch these wretched animals before they run off."

The dogs were still too scared to do anything but yelp timidly and it was the work of a few minutes to recapture them. It took considerably longer to undo the tangle that the six puppies had made of their ropes but eventually we were ready to begin our return journey.

"A very fine job Riff-Raff," Thengol congratulated me. "No mistakes, no errors, straight in and straight out. Very well done." I looked at him and wondered what a botched job would be like if Thengol was involved.

"Yes master, a work of genius," I replied as we walked into the deepening twilight.

Some way out of the village we passed a farm standing alone in the night.

"I bet they have a dog," my master whispered as we passed the sleeping buildings.

"It's late master, they won't sell it to you."

"Then I shall have to steal it. Wait here." With that injunction, he slipped into the night leaving me with six overexcited puppies and three irritated hounds. As I stood alone in the night the dogs leaped over each other and ran round and between my legs. It took great ingenuity and gymnastic ability to avoid being trussed like a maypole. Above my ridiculous performance an avenue of trees stood like sentinels along the road. Behind them the sky loomed, lit by starlight and a soft moon. Clouds crept across the heavens like enormous animals, mutant creatures stealing silently out of sight. A breeze blew down the lane and the hairs on my neck bristled. I shivered and looked round. The night was eerie, its silence broken by the scuffling of dogs around my ankles. I felt a presence in the night and peered from side to side, trying to force the nebulous darkness to congeal into a solid form. The dogs quietened and lay down; silence briefly reigned.

My heart beat in my chest, I could feel the blood rushing to my head. Nameless, formless fears arose in my soul. A nightmare of years gone by sprang into my mind. I imagined a great lizard crawling through the darkness, the Philosopher Beast come to reclaim me as his own. I heard his feet crunching on the stony track, his belly sweeping the floor as he dragged his bulk along the lane. I smelt the stench of death that hung around him, the ingrained reek of living in a house of bone. I saw the starlight reflect off his tiny eyes as he came closer; peering into the shadows I could just make out a patch of deeper blackness approaching. I felt his presence, the overwhelming weight of his mind pressing outwards, seeking his prey. I steeled myself to fight, to run. My legs felt like lead, my arms hung useless by my body. I forced myself to concentrate; I mustn't stand there like a helpless victim and yet I stood, my muscles refusing to co-operate. My master had come to reclaim me and I stood alone and alone I was unable to resist him.

A puppy growled. I looked down and saw the adult dogs waiting patiently, the pups sleeping in a heap. The nightmare was broken, the darkness was just night, the breeze just a wind. No longer was I a frightened child, great power ran through me; magic crackled at my fingertips. I drew a deep shuddering breath and banished my fears. Across the quiet of the night I heard a muffled curse and as I stared I saw Thengol half leading, half dragging a great beast towards us.

"Give me a hand then," he called.

"You know that's not a dog, master," I replied as I nudged the pile of puppies into wakefulness with my toe.

"They didn't have any dogs and I reckoned that a zombie donkey would make a
pretty fair guard," he explained. "Unfortunately the wretched creature is as stubborn as all hell. I think I'll call it Phosphor after the Courtesan."

"I'm sure he'll be touched, hold on." I tethered the dogs to a tree and grabbed hold of the donkey's halter. In response to the two of us tugging at the rope round its neck, the animal dug its heels in and refused to take another step.

"Maybe one of us should go round behind and push," my master suggested as he caught his breath.

"Go on then, I'll pull." Thengol strained, I heaved and the obstinate creature stayed as firmly planted as if it had roots.

"Come on Riff-Raff, try harder." I set my feet firmly on the rough ground and used all my weight to pull on the rope. Thengol, meanwhile, turned his back, set his shoulders against the donkey's rear and pushed with all his might. Phosphor lifted her tail and blessed the mage with a gentle rain of dung. Thengol swore with unintended accuracy.

"This is useless," he said as he tried to brush himself clean.

"Let me try something master." I formed my right hand into the fist of control and placed it gently against the donkey's flank. Scratching its muzzle with my left hand, I whispered the secret words of animal command in its ear. I felt her muscles relax as I grappled with her mind and her body slowly softened against mine. I stood there for a moment, then took up the rope and led her quietly to where Thengol waited with the dogs.

"The wretched creature seems to like you Riff-Raff."

"Yes, master," I replied as we made our way back to the covenant, an apprentice, nine dogs, a donkey and a slightly stinky wizard.

I've changed into dry clothes and I stand at the window sipping hot, spiced wine and watching the storm drench the courtyard. I smile in satisfaction as I see Braun bustle through the driving rain. He splashes through a puddle and I imagine his feet squelching in his boots as he approaches the door to the old building. A few minutes later the knock comes on my door.

"Enter." Braun is no longer a small child but an ugly and gawky youth. He is still short and round, however, and is yet to grow into the great hulking bear-man he hopes to be.

"Your chaim," he grunts, lobbing a pebble onto my bed. I turn on him and glare,

"What?" I ask. He glares back, a look of obstinacy in his eye but I feel his rebellion dying away as I maintain my steely gaze.

"Your chaim, oh Great Riff Raff."

"And don't you forget it little Braun."

"I don't see why I should bring you chaim every year," he says sulkily. "It's not written in the constitution. I checked. I should complain to my master. I should complain to the Courtesan."

"Yes, little Braun, but if you did that I should be forced to burn you until your pelt was bare and patchy and your growl had shrunk to a pathetic whimper." I take a step forward and look down on him.

"My master will protect me."

"Your master would be ashamed to have a snivelling, inadequate cub as an apprentice and would kill you himself rather than admit your deficiencies to the world." Braun takes a step backwards and feels for the door with one hand.

"I'll get you Riff-Raff."

"And I'll not forget that you said so, little Braun," I murmur as I push the door shut behind him.

Next year I am to work for Darius and he is to induct us both into the mysteries of illusion, the subtle nuance of appearance and deception. It is therefore important that Braun should start our period of collaboration with a suitable deference. I pick the flint off my bed and add it to the collection of chaim under my mattress. This year has been very profitable and my deal with Thengol has multiplied my wealth from a handful of pebbles to a veritable fortune of twigs, fur and pure magic distilled into crystal bottles. I consider my riches and decide that the security afforded by the underside of my bed is insufficient. A solid lock is required; I now have an enemy. Braun may be miserable and pathetic but it does not do to underestimate one's adversary. I lay back and gaze at the ceiling, my eyes sightless as I ponder the best way of dealing with the wretch.

The Fourteenth Year

"The COURTESAN may Declare the TYRANNY OF THE WIZARD at any Meeting of the FOUR High Mages, and requires only the Assent of ONE other High Mage for the TYRANNY to be Established. The COURTESAN'S Votes are counted throughout the TYRANNY"
                    From the Law of the Covenant of The Castle of The Lovers

The covenant groans under the Tyranny of the Wizard, Thengol Greydog groans as his source of chaim has been cut and I groan as I stand, listening to Darius who has chosen to address Braun and I whilst perched on his mantelpiece.

"I have been disappointed with the wealth of chaim collected over past summers and so you will both go out this night and compete for the precious flints. To the winner," he adds, smiling down at Braun, "shall go my favour and approval and upon the loser," and at this a sharp frown is fired in my direction, "shall fall punishment. Is that clear?"

"Yes Lord Darius," chants his sycophantic favourite. I merely keep my eyes fixed on the wall ahead of me and bark a monosyllable.

"Sir." It should be clear; this possibility has been suggested frequently over the last year; whenever I have demonstrated my superior intellect or insight Lord Falconwing has clucked his retort that I would be bested in the inaugural chaim claiming competition. Darius clearly expects that Braun's physical speed and fitness to prove decisive in what is effectively a trial of gymnastic prowess. Braun has filled out over the last year and his sneering grin suggests that he has faith in his firm thighs and sure feet.

This year has been a great trial to me; I do not find Kato's rooms a convivial place for study and he clearly knows little of the gentle art of illusion. Darius prefers reality and his reality is that of the hunt; cold air on his face, wild country beneath his feet and his quarry fleeing hopelessly before him. His rooms are decked out as a cave; the walls are decorated with the heads of wild creatures and their pelts are strewn across the floor. From the roof hang bunches of herbs and ingredients for the wild magic Darius prefers. There is no furniture and the few books are hidden in a corner beneath an old tree stump. Much of our study has been conducted squatting amongst the filthy skins as our teacher perched in an alcove above the fireplace. The work of assisting the wizard's work has been no better; most mornings, we have been roused before dawn and have hiked into the wilderness. Once out of sight of civilisation my companions have transformed into hawk and bear and have sped off ahead of me; their speed across rough ground or through the air too great for me to match.

The first expedition saw me attempt to keep up, running and stumbling over rocks and through streams until I lost sight of them. By now, I was exhausted and lost; we had left all traces of humanity behind us and I was alone in the wild. I stopped and drew my breath before turning resolutely on my heel and attempting to retrace my steps. Unfortunately the hillsides all looked the same and it was impossible to follow a straight line down cliffs and across ravines. I grew thirsty and drank from a mountain brook; I grew hungry and walked onwards, my belly grumbling. The sun rose and fell as the day passed and it was clipping the horizon to my right when I saw a rough track in the valley ahead of me. I reached it before the last segment of sunset was obliterated by the dark hillside and, turning into the darkness, I followed it along the valley and through the gloomy hills.

Tramping alone through the countryside was an eerie experience, the sounds of night-time echoed hollowly from the unseen rocks and the thin light of the moon bleached the landscape into shades of ghostly grey. For a while I conjured a flame to dance on my palm and light my way but the shadows that flickered beyond the reach of the firelight formed themselves into bandits and evil creatures of the dark. My courage began to fail and I found myself constantly looking behind me and peering into the darkness trying to catch a glimpse of what I hoped wasn't there. Finally I came to my senses and extinguished the flame, threading my way along the moonlit path. Even being alone and in the dark is better than being surrounded by enemies.

Eventually the path met a broader trail and, after a few miles, the trail ran into a road and soon afterwards I caught a glimpse of the tall tower of the Castle of Lovers silhouetted against the pale sky. Almost exhausted and famished from my long trek I trudged up to the gatehouse, my feet complaining with each step. In answer to my knock came the familiar call,

"Stranger or Lover?"

"Lover," I replied, too tired to engage in discussion. The gate opened,

148

"I see you have got lost." Behind Siero I heard a smothered giggle. Ignoring both of them I shuffled past, my feet barely lifted above the cobbles.

The night passed swiftly and it seemed no more than seconds after collapsing into my bed that I was awoken by an absurdly cheerful Braun to go on another expedition.

"Try not to get lost this time," he laughed. My head ached from lack of sleep, my feet protested when I bound them into my boots and my belly was still empty. Fortunately one of these handicaps was alleviated when I struggled into Darius' rooms as a generous plate of venison was lifted from the fire and placed in front of me. As I chewed, Darius explained that the next journey would have to range further into the mountains to appreciate the true magic of the wilds. I nodded my agreement with this insane plan and decided to find a more productive employment.

My opportunity came when Braun and his master transformed into dumb beasts and sped ahead of me. I made a brief show of struggling to keep up before turning round and heading for a sheltered copse not far from the covenant road. I made myself a comfortable nest between the roots of a great oak and slept soundly. Above me the day passed and presumably the bear and the hawk hunted happily in the wild hills. I awoke as the warmth of the afternoon began to fade and the sun dip swiftly between the trees. I brushed the leaves from my tunic and strode back towards the Castle of Lovers. A little ahead of me I saw Braun and Darius, transformed once more into their human forms, limping along the road and I quickened my pace to overtake them.

"Had a good day?" I asked, innocently, carefully ignoring the bloodied gash in Braun's thigh.

"We encountered a fine griffin," replied Darius haughtily, nursing his left arm beneath his jacket.

"Very edifying," I smirked.

"Well, what did you learn?" asked Braun, cheekily. "I see you have at least managed to avoid getting lost."

"I studied the ways of wild creatures and I learnt, little Braun, that it is not always wise to anger those more powerful than yourself." Braun huffed and puffed at this but could produce no good retort.

"A useful lesson Riff-Raff," Darius growled darkly, "and one I hope you will take to heart." I smiled to myself and took no notice of the admonishment.

I smile again now as Darius announces the start of what he thinks will be a race.

"The storm is beginning to build and will shortly break over the Fire Hills. I suggest that you make your way there swiftly."

"Yes, great master," grovels Braun and fairly sprints out of the room. I bow deeply and leave more decorously. By the time I reach the gatehouse, Braun has established a lead of several hundred paces but his gait has slowed to a loping jog. As I stride swiftly along the path, my gaze is fixed on the hills ahead and the thin strip of orange sky between the boiling clouds and the rocky horizon. I've watched the midsummer storm before and I know I have time to reach the summit before it will break. I slacken my pace marginally and shift my view to where Braun is struggling up the hillside ahead of me, his hands reached out in front of him, almost going on all fours as he strives to maintain his speed.

Darius' affinity for the wild outdoors and his clear preference for hunting alone with his ursine apprentice have provided me with many days of solitude and I have been careful not to allow this opportunity to slip through my fingers. By sleeping through the day I have liberated my nights for study and have found in the library great knowledge. I have also had the opportunity to conduct experiments of my own and have furnished a cave in the woods as a makeshift laboratory. There I have delved an alcove in the rock and now use it to store my chaim, keeping the opening hidden and closed by an enchantment used by the great Danielli during his stay at the Venetian court. Time alone has been time to plan and I've spent hours thinking through my situation. Just as I once planned to escape from the Philosopher Beast so I've racked my brains for a way to beat Braun to the chaim. The difference is that the Philosopher Beast was far more powerful than me whereas Braun is a much less impressive opponent. I have therefore searched the covenant library for a spell that would grant me the advantage of surprise. Unfortunately the dusty tomes contained no suitable enchantment and so I have rehearsed and practised a simple charm of my own.

The process of invention has been an exciting revelation; for the first time in my life, I have been creating magic of my own rather than emulating the spells of others. I have carefully choreographed the gestures and refined the words of power that initiate the enchantment. I have searched the ancient pages of the library for magical resonances that would increase the power of my spell and have contemplated the depths of my gift, seeking to align the sorcery with my own strengths. I have practised, refined and practised again and soon my work will be unleashed upon an unwary world or, at least, upon an unwary Braun.

I finally reach the summit and stand there panting, hands on my hips, sucking the air into my lungs. The moment of truth has arrived, our contest has begun and as soon as I regain my breath I shall be ready. Braun is waiting for me, twenty yards away, and as the first, heavy drops of rain begin to fall he shakes his fist at me.

"You were lucky, bookworm," he growls. "Any slower and you would have missed the first thunderbolt." I have neither breath to respond to this inanity nor time in which to do so as a bright light flashes from the heavens and cracks into the rocky ground not feet from where I stand. I step swiftly over and pick the glowing flint from its gravelly bed.

"One to me, methinks," I smile as I drop the chaim into my pouch. A glower crosses Braun's face but this time it is he who has no time to respond as a second lightning bolt follows hard on the thunderclap the first caused. This time the heavens strike the ground fifty feet to my left and Braun springs into action, his muscles uncoiling, his feet pushing hard against the ground. There is no competition between us, no way that I can reach the white-hot rock before him. I take a deep breath, form my right hand into the fist of control and fold the fingers of my left holding my fist out towards the glowing stone. Swiftly, I recite the syllables I know so well and finally, holding both arms in front of me as Braun bends triumphantly to claim the second peg, I call the word of initiation.

"Chaim!" From between my opponent's outstretched fingers the flint flies fast and true into my left palm. My spell works. Braun looks towards me forlornly as I drop the chaim into my pouch; I suppress a smirk as I see his eyes register defeat. He had expected that his physical prowess would suffice to overcome my guile but had underestimated my preparation. Tonight will be the night that Braun learns an important lesson about the relative strengths of muscle and magic. I plan to emphasise this lesson every time lightning strikes. Poor Braun, it looks like being a long night.

Darius' expeditions provided me with welcome opportunities to study and to develop my own magic but they have been punctuated with periods of recuperation during which the two heroes recovered from their injuries and I was left to do the chores. As I brushed, swept, polished and picked lice from the furnishings I had the dubious pleasure of hearing first hand accounts of my colleagues' exploits in the wilds. Consequently I was keen to offer my services when the Courtesan commissioned an expedition to buy rare spices from the traders in Barcelona.

"Normally, I wouldn't be keen to allow you such freedom." Darius was at his haughtiest when I came to seek his permission. "However, as Braun and I are preparing to seek out a fire drake, I think you might be safer in the city than you would be if you were to accompany us."

"Yes, Riff-Raff," Braun interjected. "You won't get hurt if you go to the city."

"Well," I replied, controlling my anger. " I can only consider that an advantage to the plan. Do I take it that I have your permission Lord Darius?"

"Yes, now go." Darius answered slowly, seeking for some offence in my answer.

The Castle of Lovers was busy preparing for the great winter feast and I was accompanied on my mission by only Antonio and M'Benga as all the warriors were in training for a festival of arms they had planned by way of entertainment. I was content by this arrangement as I had no intention of seeking combat and we were more than capable of defending ourselves against footpads and common bandits. Antonio carried a slim dagger sharpened to a lethal edge and M'Benga wore a wickedly curved knife in his belt.

"The kris swerves like a snake and strikes like a cobra past the defences of the ungodly," he told me when I asked why he used such an unusual weapon. He is no match for Mongrol or Lopez but looking at him holding the mesmerising blade in his hand, his weight balanced on the balls of his feet, I felt that he would be a doughty opponent. I put my hand on the hilt of my sword and felt confidence in the hard steel of my weapon and the courage of my comrades.

Antonio led us along the riverbank, keeping out of sight of the hillsides, hidden amongst the willows and we made good progress, sidling through thickets and tripping lightly across the wet grass. At night he insisted on burning only the driest wood in order to avoid a smoking fire and M'Benga cooked a delicious stew; menservants have certain advantages over warriors as travelling companions.

"Tell me, M'Benga," I said as we lay by the fire digesting our fine supper. "Why did you leave your own lands and come to work for Señor Phosphortube?"

"'Tis a long story," he replied, "but told briefly it goes like this. I was born free and fortunate in God's own land where he gazes down on the dry grassland throughout the day and leaves the night in the care of the true stars which tell no lies. My tribe followed the path given to us in the old days when God walked with man upon the earth; we hunted the antelope and enlivened our feasts with the roots and grasses that bless the plains. It was a fine life but I was young and did not appreciate what I had been given. I roamed far and wide seeking adventure and danger. Of both there was plenty to be had for men are not the only hunters in that land; snakes stalk through the shadows and great cats prowl at night."

"Like Cleopatra?" I asked.

"Aye, but larger, finer and more fearsome than even the devil-cat of Greydog," I smiled to hear M'Benga shared my affection for the panther. "I'll spare you the tales of high adventure as I explored far from my folk and gained the name M'Benga, the wanderer. Instead you shall hear of my pride and the fall that brought be into the clutches of the devil. One day, as I wandered, I came across an encampment. A foreign tribe had strayed onto our lands. I should have run immediately to tell my headman but I was curious and had no desire to flee before I had information to share with my people.

"Silent as a shadow and invisible as the night I crept over the rocky ground until I could see more clearly. I lay, hidden behind a patch of long grass and watched as the women lit campfires and prepared the evening meal. I was close enough to hear their voices, strange syllables carrying on the evening air. It seemed to me that they sang as they went about their business, their voices firstly high and then low, the rhythm of their talk a strange, syncopated beat. In truth, I was entranced, and not by the song but by the beauty of one of the women. Tall she was, and well formed, her skin smooth and her limbs lithe; I stared, my eyes captured, my heart won. So fiercely did I follow her every movement, the subtle shift of sun and shade as she worked, that I heard not the approach of men behind me. They grabbed me and lifted me to my feet shouting and sneering. I was taken into the encampment, bound and tied to a tentpole. I strained to free myself but to no avail. I lay there cursing myself until morning when I was released from my prison only to be tied to the harness of a camel. For days we walked across the lands, leaving my home far behind and, as we travelled, I was joined by further captives, a merry gaggle of loners and runaways stumbling behind our masters across the desert. Throughout that miserable journey I kept watch for the girl whose beauty had cost my freedom but I never saw her again.

153

"I was a slave and now I realised what I'd lost, what I'd never appreciated before; my freedom was forever gone and with it my right to walk across God's land beneath his sun and his true stars. And yet I'd not exchange my life of exile for a free and happy life in which I'd never set eyes on the perfection of God's creation, for so she must have been. Those short minutes lying in the evening sun were the reason for my existence and never can they be taken from me.

"I was sold to a trader who put me to work, beat me and sold me again. Eventually I reached the coast and was put on a slave ship where I was chained to an oar and whipped to pull harder as we ploughed our stinking way across the ocean. There I was in hell and the devil himself stood in the prow and beat his drum. The ship leaked as it stank and stank as it leaked and the timbers were rotten and loose. Eventually the time came and God reached out his hand to put an end to the evil of that ship; he called up a great storm and blew the sea into a fearsome mountain range of white-topped waves and sickening drops. The captain ran before the storm, unfurling a ragged sail and steering out into the open sea. The wet cloth swelled as the violent winds filled it and the ship groaned as strain filled the timbers. All through the night we sped across the nightmarish seascape, the cries of the men drowned by the thundering crash of the waves and the incessant shriek of tortured wood. As morning came a harsher note was added to the din, that of stone grinding against stone. The captain tried to steer us to safety but the ship was too weak, the storm too fierce and the sail was blown away, dragging spars and much of the mast with it. We turned round so that the winds blew direct against the side of the ship, a moment of calm and then blue chaos as a wave crashed against us, tumbling the ship over, rolling us towards the cruel coastline.

"In that first, dreadful moment the timber beneath my feet crumbled and my feet were loosened from their shackles. The world span round me, water gushed over me and my shipmates were swept past me. Only the grip of the iron manacles round my wrists kept me from being swept into the whirling blue sea. The wave passed and I found myself coughing, spread-eagled on top of one of the remaining cross-beams of the boat. The respite was momentary and another wall of water smashed across us firing a spiked iron boathook into the beam just in front of me. A further wave capsized us once more and my chains, rusted, old and now caught by the boathook came apart under the forces that dragged me from my repose. The torrent swept me through the turbulent water and across a wide beach of sharp shingle before slamming me into a small boulder and retreating. I had just the wits to drag myself a few feet further up the beach before falling into a dead faint.

"Señor Phosphortube found me there, nursed my wounds and, when I was well, offered me a place as his servant. I accepted for I knew that evil had dragged me far from God's country and that I should never look upon it or walk free across the grassland again. I went with my new master back to the covenant and have served him ever since."

"And you never saw that girl again?" I asked.

"Only when God takes pity on me and blesses my dreams," he smiled to himself as he made himself comfortable for the night.

The next day dawned bright and clear and Antonio led us once more along his secluded route to the big city. As we walked, I considered the story M'Benga had told and wondered at the stocky figure that strode alongside me. For years I have shared a home with this man and yet have known so little of him. I glanced across at Antonio and wondered if he too bore a story as fine and moving; I knew a little more of his life but much of his past remained a mystery that only Antonio himself could unlock.

We made our way steadily along the wooded valleys and camped comfortably at night, our fire burning clean and bright; our suppers tasty and wholesome. I listened to my companions carefully but learned little more about them; M'Benga is by nature dour and Antonio by habit secretive and neither of them wished to share any further secrets with me. Despite their reticence we grew closer as we walked through those fine sunlit days and huddled by the fire in the cold, dark evenings and I began to wish that our journey could last forever.

Unfortunately, not even Antonio's route could make this so and, a little over a week after we set off, we camped within sight of Barcelona. The next morning we joined the busy highway and slipped through the crowd, Antonio making even elbowing a fat merchant out of the way seem an act of stealth. When we reached the richer quarters of the city I saw again the great house that had so inspired me on my last visit and stopped to gaze up at the coat of arms. I smiled at my naivety and wondered at a youth that could equate a showy mansion with the power of a great mage. I had not yet reached my ambitions but I was making progress; I led my own mission and would see it end in triumph rather than humiliation or disaster. Thus resolved, I turned once more towards the city centre and followed Antonio into the crowd.

"What's the plan, sir?" asked Antonio when we reached the market.

"I'm not sure," I replied carefully. "Just keep your eyes open and your hands to yourself, we can't afford trouble." Antonio looked hurt but nonetheless placed both fists firmly in his pockets. M'Benga followed us wordlessly.

As we wandered the streets of the markets, looking at the stalls and listening to the traders, I felt a sense of disappointment; this was really nothing more than the fair that had come to the covenant. The goods were the same, the sales pitch identical and I even recognised some of the traders. I felt let down, I had expected that in the great city of Barcelona I would find greater sophistication and skill, that the city folk would demand more than mere trinkets and nonsense in exchange for their silver. On the contrary, it seemed that if the market here was rather bigger than our fair it was only made so to accommodate the most inferior stalls trading worthless rubbish for coppers.

"Where is the real trade being done?" I wondered aloud.

"What's that sir?" Antonio asked.

"Paulo wouldn't be seen dead in this place," I said. "Where would he set up his stall?"

"We haven't seen all the stores down that street."

"No, Antonio, I doubt that great commerce is being done in a darkened alleyway lined with scruffy men selling oddly shaped vegetables. We must look further afield."
I led Antonio and M'Benga away from the jostling crowds and cries of stall-holders towards the docks.

"Goods arrive here in ships and leave by mule. This is where we'll find the real merchants and where we must look if we're to sniff out the spices." We walked behind the great warehouses and down the fishing quays; we peered through windows and climbed onto roofs but found no sign of the commerce I knew must be going on. Eventually, it grew dark and we found our way to an inn in which to spend the night.

"The Merchant's Purse," I read to my companions as we entered. "Keep your ears open, we might learn something to our advantage." A handful of copper coins equipped us with two rooms and large helpings of a tasty fish stew. After we had dined we circulated the public bar, listening to the gossip of the day. The inn was well named, there were dozens of merchants staying, eating or merely drinking there; unfortunately they were of the common market variety and the talk was of trinkets sold to gullible peasants rather than of rare spices from the east. Tired and dispirited we went to bed early.

I was woken by a strange premonition and saw Antonio sidle into the dark room. The air felt strangely alive, the hair bristled across the back of my neck.

"What is it Antonio?" I asked, but it was M'Benga's deep voice that answered

"The wind has shifted." I thought of returning to my slumbers but I was filled with a strange energy, all sleepiness had dropped away.

"Let's see if this breeze brings trade to the docks."

"The inn is locked up against brigands. We'll have to wait for first light," M'Benga remonstrated.

"I hate to suggest it but I'm sure Antonio can find us an alternative." I looked across at the Spaniard who was already unravelling a rope from beneath his cloak.

We let ourselves out of the window, crept across the courtyard and waited while Antonio hurled his rope over the wall. The iron claw chinked loudly in the still night and a dog barked in the distance but there was no stirring from the inn. Antonio climbed the wall first, I followed and M'Benga coiled the rope up behind him. We dropped down the far side of the wall into the quiet street and crept silently towards the shore.

"Why are we creeping silently," I whispered.

"To avoid alerting our enemies," Antonio hissed back. I shrugged, who knew what enemies Antonio might have in a city the size of Barcelona? Safe passage into the harbour was marked by lanterns on the shore but these lights were dim beneath the crescent of a yellow moon, its reflection broken by a thousand ripples. In the clear light we saw a tall ship drifting into port, its white sails catching the breeze high above the water that gushed round the prow. Despite the apparent effortless drift, the craft was nearing the shore at a surprising pace. I paused to think as the ship slipped towards us and quickly made a plan.

"Antonio, you need to get on board that ship as soon as she drops anchor. Find out what cargo she's carrying and report back here. M'Benga you're to be my mysterious African companion; find out if there are any other traders out here tonight. Say as little as possible." Antonio faded like a ghost into the greyness and M'Benga stepped into a patch of shadow and was gone. I stood alone by the side of a warehouse and watched the beautiful ship sail gently into the harbour. A flurry of activity on deck saw the sails furled and an anchor dropped. In the pale light of the moon I saw a fleeting shape row silently across the water and into the shadow of the great ship. I waited in the darkness.

"Sir," it was M'Benga's gruff voice, not Antonio's hiss. "There are three other merchants on the docks; they seem to recognise the ship but don't know what cargo it's carrying."

"They recognise the ship, you say?" I asked. "Who do they say it is?"

"They don't use a name but it's clear they're expecting a great trader."

"And the merchants on the dock? Are they the half-florin relic salesmen we saw in the market yesterday?"

"These seem to be men of substance."

"I wonder about that ship; I wonder if I could put a name to its owner," I murmur. As we talked I saw more activity on the ship; boats were lowered into the water and bales of goods bundled into them.

"C'mon Antonio, where are you?"

"Just here sir, sorry about the delay sir," answered my breathless and dripping companion. "They're carrying cloth from Marseille."

"Thank you Antonio," I replied, gratefully.

"But hidden in a secret compartment they've got fine bronze statues from Italy." I turned to him and smiled.

"Come M'Benga, let's trade." We walked towards the jetty where a group of men had gathered. They turned to look as we approached.

"French textiles M'Benga," I said conversationally. "They'll make a fine profit when we bring them up to Leon."

"Yes Oc'hacha," he rumbled in reply. I raised an eyebrow.

"I understand the court in Madrid is also keen on the fabrics of Provence," I added, "Do you think we should take them there instead?"

"No Oc'hacha." Fortunately we were interrupted before I had to manufacture any more one-sided trader talk.

"Forgive me for interrupting, but do I take it that you know what goods he's carrying?" I assumed an irritated tone,

"Of course," I turned my back on my questioner and frowned at M'Benga. The merchants began to babble, excited by the news. An auction broke out and was stopped only by the arrival of the first boats.

"Twenty florins," shouted one excited merchant.

"Twenty four," cried another.

The bemused captain stepped from the boat onto the shore.

"I have fine linen from Marseille worth," but he was interrupted.

"Twenty eight florins a bale," called out a voice.

"Thirty eight," I found myself saying. Six pairs of eyes turned to me and I felt a prickle of sweat form between my shoulder blades. After an uncomfortably long silence one of the merchants accepted the challenge,

"Thirty nine florins a bale."

"Forty."

"Forty one."

"Fifty," this time it was M'Benga raising the stakes but by now the merchants were too excited to give in, even for a moment.

"Fifty five."

"Fifty six."

I placed a hand on M'Benga's shoulder and led him quietly into the shadows.

"Oc'hacha?" I asked.

"Means watering hole, very mysterious," he answered gruffly. The sun was beginning to rise and the deep blue of the harbour was suffused with fiery light as we returned to Antonio.

"Let's go and have breakfast," I suggested, "and then, Antonio, you can deliver a message for me."

The innkeeper was surprised to find us at his gate that morning but let us in without comment and served us a fine breakfast of cold ham and bread. When we had finished I turned to Antonio,

"Wait until the unloading is over and then find the captain of the ship," he nodded his comprehension. "Tell him that your master doesn't want to buy any linen but that I am interested in his other cargo."

"Yes sir, the other cargo," echoed Antonio, putting a careful emphasis on the word "other". As he slipped out of the inn I leaned back in my chair and smiled warmly.

"Another jug of ale, I think, M'Benga. It's going to be a glorious day."

We waited all morning in the inn and Antonio returned shortly before lunch. As the afternoon drew on and the sun began to sink towards the horizon he began to look a little disturbed.

"Don't you think we should go out to look for the spices, sir?" he asked.

"No, Antonio, I think that any spices there are may just be coming in to look for us." A well dressed servant had just entered and exchanged a few words with the innkeeper before being directed to our table.

"My master says that you should come with me." I looked him over, a fine capable young man with a scribe's fingers and a warrior's scar. I rose from my chair.

"And what is your name?" I asked.

"Jorge," he replied.

"Then lead on, Jorge. Let's see what your master has to say."

We walked quickly through the streets of Barcelona towards the richer areas until we found a large, unmarked house of white stone. We entered the gate and followed Jorge up the stairs where we were led into a clean room with a polished, wooden floor.

"Wait here." The walls were decorated with fine paintings and I was admiring a map of the world marked in exquisite detail when I heard a voice behind me.

"Riff-Raff." I turned,

"Paulo," I smiled warmly and we embraced.

"I think I owe you about forty florins a bale for this morning's work," he smiled. "How can I repay the debt?"

"I've been commissioned to buy rare spices from the Orient but I can't find any," I replied.

"No, you wouldn't. It's rare that a cargo reaches Spain and rarer still that it hits the open market." My face fell. "However, a fool outbid me in Venice a month ago and he's following the coast round to the Moorish ports in the south. We could engage in a spot of interception if you were interested. I could do with three young men who were handy with a cutlass." I pondered the suggestion.

"Interception?" I asked. Paulo nodded. "How would we share the intercepted goods?"

"We split the cargo evenly, you get half, I get half. I get to keep the ship and any prisoners we take."

"That sounds very generous," I said slowly.

"As I say, I owe you and I like to keep short accounts. Life's simpler that way," Paulo grinned. I turned to my companions. Antonio's hand had slipped to his dagger and a wolfish grin had crept across M'Benga's black face.

"Let's do it," I decided.

The last glimmer of sunlight shimmered through the water streaming from our oars as we rowed across the harbour to Paulo's ship. Antonio had suggested we wait for dark and then edge our way round the harbour beneath the sheltering shadow of the breakwater but Paulo insisted that it was perfectly normal behaviour to row out to one's ship in the evening. We sat in the stern of the little boat and watched as a muscular sailor hauled his oars through the chuckling water. Slowly he heaved us towards the high sided ship and finally rested on his oars as we drifted gently against the solid wood.

"Gentlemen, I give you the Santa Anna. The fastest cargo ship in the ocean." As Paulo spoke, a rope was thrown down and we climbed up the side with varying amounts of grace. My efforts raised a hastily concealed chuckle from the watching sailors whilst Antonio was on deck before anyone had noticed his approach. After M'Benga had heaved himself up by brute strength and the sailor following him had used less energy to achieve the same end, the rope was untied and coiled neatly. At a word from Paulo my companions were led beneath the decks to where they would be safely out of the way during our voyage and I followed my host to his luxuriously appointed cabin.

Against the side wall a cot was slung from the ceiling so that it rocked gently as the small harbour wavelets lifted the ship beneath our feet. Along one side of the cabin, portholes allowed us to see across the dark seas to where the paler sky remembered the daylight. The room was richly appointed; the cot was decorated with a finely embroidered coverlet, the portholes were bounded by gleaming brass and the space was dominated by a large desk of light and dark wood intricately inlaid onto which Paulo unrolled a strange map. Unlike the ones in his town house this map was strangely plain with large blank spaces and cities neatly marked with small black circles. The greatest detail was reserved for the coastline with cliffs, beaches and even underwater rocks marked and carefully labelled.

"We are here," he said, pointing at a bay on my side of the map. "Julius set out from Rome in the Athene three weeks ago and will be following this coastline here."
"So we just sail along here and intercept him about here?" I asked pointing to a likely spot.

"That's inland and it might be a little more tricky than that but your theory is sound," answered Paulo looking out of the window. "Darkness falls, I think it might be time for us to make sail," he added ringing a bell which summoned a tall, bald man to the cabin. Some incomprehensible commands, a few loud shouts and lots of stamping later heralded a lurch to starboard and the ship began to turn slowly away from the shore.

161

"I doubt we'll reach him for a few hours yet, you can use my bunk if you're tired or come up on deck with me." I turned towards the cabin door but felt suddenly weary. It had been a long day and I would need to be rested if I was to indulge in piracy. Despite the occasional jolt the strange bed was surprisingly comfortable; the ship rocked wildly as it rode the swell but the cot, suspended from the ceiling merely swayed, gently lulling me to sleep.

When I awoke, I found myself in darkness; the last light of day had long gone and no moonlight illuminated the cabin. I rubbed my eyes and carefully felt my way around the room to the door. Once there, I stepped outside and found myself in a dark passageway. Not fancying my chances of stumbling blind round a strange ship I called out

"Hey! Any chance of a light down here?" A strange cackle served as my answer but it was soon followed by the arrival of the bald sailor illuminated by a sturdy lantern.

"The captain says you should come up on deck." Shrugging, I followed my guide along what I now perceived to be an open walkway. Peering over the handrail I saw the foaming water speeding along the side of the ship. Turning my back on the waves I climbed a ladder and found myself on a raised deck at the rear of the ship. Ahead of us the great sails soared high into the night and beneath them men toiled to ensure our course remained steady. Beyond the ship I could see nothing but blackness; it seemed that the inky seas stretched forever, swallowing what little light was produced by our lanterns or shone from the few stars that peeped between the thick clouds above. I peered keenly into the dark.

"How are we to find anything in this?" I asked, only now realising the difficulty of our task.

"Watch," answered Paulo taking something from his coat. He placed it in a bowl of water on the deck in front of him and gestured that I should take a closer look. A long, thin piece of wood as thick as my thumb and a span in length had been carved into the shape of a tiny boat with a dragon's head at the bow and its tail at the stern. The inside of the boat was inlaid with a single piece of black stone.

"Pick it up and turn it round." I did as I was bid. The boat was heavy from the weight of the stone and water dripped from its keel as I gave it a half turn. When I placed it back in the water, a strange thing happened. Very slowly and without any external force, the boat twisted round in the bowl until the dragon's head was again facing the direction it had started.

"An old sailors' trick," Paulo said in answer to my astonishment. "It's called a lodestone and points towards true north. This one, however, is a little special. I bought it from a Northern wizard who'd fallen on difficult times." From his pocket he took a soft leather pouch and shook a sliver of wood out into his hand. "A splinter from the Athene's figurehead," he explained and placed it carefully in the little boat. As he moved his hand away the lodestone twisted an eighth of a turn anticlockwise. "Now it points towards the Athene and it seems that we are getting close. A quarter turn to port please Diego," he bellowed.

"A quarter turn to port," echoed the helmsman and the sailors scurried across the ship pulling ropes and turning the sails. Slowly the great ship turned and as it did the little boat appeared to spin in its bowl, now pointing towards the starboard bow.

"We'll plot a course to intercept them," explained Paulo pocketing the lodestone and carefully replacing the splinter of wood in its pouch.

I positioned myself on the starboard side of the stern deck and peered into the darkness. I could see no sign of a merchant ship or, indeed, of any other kind of disturbance on the broad sea but maintained my position patiently, huddled inside my cloak against the cold and stamping my feet occasionally to renew the flow of blood. Eventually a cry came from the top of the mast.

"Sail ahoy!"

"Extinguish all light," ordered Paulo urgently and added as the men moved to obey his command, "and move quietly, we don't want to give them any warning." The Santa Anna sailed on through the darkness, its timbers creaking eerily in accompaniment to the splash of the waves on her bow. From my vantage spot I could see nothing of the rumoured prey but continued to peer across the ocean ahead of us. As I was beginning to doubt the existence of another vessel in these waters, I saw a glimmer of light on the horizon. I blinked and rubbed my eyes and could soon make out two bright pinpricks. I watched the lights and saw the form of a sailing vessel emerge from the darkness. Still we hurried towards it with as much stealth as possible. By the time the lookout on the Athene saw us we were close enough to hear his cry,

"Pirates!" I felt a hand on my shoulder,

"Get your men ready Riff-Raff, they can't get away now." I hurried below and roused M'Benga. Antonio was awake and looking distinctly green,

163

"It's the swaying sir." He paused for a moment and then corrected himself. "The swaying and the rocking, sir. It disagrees with me."

"You'll have more to worry about than the swaying in a minute Antonio, we're going into battle." We took our positions at the starboard rail amongst a band of bloodthirsty sailors bearing vicious cutlasses and long pikes. On the Athene we saw a similar rank of defenders waiting for us with weapons drawn. The two ships collided. Ropes and grapnels were hurled to make the ships fast and the sailors swarmed across from the Santa Anna. I looked queasily down at the foot of black water churning between the ships, gulped and, drawing my sword, vaulted across the gap into the press of bodies. I landed awkwardly with my sword arm inside the Athene and the rest of me scrabbling outside. After an age of panic, my foot found a purchase and I was able to heave myself into the enemy ship in time to roll out of the way of an angry defender's axe. The weapon splintered the boards by my head and I stumbled to my feet and half parried a second blow. The clang of crashing blades rang in my ears as a shock wave numbed my arm and I took a step backwards. Two more blows followed quickly and I found myself pressed firmly against the solid wood of a mast. I held my sword firmly, desperately recalling Mongrol's lessons. I fixed my eyes on those of my assailant and found I could read his stroke. A firmer parry kept him at bay and I found the strength returning to my arm. The blows came in quickly but I was able to push back, away from the mast and began to drive him backwards. My breath was coming quickly and I saw the sweat dripping from my opponent's straggly beard. I saw an opening in his defence and lunged towards his belly. A reflex defence caught my sword in the angle of his axe. As he twisted free, my grip loosened and my sword flew out of my hand, slid across the deck and fell into the ocean. The sailors glance flickered towards my disappearing weapon and then returned to me; he drew his arm back to strike. I held my hands out in defence and stepped backwards. As I retreated, I drew my breath for my last gamble. My opponent stepped forwards, his eyes showing his delight in my helplessness. I felt the mast at my back once more and, holding my palms towards him cried out

"Fire!" The flame that sprang from my hands could not really be called a fireball but it was enough; the bearded man let out a cry of terror and flung both arms up to his face. A voice called from my right;

"Oc'hacha!" I turned and saw M'Benga toss me a cutlass, its blade red with blood. I smiled my thanks and then turned to my adversary who, partially blinded by the flame, stumbled away from my new weapon. I let out a joyous cry and pursued him. He turned to run, tripped on a coil of rope and tumbled towards the rail. He scrabbled weakly for a grip but the ship lurched beneath a large swell and he was tipped into the dark seas. I turned towards the melee and found that our opponents were trying to give up. Paulo strode across a gang plank to take formal surrender of the ship and I found Antonio had recovered from his sea-sickness sufficiently to master three opposing sailors. M'Benga was cleaning his kris on the shirt of a fallen foe and was once more grinning broadly.

"A fine fight Oc'hacha," he said. I put one arm around each of my comrades. Exhilaration filled my body, a mixture of relief at my survival and joy in the victory. A breeze fluttered across the ocean filling my lungs with clean salt air and I realised that I had finally found the freedom I'd been seeking all my life. We could stay with Paulo, a life of trading and piracy, of excitement, adventure and comradeship. I need never be alone, I need never call another man master. I need never return to the thrall of Darius Falconwing or Thengol Greydog.

"A fine fight indeed," I replied as Antonio scrambled out of my embrace to retch over the side of the captured vessel.

The storm dies with a flourish, three thunderbolts falling almost simultaneously on the hill between us.

"Chaim!" I call and, gathering myself turn to the second glowing flint, "Chaim!" Two more pegs of pure magic find their way into my pouch but before I can recite the spell a third time Braun has reached the final magical stone. We both look up at the receding clouds.

"I think that may be all, little Braun, don't you?" Braun cuts a poor figure. His clothes are soaked and water runs from his thick hair. His hands bear scratches from the times he dropped to all fours, confused by panic. His shoulders have dropped and three lonely fragments of rock lie in the pouch at his waist. He nods and I turn to climb back down the hill. This is the moment for which I returned to the Castle of Lovers. I've come too far to sell my apprenticeship for the freedom and friendship of the sea; instead I shall complete my fifteen years, shall pass my gauntlet and shall gain freedom of a different kind. My plan for tonight has worked, my magic is triumphant and I am eager to face Lord Darius Falconwing with eleven pegs of chaim to his protégé's three. I do not anticipate the promised great favour but am eager to see what punishment will be meted out on the hapless Braun. I have no need of Darius' favour; my piracy has left me ludicrously wealthy and the success of my mission has endeared me to the Courtesan.

The three of us returned from Barcelona in fine spirits, dressed in fine clothes and with heavy money belts. In a small leather bag I carried a large sample of the finest spices of the orient; the rest having been sold for cash. Paulo had bought the surplus cargo from us for a fair price and had recommended a good tailor before setting out for Grenada to maximise his profit.

"I see you have had a successful journey." I was so pleased with myself that I couldn't be bothered to berate Siero for his useless fortune telling.

The night after we returned was the solstice and the night of the Covenant feast. At sundown we gathered in the courtyard and joined hands to form a great circle. I stood between Antonio and M'Benga as the Courtesan read the Covenant spell from an ancient tome held by Thengol. Holding chaim in each hand he called upon magic from deep in the earth to keep the Castle of Lovers safe and to protect it from its ancient enemies. Then he called upon us all to answer,

"Lovers, will you be faithful?"

"Yes, to our love," we called back. I glanced sideways at Antonio and M'Benga and, as I felt the warmth of their hands in mine, I felt a strange thrill shiver down my spine. The ceremony continued, solemn but exciting, familiar but challenging.

"Lovers, will you be true?" Again, we responded,

"Yes, to our love," and I looked round the circle at the faces around me. All of us were there, wizards, apprentices, warriors, servants and guests; even Juan had descended from his pole to join the pagan rite, part of an agreement by which the Courtesan attends mass on Easter Morning.

"Lovers, will you defend your beloved?"

"Yes, from foe or fiend, from any who threaten or dare to cross the unseen boundaries of love." I gripped my neighbours hands tightly and looked once more round the circle at the community that makes this strange and lonely castle my home.

Then the celebrations began. Lopez, Mongrol and Pedro performed a choreographed demonstration of their fighting prowess, Romario sang a great ballad of true lovers separated by fate and, in the centre of the courtyard, Thengol lit an enormous bonfire round which we danced and drank and sang. Sparky provided some amusement by

166

bringing Augustus to the party and getting him to perform a vigorous but rather uncoordinated jig. Conchita had been working all day to provide us with a feast to which we added two great boar, caught by Hawkeye and Darius and roasted over the flames of the fire. As I wandered through the crowd I saw Antonio retelling the tale of our piracy with increasing exaggeration as alcohol gained the upper hand. I settled down to listen to the tale of how we had single handedly fought off a fleet of Persian warboats manned by the damned.

"Did you really conjure a firestorm that incinerated four ships?" asked Thengol, sitting down beside me. I grinned,

"How are you getting on with the zombie dogs?"

"Well," he nodded. "It's a little more tricky than I'd hoped; they seem curiously reluctant to be resurrected once I've killed them."

"I can see how that might be the difficult stage."

"Still, I'm making progress thanks to Adriel. I owe you some chaim, by the way."

"Excellent," I smiled.

The party continued until the sun rose on the embers of a fire and clusters of drunken revellers trying to summon the strength to find their beds. As I stumbled past Antonio's slumbering form, I stooped tenderly to pull his cloak round him, then straightened and staggered up to Thengol's rooms to claim my dues before he forgot his generosity. Armed with eight pegs of chaim extracted from a sleepy and rather befuddled wizard I struggled across the courtyard and up the stairs to where my own bed awaited me.

The next council meeting proved rather significant and Darius recounted events gleefully as I scoured the flesh off an antelope's skull for him. Apparently Thengol had gone to the council to demand another enormous grant of chaim in order to continue his experiments on the dogs but, before he was able to vote himself the fifty pegs he needed, the Courtesan stopped him by hammering on the table. With all eyes upon him he said in a firm voice,

"I propose a Tyranny of the Wizard."

"A what of the what now?" asked Thengol. At that Señor Phosphortube unravelled the Law of the Covenant of the Castle of Lovers and pointed to the passage detailing the awful consequences of the Tyranny of the Wizard.

"It says here you need the assent of one other high mage," my master pointed out.

"Yes, Pato, do you assent?"

"No, I certainly do not. You don't deserve four votes. That's not reasonable."

"I have four votes anyway, I just use them sparingly."

"Well, I think it's a ridiculous idea," and Darius made a great play of impersonating Lord Greydog's petulance.

"Very well, Lato, do you assent?"

"I will have nothing to do with this nonsense," Adriel replied. "The Law is ridiculous and petty."

"I'm sorry you feel that way. Kato, do you assent?" This, of course, was Lord Darius' great moment. His single vote had suddenly gained a real significance and he seized his opportunity.

"Yes, Courtesan, I assent. Let the glorious Tyranny begin!"

"Thank you Kato," replied Sparky gravely. "Now, back to business, I believe the Chaperone wanted us to vote on a grant of chaim."

"Fifty pegs, needed for the defence of the covenant."

"And it will be used in what way to defend the covenant?"

"It is to continue the project of building a ditch round the castle walls and filling it with ravenous zombie dogs to fight off any invaders."

"Very well. Pato, how do you vote?"

"In favour."

"Kato?"

"Against, as always."

"Lato?"

"I shall not vote on this measure."

"And, considering the current state of the castle's defences, the likelihood of attack and the resources already dedicated to this project I shall vote against. That makes a total of three votes in favour and five votes against and the chaim is not granted." I can only imagine the look of hatred and anger that crossed Thengol's face when he realised that he could no longer help himself to the covenant resources but Darius' exultation as he crowed about my master's defeat will remain with me forever.

Three more times during the year Thengol requested another grant of chaim and each one was defeated by the same margin. As spring brightened into summer and his reserves began to fall low so his mood blackened and cast a shadow across the whole community. Now, as I turn towards my master's rooms to begin my last year of apprenticeship,

I look around at the castle walls. We are a house at war with itself and the next twelve months could be very interesting.

The Fifteenth Year

It is midsummer and I stand upon the roof of the old tower and watch the storm striking the Fire Hills to the west. I have completed my training and now need only to fulfil my master's challenge in order to gain my freedom. The challenge was laid down hours ago in Lord Greydog's rooms and I have six months in which to fulfil it or my life is forfeit. I have climbed up here to take pause and to reflect on the coming six months which will see the end of my apprenticeship one way or another.

Lightning flickers between the clouds as the storm builds to its crescendo. The past fifteen years of my life have built to this moment and I stand poised to grab hold of my destiny. If I complete Thengol's challenge I shall be a Full Mage of the Covenant and, whilst I shall be the most junior mage with no vote on the council, I shall be free of my apprenticeship and one step closer to my dreams of glory and power. This moment is the fulcrum of my destiny; success will lead to greatness, failure to death. All my life so far has led to this hour, all my plans, struggles, hopes and fears and, as a great river flows from the pool beneath a waterfall, so the rest of my life will flow from this challenge.

The last year has been very busy. I have studied hard to complete my knowledge of magic and to understand every last aspect. I still have much to learn but there are no secrets of sorcery that remain completely hidden to me. I have also been hard at work in my cave and, in the depths of winter as my master worked alone in his rooms, I started work on my greatest treasure. Since my adventure with the Kernelwyrm one flask of the dread creature's blood has lain safely with my store of chaim and now I began to experiment with the precious fluid. Carefully, I diluted a few drops with clear water and mixed it carefully with other magical ingredients. I noted the results on a clean roll of parchment I had bought with my new wealth and tested the liquid on a captured rat at each stage. Most of the mixtures had little effect but I did discover that by adding olive oil, sea salt and charcoal I was able to produce a green vitriol that ate through the flask and my table before burning a hollow in the stone floor of my cave. I cleaned away the damage and washed the floor thoroughly before continuing carefully with my experiments. Most of the rats survived the tastings I inflicted and presumably found that their spells of destruction were doubled in power and I grew quite fond of the rodents I kept in an iron cage.

I was therefore rather sorry when I tested a potion on the eldest rat and it dropped dead. I had mixed equal measures of brimstone and blood and found the resulting reaction had boiled furiously before subsiding into a clear, odourless liquid. I was fascinated to discover the effects of this new magic and reached for the well-fed creature I had nicknamed Toad. Knowing that partaking in my little experiments was always rewarded with food, Toad was keen to taste what looked like water as I poured a little into a bowl. As soon as he had begun to drink, Toad's eyes swivelled in his head, his legs buckled and he collapsed on the ground. I could find no sign of life in the creature and feared I had been the victim of a dreadful coincidence. To ensure that I properly understood the effects of my sorcery, I reached into the cage for a vicious moth-eaten specimen.

"Here, Braun," I said to the rat. "Try some of this yummy drink." The creature drank thirstily and swiftly suffered the same fate as Toad. "Oh dear," I sighed as I noted this second death. "If only it were as easy to dispose of your namesake. Don't worry little ones," I added, turning to a rather empty looking cage. "I'll find you some new friends to play with." I made a last couple of notes and then began to try to replicate my creation.

Over the next few weeks I tested my potion thoroughly and found that whilst it was certainly efficacious for the slaughter of rats I could not find a spell powerful enough to reveal it as poison. Whenever I passed a pearl over the clear liquid, it remained as lustrous as if it had been used to check on clear spring water. It seemed that my experiment had been successful and I had to concentrate to subdue the triumph that built in my chest. This was just the first stage in my plotting, there was more to be arranged before I could put my plan into action and even this, first stage was incomplete. One more test remained to be performed and, for this, I would need a suitable victim. I could not afford discovery or trial and so needed an excuse to journey far beyond the covenant walls. I needed a human victim and a tremor of horror crept over me as I contemplated the conclusion to which I had come. I had heard Juan's words on the sanctity of human life, heard him say that save for the bread and wine of the holy sacrament, our fellow humans are the greatest exhibition of holiness we will see before we come face to face with God himself. The tremor passed, I knew the value of human life and needed no priest to emphasise it. Destiny drove me onwards. Juan also said that the finest act is when a man sacrifices his life for another. How much better it must be if a wizard should sacrifice another life for his own greatness?

A crash of thunder follows a jagged burst of fire from the skies. The lightning strikes again, blind and ruthless in its ambition to reach the earth. I see a flicker of orange flame and a wisp of smoke where a tree has come between the lightning and its destination. The tree is far from me but I smell the smoke in the sultry air. The storm has imprisoned the fumes and vapours of the earth and there is no escape from this heavy burden until the crisis is passed and clear calm rules once more. Thunder bellows again; lightning feels no pity.

"Antonio," I said one morning on finding the handyman sweeping one of the workshops. "How is the weathervane market this year?"

"Slow sir," he replied. "It's difficult to find suitable merchandise. For instance, the vane upon the church at Monzon is said to be enchanted and highly valuable but the spire is dizzyingly high and the vane rusted firm onto the roof. There's no way a single weather vane tradesman could harvest it under such circumstances."

"Highly valuable you say?"

"Yes sir, extremely so."

"And rusted firm onto the roof?"

"Sadly yes, sir."

"How infuriating for you Antonio."

"Indeed sir."

I strode off to continue my studies and mused upon Antonio's problem. He deserved some success in his enterprises and I felt I owed him something for the courage he had shown on board ship last year. Impossible for a single tradesman to harvest he had said and although I felt that the word tradesman was a little generous I wondered if a single weathervane thief might manage the task if he had sufficient assistance from a talented comrade.

As I studied the deepest secrets with which I have grappled to date: the very magic of magic, I found my mind straying to Antonio. An odd-job man and part time felon deserved an occasional success and I felt that I had the opportunity to present him with one. I shut the book, my chapter unread, and rehearsed some small enchantments that might be useful. There was no time to develop a new spell but a little practice in the spontaneous manipulation of magical power gave me confidence that we could be successful.

By the time the dawn broke the next morning, flooding the sky with crazy shades of pink, I was exhausted, having worked through the night on my intonation and gesture. My eyelids flickered as I fought to stay awake and I felt a strange, uncomfortable wakefulness in my muscles. I closed the door to my cave and made my way back to the covenant. I passed Antonio as I stumbled bedwards in search of some well-earned rest.

"Antonio," I murmured as I walked by. "There's a mission. Sundown tonight. Be ready." He turned to me, his face full of questions but I never broke stride, my exhausted legs carrying me inexorably onwards.

As I lay on the bed, the last rays of coloured dawn fading on the wall of my room, my eyelids continued to flicker; having been forced open for so long they were unwilling to close. My thoughts flit from the words of my incantations to the challenge of the evening to my need for sleep. My legs twitched nervously, my body continuing to fight against sleep. Finally, however, tiredness overcame me, my muscles calmed, my mind relaxed and oblivion covered me.

When I awoke the room was dim; the sun was starting to set on the far side of the tower and little of its gentle light made its way through my window. I arose with a jolt, remembering the preparations I needed to make and changed into a sensible hiking outfit. I packed a bag and filled a small silver flask with brandy then went over to the window and looked out. Sunlight still warmed the gatehouse but the shadows were lengthening quickly; I pulled my boots on and slipped quietly down the stairs.

As I emerged from the front door I saw the courtyard like a tableau set before me; Siero was on his way to relieve Hawkeye who was standing by the open gate ready to perform the familiar charade. Antonio was lurking in a doorway close by. Nobody else paid them any attention; it was a busy moment as everyone worked to get their last chores completed before dark.

I strode purposefully across the cobbles, passing unremarked through the busy courtyard. I felt rather than heard Antonio fall in behind me and then we had reached the gate.

"Stranger or Lover?" came the challenge and I felt myself tense.

"Guardian and sentry of both." As the answer was given I felt myself relax; Hawkeye had no interest in Antonio or I and we passed unmolested through the gatehouse as the sentries voices sang out behind us.

"Know you the secrets?"

"Of lovers or friends?" The performance died away as we walked swiftly to the river.

"Where are we going sir?" asked my companion.

"To Monzon to liberate the weathervane?"

"Truly sir?"

"Yes, the Courtesan requires its magic for a deep enchantment and will pay us generously if we acquire it for him." Antonio nodded approvingly. "I think that between us we have the skills to do the job."

"I agree sir. Weather vane acquisition is a speciality of mine."

"I know Antonio, I know."

As we walked through the deepening gloom Antonio told me of the difficulties presented by the enchanted weathervane of Monzon.

"The churchyard is surrounded by a high wall blessed by the bishop to deter devilish intruders."

"We've been over churchyard walls before and I don't consider either of us to be particularly devilish."

"No sir. Enterprising certainly, devilish no." In the short pause that followed, I was struck by the silence that had fallen with the night. The breeze had stilled, the birds quietened and the only sounds were those made by ourselves, the intake of breath and the fall of booted foot. "The church itself is vast with the weathervane proudly displayed upon the highest tower."

"You have your rope?" I checked.

"Yes sir, climbing the tower will be no problem for me." He looked doubtfully at my generous bulk.

"I'll manage Antonio, trust me I'll manage."

"Very well sir. Well, once we get to the top of the tower we'll have to find a way to liberate the treasure. There are eight great bolts and each one was fastened by the village's strongest man and has since become corroded with rust. It's said that the devil himself has tried and failed to pull the weathervane off the church at Monzon."

"We shan't be relying on brute strength. I suppose you've considered oiling the bolts?"

"Yes sir, two summers ago. Three nights of patience and a hogshead of finest olive oil it cost me and to no avail. The rust is too thick sir and the bolts too old."

"Then we must try something else."

"Yes sir, but even supposing you manage to undo the bolts we're left with the problem of the weathervane itself."

"I thought it would be an asset rather than a problem," I wondered.

"Well sir, rightly speaking it will be an asset, once we get it back to the Castle of Lovers, that is. The problem is that the enchanted weathervane of Monzon is made in the shape of a bull and stands as tall as a man. Half a ton of solid copper is a bit of a problem sir, as well as being an asset as you say." I gulped. I hadn't realised the size of the undertaking.

"I can see that would be a challenge. Still, " I mused, "if we have the skills and ingenuity to get the thing loose I'm sure that we'll think of a way to transport it. It's just a question of force and power."

"Yes sir," replied Antonio, by no means convinced by this answer.

We walked through the dim countryside, our way lit by the stars and the misshapen remnants of a moon. The locals called the end of a waning moon "the devil's light" and considered it a bad omen. I wondered whether a bad omen could be a good thing if you were attempting to sin in a way that had defeated the lord of darkness himself. My musings were interrupted by Antonio who had been acting strangely for a little while. Every now and then he would half turn suddenly to look over his shoulder and peer into the gloom behind us. Now he stopped completely and turned back to harangue the darkness.

"What is it? What do you want?" The silence was broken by a faint wind blowing through the branches and the rustle of small rodents scurrying through the grass. Antonio's strange conversation continued; the replies to his questions audible only to him.

"What?"

"No, I won't."

"Not trust him? Rubbish!"

"Leave me alone. Let me go!"

"Antonio," I interrupted, "what is it? Who are you speaking to?" He appeared to pull himself together and turned to face me.

"It's like this sir," he explained. "It's the ghost of my uncle Carlo, sadly drowned in poaching accident. He haunts me sir, he won't let me be alone." I wondered briefly at the exact nature of the poaching accident but dismissed the idea from my mind and asked,

"What's he saying?"

"He's telling me to turn back. He say's you're not to be trusted." I pondered briefly.

"Is his advice normally good?"

"No sir, it's terrible. He deliberately gets me into trouble."

"Then I should ignore him if I were you. When we get back to the Castle of Lovers I shall find an exorcism spell and rid you of this foul shade."

"Yes sir. Sir?"

"Yes Antonio?"

"That's probably why he doesn't want me to trust you isn't it?"

"That's probably it." I nodded wisely.

The moon had set by the time we reached Monzon and a flame danced in my palm to light the way. It provided us with little enough light but we didn't want to attract attention, at least not until after our nefarious purposes had been fulfilled. We skirted the village to where the great church loomed in the darkness. Antonio scaled the rough wall and then lowered the rope for me to follow him. My muscles strained as I hauled myself upwards and by the time I reached the top my breath was scorching my lungs and my arms were iron bolts of pain. I lay breathless across the mortared stones and felt my heart hammer against my ribs.

"The church is much higher sir," Antonio pointed out, a worried tone in his voice.

"Mmphrh," was all I could reply as I slithered off the wall into a breathless heap in the churchyard.

We picked our way between gravestones, ancient and modern, each one a witness to a lost soul taken by God. In the darkness the simple crosses and rough slabs seemed eerie, a jumble of stunted dwarfs whispering to each other as we passed by. I shivered and hurried onwards towards the safety of the church tower. Antonio followed and hurled his grappling hook upwards towards the crenelations above. The metal barb flew upwards, the thin line snaking after but it fell short and, with a dull clank, bounced off the unseen stones above and fell to earth. Eight times

Antonio hurled the rope and eight times it bounced back. I looked around nervously.

"You said this part wouldn't be a problem."

"Patience sir, it's a long throw and I'm out of practice."

I turned my back and peered into the darkness. The flame in my hand danced brightly but cast long shadows where it hit the gravestones and in the flickering light the memorials looked more alive than ever. In the darkness beyond the first rank they seemed to gather menacingly, an army of petrified soldiers ready to defend their territory. I deliberately turned once more, refusing to be drawn into a nightmarish fear of pieces of rock and the darkness. Above me I heard a solid clank as the hook hit the wall above but this time there was no answering thud; the metal had lodged somewhere far above us. Antonio pulled sharply on the rope but it held firm and so, wrapping his legs around it, he began to haul himself upwards. I followed his progress upwards until his feet faded into the darkness above and I could only track him by the soft grunt of exertion and a rhythmic twitch of the rope at my feet. After an eternity of waiting the rope fell still and I heard Antonio's voice above.

"I'm up sir," he called. "It's quite safe to follow." I looked upwards along the rope and shook my head. There was no way I could pull myself up the tower; my strength would fail and when it did, nothing would stand between me and the ground but tens of feet of insubstantial vapour. I shook my head again; no sane wizard would attempt the feat. Fortunately I had anticipated this situation and had practised an enchantment that would render me effectively weightless, allowing me to float gently to the top of the tower. I formed my right hand into the fist of control and curved my left into a claw pointing towards my belly. I took a deep breath and began to recite the syllables that would free me from the earth's pull. As I chanted I felt a strange resistance and saw in my mind's eye the stone gravestones flaming brightly. I struggled to concentrate on the words I spoke and wrested my mind from the horror behind me but the thought of a thousand burning crosses haunted me and I felt the power drained from me, away from the spell. I completed the incantation and looked around; behind me, the gravestones stood innocently in the darkness. I turned back to the rope; the interference I had felt had weakened my spell and I would be unable to float demurely upwards. I took the strain in my arms and pulled myself off the ground. I was elated to feel the load was less than I had expected; the magic had clearly taken some effect. I pulled myself rapidly upwards but soon found that even my supernaturally reduced bulk was taking a toll on my muscles. I growled and forced myself to continue, hand over hand, foot by foot. The wall seemed to be endless but I dare not pause or rest for fear that I'd find myself unable to continue and would hang helpless above the floor until my grip relaxed and I fell to my doom. My breath came in gasps, my knuckles were skinned from collision with the rough wall and my arms were solid cylinders of fire. At last I felt Antonio's grip on my tunic and hurled an arm over the top of the tower wall. Together we forced our muscles into one last exertion and then lay, gasping on the flat roof, looking up at the stars.

"Well done sir, I didn't think you'd make it all the way up."

"Erghmhth" I replied incoherently. My head span and my arms shook as the acid drained from them but I was elated. We had made it so far; I now felt sure of success. It was only then that I glanced sideways and saw the enormous copper sculpture I had vowed to steal. I turned my head back sharply and closed my eyes but the shape of a giant bull was etched into my brain. In the darkness it loomed above us, glowing greenly in the dim light of the stars. I took a deep breath and, feeling the air burn my lungs let it out gently before taking another; I'd need all my energy before I dared to face the monstrosity above.

The bull was cast from a thick sheet of green copper and was mounted on a great spindle the thickness of a man's thigh. Four of the great bolts held the spindle firmly attached to the tower roof and the other four held the bull in place. The light breeze shifted slightly and with a creak the vane twisted round knocking Antonio a pace towards where I lay. A smile flickered across my lips and I pulled myself to my feet; I had not come unprepared and nothing would stand in my way.

I ducked underneath the bull's forelegs and placed both hands on the spindle, sizing up the challenge. Then, with my right palm towards the ground and my left fist braced against one of the giant bolts I began to chant. Again I felt resistance but this time I was ready for it; the power of the divine was strong but not great enough to stop me, not here and not now. The huge bull filled my mind, its eyes glowing, a scarlet cross emblazoned across its flank. The target of my spell was larger than I'd hoped and I hadn't rehearsed the enchantment on holy land but I only required a small change. The beast resisted me; it had no intention of changing shape or size but there was just space in the gap between my abilities and its inertia to slip a small enchantment and I focussed all my energy on that gap. I blurted out the last syllables and stepped back, breathing heavily. The wind swung back a quarter of a turn and the weathervane followed it in silent obedience. Still the great bull hung there, black and ominous in the darkness but I knew my spell had taken effect.

"Let's try those bolts now Antonio," I said. The great hoops of metal that had held the weathervane firm for so long were still in place but years of exposure had taken their toll. Now, with their protective patina of corrosion magically removed, they were merely enormous bolts tightened by a muscular giant. Antonio and I had to combine our weight on the end of a long lever to release them but soon all eight bolts were loosened and the bull leant dangerously towards us.

"I think another enchantment is required," I said, leaning across Antonio to stop him further loosening the massive device before I'd cast a further spell I'd devised to make manipulating the monstrosity less difficult.

Facing a reduced weight, we were able to remove the bolts and lean the weathervane against the stone wall. We tied our rope through the bull's eye and looped it twice around what remained of the spindle. Antonio heaved our prize over the precipice and I braced myself to take its weight. I was pulled two steps forward but managed to control myself and the rope in my hands. Together we slowly lowered it to the ground, the metal clanking against the solid masonry. When it settled amongst the nettles at the foot of the tower, Antonio lodged his grappling hook in a crevice and heaved himself over the edge. I slithered after him, doing just enough to maintain what might be generously referred to as a controlled descent, and landed heavily.

"Ouch," I said sucking my stung hand.

"Come on sir, we're not out of the churchyard yet," Antonio reminded me, flicking the rope upwards in order to release the hook far above us. He grabbed the metallic beast round the neck and I found a grip round the rear legs and, with its tail under my right arm, we staggered between the gravestones to the wall. Once there, we used the rope to climb to the top of the wall before combining our weights to pull the weathervane after us. Unfortunately the stonemason had not finished the stones carefully enough and our burden caught against an irregular protrusion just before the summit. We pulled and strained but to no avail and so I leant backwards to take the strain while Antonio scaled the wall to free the weathervane. The rope pulled on my arms and I felt the blood throbbing in my hands. I considered a spell to make myself heavier but I hadn't practised one and this was not the time to attempt something new when both hands were occupied and I had no breath for speech.

179

"Relax it a little sir," came Antonio's voice and I took a quarter step forwards. "Good. Hold it." I heard a muffled grunt and a clank.

"Right sir, take the strain."

"Pull sir, pull!" Antonio had hold of one leg and was levering it over the wall above me as I hauled on the line. For a few heartbeats we stayed frozen in place, fixed in equilibrium and then the balance shifted. The bull scraped half an inch towards me across the wall; Antonio was able to slither backwards; the balance tipped and I felt myself stumbling backwards.

"Watch out sir!" cried Antonio leaping clear of the falling metalwork. I looked up and saw the bull tipping over as it fell, still propelled by the length of rope in my hands. I let go and hurled myself to the side, rolling through the rough grass. The bull's forelegs touched the ground first and momentum took it and it toppled forwards to land with a muffled clang on the ground in front of us. Antonio and I looked at each other and I saw he shared my sense of joyous disbelief. We embraced, sharing our delight and then lay back against the wall, too tired yet to get up. I reached into my pack and pulled out my flask. I unscrewed the lid and handed it to Antonio.

"I think we've earned a drink," I smiled. "Brandy from the covenant cellars." My companion took a deep draught and a smile of contentment spread across his face. I felt his muscles stiffen next to me and looked over at him. The soft smile on his lips had hardened into a rictus and his eyes were staring and sightless.

"Antonio!" I called, shaking him. "Antonio!" but I got no response. I prised the flask from his nerveless fingers and held it up to his face; no breath clouded the cold metal, my comrade was dead. A slow smile of contentment now spread across my features as I carefully restoppered the flask. The final test had been successful, the poison was as deadly to humans as it had proved to be to my rats.

I gaze across the dark land reflecting on my triumph. I chose the perfect victim. As far as the world is concerned, Antonio has disappeared without trace; his body has never been found. It will never be found; I spent a grisly hour magically destroying it chunk by chunk, forced to rest between incantation as the spells gradually removed the evidence of my crime. I hear that the folk of Monzon blame the faeries for the strange relocation of their weathervane. I smile to myself, sure that the Comptessa would have taken great delight in the whole affair. If she'd been in charge, however, Antonio's rotting corpse would have been left to protect the burnished copper statue. This I could not afford. I needed secrecy for the trial of my potion; none may suspect me experimentation. Nothing must stand in the way of my quest and if I must make a sacrifice from those dearest to me then I shall.

The journey home through the dark was lonely; I kept turning to Antonio to replay part of our adventure or to rejoice in our success but he was gone and I saw only dark empty gaps between the trees. Occasionally I heard the crack of a twig behind me and spun round, spooked by the night and a strange weight on my conscience. I saw nothing but became convinced of a presence on the path beside me, dogging my footsteps, its voice just out of earshot.

I've felt that presence occasionally since and I feel it now on the roof beside me. I've concluded that it's the ghost of Antonio's uncle trying to haunt me now that his nephew is gone. I won't let him. I won't be driven mad by the shade of a fish thief. I look back over the dark hillside and up at the stars above, shimmering in the gaps between the thinning cloud. I look up at the familiar constellations, partially occluded and occasionally invisible as a thin wisp of cloud is blown across them. The stars look down on the mortal world, unaffected by love or death. Unaffected by magic itself, they are fixed to the heavenly spheres above us and watch, unjudging, the scenes played out below.

Antonio wasn't missed for several days and when, finally, someone wondered why the courtyard hadn't been swept, nobody could quite say where he'd gone or when they'd last seen him. A mild ripple of worry flowed through the covenant and the local inns were searched for an inebriated odd-job man but there was no sign of him and soon the castle returned to its routines. Antonio had left, found something better, or worse, and good luck to him, or good riddance. He had made little lasting impression and his disappearance was overwhelmed by the quarrel that was brewing between the Courtesan and the Chaperone.

Thengol's experiments on the creation of zombie dogs have not gone well. He started with high hopes and a pack of nine dogs and one donkey. He worked for some time on a suitable method of killing the creatures that would allow them to be resurrected effectively; it seems that a simple fireball would not answer as an animated heap of ash would be unable to defend the covenant from attack. For many months he studied ancient tomes seeking an answer to this vexing problem and eventually concluded that a sharp knife across the throat would be ideal.

Having messily slaughtered one of the hounds and acquired several puncture wounds in the process, he started on the enchantment that would animate the corpse and endow it with a rudimentary intelligence. Unfortunately for my master this particular effect required him to use magic to control the animal's body and this has never been one of his strengths. The sorcery took two whole seasons, used up a wealth of chaim and nearly destroyed the new building but when Thengol staggered from his smoking room, the dog remained within.

He decided that the problem was with the particular dog he had chosen and slit the throat of a second in order to repeat the process. This time he took a great many precautions to ensure that the magic remained under his control. His cautious approach was no more successful at canine reanimation than his previous attempt and the poor creature remained resolutely dead. There was nothing for it but to bury the corpse and start again.

By now, Señor Phosphortube had lost patience with the drain on covenant resources and declared the Tyranny of the Wizard. My master's research continued on a more modest budget and with a similar level of success. Since Antonio's disappearance I have done little but study and assist Thengol in his work and I have seen the last two dogs experimented on. Salves have been applied to their corpses, potions forced down their throats, enchantments and incantations of all sorts have been devised but only the weakest of tremors has shaken their sinews. My master's personal stores of chaim have dwindled and every time he has opened his cupboard to withdraw another peg he has cursed the constitution and the Courtesan it has exalted.

"Damn him." I looked up. "Damn bloody Sparky Phosphortube and his insane laws. That spell would have worked if it'd had enough power behind it." I listened attentively as I scrubbed the bloodstains from the floor. "Does he want to leave the castle open to attack?"

"Maybe he does master," I reply comfortingly.

"What's that?"

"Maybe that's why he won't deliver your chaim." I began to warm to my subject. "Maybe this tyranny is the first step in his endless quest for power. Maybe he's waiting for the opportunity to get rid of you and to call in his friends from outside."

"What friends?"

"Evil ones, master. He can't afford to let you create a pack of zombie dogs or his assault on the covenant will fail. He needs to leave us weak so that the attack succeeds. You will be killed in defence of the castle or put to death once it's captured and the Tyrant will rule unopposed."

"Damn him."

"Indeed, master"

"Well, I shan't let it happen," he said resolutely, his feet placed far apart, his arm held aloft. "I shan't let him destroy our island of safety, our home, our refuge from the evils of this world. Whilst I have blood in my veins and sinews in my limbs I shall work to oppose his evil schemes and to protect our paradise, our covenant, our golden charm." I nod approvingly.

"I shall help you master."

"Good and faithful apprentice, together we would have worked a mighty enchantment the like of which has not been seen."

"Would, master?"

"I have been thwarted Riff-Raff. I have nothing left but seven pegs of chaim and a donkey."

"Then, master, we must work cunningly to create a valiant zombie donkey to defend our inheritance."

I pored over my master's notes and read through the ancient books on his shelves. I corrected his pronunciation and harvested herbs during the appropriate phase of the moon. We worked day and night whilst the donkey lived in a corner of my master's rooms so that she would be safe from the machinations of our enemy. The name Phosphor hadn't stuck; the light humour now seemed inappropriate as we struggled beneath Sparky's tyranny. Instead, finding the donkey female, we had named it Beatrice. Every morning and every evening I took her down to the river to drink and to exercise. For the rest of the day she watched us work, chewing docilely on a wisp of hay and braying in outrage if Cleopatra stalked too close.

My master's pet has decided to tolerate me now she has seen me at work with him. I have found her a useful assistant, able to react quickly to approaching disaster and with a marvellous sense for finding the right ingredients when I went out into the woods. The days passed and my confidence grew; Beatrice had been well prepared for the magic we would work on her corpse and I knew the incantation was within my abilities. Everything I had learned over the last fifteen years was coming together as I fitted the last few pieces of knowledge into my understanding of magic. There is still much to learn and a great wizard is always open to new insights but my foundations are now firm and no mysteries lie hidden from me.

This morning my master declared that we were ready. He returned from another fruitless appeal for chaim at a Council meeting in a foul temper. After the vote, the recriminations had descended into a screaming row and Thengol had almost challenged Señor Phosphortube to combat according to ancient custom. He explained that only a sense of responsibility had prevented him from making this rash move. I nodded in the knowledge that my master also had the sense to know that he would lose such a combat for the recipient of such a challenge has a right to set the types of magic that can be used. Ancient Custom would therefore ensure that my master was prohibited from fireballing his adversary and would thus render him effectively defenceless.

"Damn the Tyrant," he declared. "Let's act now before his army attacks. We have little time."

"Indeed master," I agreed and so we prepared for the great enchantment.

I laid my hand on Beatrice's head to comfort her as Thengol approached her with his knife. She leapt as the blade cut her skin but quickly collapsed in a pool of blood as her throat was slit. I collected a bowlful of the thickening fluid and Cleopatra licked hungrily at what remained as we dragged the heavy corpse into the centre of the room. I placed the bowl over a low flame and added quicksilver and rosemary to the blood, stirring with a silver rod. Soon the liquid began to bubble and I scattered holly blossom over the steaming surface and cut my finger to allow drops of my living blood to infuse the potion. I now began to chant the syllables we had crafted, drawing magic from the world around into the cauldron before me. I held my right hand in the fist of control and touched my left thumb with the middle finger, summoning the fluttering spark. I smiled at Danielli's overblown prose and relaxed as I completed the incantation. I took the bowl in both hands, steeling myself to ignore the scorching pain and poured it over Beatrice's body. Thengol rubbed the liquid into her corpse and then heaved her over so I could anoint the other side. Gratefully I returned the bowl to the table and plunged by hands into a bowl of cold water as my master coated the donkey's body, rubbing the potion into her bristly flanks.

When the corpse was prepared I held the seven remaining pegs of chaim in my right fist and began to intone the charm of animation. As I chanted, I felt the power leach out of the handful of dried vegetation and spread along my forearm and up to my shoulder. The syllables continued, my voice working almost of its own volition as I became intoxicated by the magical forces that spread through my torso and into my brain. I felt a golden aura surround me and saw before me Beatrice's solid body. The room faded away until all that was left was the corpse and my glowing form. I chanted the last few words of command and placed my hands on the donkey's head. The golden halo flowed from me like a cold shower as the last sound left my lips and I became aware of Thengol and Cleopatra watching in awe. I straightened up and staggered backwards and at the same moment Beatrice's legs bent and she dragged herself clumsily to her feet. Her eyes glowed red in the firelight and she brayed, an eerie hollow sound in the back of her throat. Trembling with elation we led her down the stairs and out through the courtyard to the gatehouse. We tethered her to a wooden post driven deep into the ground and left her there to guard our home from enemies. She looked a fearsome sight, eyes still glowing red, flanks damp and matted, her teeth unnaturally sharp and I felt a surge of pride as Thengol congratulated me.

"What a great success. You were of some assistance my apprentice."

"Yes, master," I agreed as we returned to his rooms.

"I still have only one zombie dog to defend the castle."

"Yes, master."

"And now we have no chaim left with which to work."

"No, master."

"If only Sparky didn't frustrate my every move."

"If only Lord Phosphortube was unable to frustrate you, master." Thengol paused and considered this delightful possibility. "If only Lord Phosphortube was out of the way, master," I added. "You would be free."

"Yes, but he's still here and he'll still vote against me. Maybe I could persuade one of the others to vote for me?"

"Darius Falconwing and Adriel the faerie? Vote for you to have extra chaim to continue the vital work of defending the covenant?" I laughed hollowly and Thengol shook his head. We climbed the stairs to his room in silence and sat in thought on the high stools my master used as chairs.

"My fifteen years is complete, master," I reminded him.

"Yes, you have grown fast, my apprentice."

"You must set me a challenge."

"Yes, I must think of something suitably testing."

"It must be a difficult thing to decide on," I prompted sympathetically.

"Yes."

"The best thing would be if it was a challenge you wanted completing anyway and then you got me to do it."

"Yes, I suppose so," he nodded thoughtfully.

"Maybe if there was a job you wanted doing I could do it for you."

"Exactly right."

"If there was something you wanted fetching," I paused, "or getting rid of."

"Yes, I'm sure I'll think of something."

"Something, or someone," I added and saw a flash of inspiration hit Thengol. He jerked and glanced sideways. I looked away demurely.

"Maybe," he said, "maybe you could..." and he trailed off.

"What, master?" I asked.

"No Riff-Raff, it would be unfair."

"What would, master?" I pressed him.

"Well, I was thinking that I really want Sparky Phosphortube to be got rid of and when you said that I might want you to do a job for me I just thought you could do that."

"Sparky Phosphortube the Courtesan?"

"Yes," he smiled. "But I think that might be rather unreasonable."

"Are you saying that as my Apprentice's Challenge you want me to kill the Courtesan?"

"Yes, but you'll never get away with it so I'll think..."

"I might know a way, master," I interrupted swiftly.

"You do? Oh clever apprentice, how well I taught you. Then go, and go swiftly. He must be dead in six months or your life is forfeit."

I gathered my few belongings and left the room, turning only to look once more at my master. A smile spread across his face as the beauty of the solution dawned on him. If I was successful he would be free to delve into the covenant chaim supplies whenever he wished and if I failed then my death would absolve him from any provable guilt. From his point of view, it's almost the perfect plan but Thengol's point of view has never been well informed and he has failed to notice a number of important points. It will be the perfect plan, if I get it right, but it isn't quite the plan that Greydog believes it to be. I left the new building and climbed to the top of the old tower from where I stand to look over the world below and to gather my strength for the challenge ahead. I feel a presence at my side and almost hear a voice in the wind. I ignore it, turn and descend to my room. I have no time for ghosts, the challenge has begun.

The Sixteenth Year

"On the Winter Solstice, also after the casting of the Covenant Spell, shall the Courtesan appoint a JUDGE who will take responsibility for the Fair Interpretation of Mundane Law and the Dispensation of JUSTICE."

From the Law of the Covenant of The Castle of The Lovers

I took my cloak and a bottle of good brandy from my room and left the covenant the next morning. Everyone in the castle knew that my Challenge had begun but the details were a secret between Thengol and me. For the next few weeks, I lived a life of contemplation in my cave in the woods, running through my plans and rehearsing the task in my mind. My preparations had long been made for the nature of the Challenge was a surprise only to my master. I needed time only to calm my mind and to plan for contingency.

My days passed in meditation and I felt the presence of a ghost beside me as I focussed my mind on the task ahead. The invisible spirit had grown slowly stronger since the night in Monzon and was becoming harder to ignore. It caused drafts to blow through my cave, fluttering the pages of my books and when I lay down to sleep I heard its voice murmuring dimly on the edge of audibility. I vowed to exorcise it as soon as my challenge was completed but until then I decided to take advantage of the intangible presence; I explained my plans to it. I ran through every detail and every contingency and found the process strangely helpful. The ghost made no suggestions and may not have been interested in my project but I found that I noticed minor flaws in my schemes that had been hidden from me in the crevices of my imagination. I worked on my ideas and developed them until I was sure that my plan was infallible, that only success was possible.

I moved back into the castle and involved myself in its life in a way I had been unable to do for the past few years. I followed the rhythms of the community, watched the warriors practice and the servants work. I lazed in the courtyard and ate beneath the shade of the faerie tree. As afternoon drew into evening I would move to the kitchen to watch Conchita prepare the evening meal and to wonder idly as her plump body shifted beneath her simple dress. I would sit in pleasant reverie as she poured wine into a small pan for the Courtesan and smile as the pungent steam curled off the surface of the liquid. The drink would be ready and poured into a glass just before M'Benga came into the kitchen to collect it. Years of practice had made their timing perfect.

"Oc'hacha," he would greet me gravely

"M'Benga," I'd smile my reply.

Even the most perfectly oiled systems occasionally break down and one evening Conchita had readied the meal and the wine stood cooling in its glass but M'Benga failed to arrive. Conchita seemed unconcerned but I had time on my hands and so volunteered my assistance.

"I'll take it up."

"If you like," she replied, smiling at me. I took the tray from the table and carried it out of the old tower and across the courtyard towards Sparky's rooms. Just inside the new building I ran into M'Benga hurrying to the kitchen.

"Thank you Oc'hacha," he said, holding out his hands to take the tray from me.

"I'll take it to him M'Benga," I offered.

"No. I take it to him," he replied firmly.

"Maybe not today?"

"Every day," he insisted, taking the salver from my hands. His expression of tolerant insistence changed to one of shocked disbelief as I forced my short dagger under his ribs. I held it firmly in place for a heartbeat and then let go to take back the tray as the manservant's legs buckled underneath him. Leaving him there with blood oozing from his wound and trickling from a corner of his mouth I stepped briskly over to the door of Sparky Phosphortube's rooms. I took a small glass vial from the pocket of my tunic, removed the cork and emptied the poison into the glass of wine. Then, trying desperately to still the hammering of my heart, I pushed the door open.

Following the routine I had observed so many times, I walked quietly over to the wizard's chair and placed the tray on a table at his side. Beppo looked up at me and sniffed curiously but Sparky paid me no attention. I then moved silently towards the door and waited, careful not to betray by sound or movement the excitement that thrilled my soul. Acting almost by instinct, the Courtesan pulled a pearl from his pocket and passed it over the steaming wine as he cast the spell of detection. I had to force myself to breathe; Señor Phosphortube was a far greater wizard than I and his spell would be proportionally more powerful. The pearl retained its lustre and he raised the cup to his lips. I heard the ghost at my side scream wordlessly and I felt my teeth bite into my lower lip;

Beppo shifted to turn his other side to the fire. Then the tension was broken as my victim took a long sip of the deadly vintage. His muscles stiffened instantly and his eyes glazed over, fixed forever in a contemplative stare. Beppo turned, the mystic cord that had bound him to his master broken. I stepped quickly to his side and felt for a pulse, for breath, for any response but found nothing. I walked quickly to the door, keen to report my success to Thengol. Beneath the corpse's chair the dog howled.

Upstairs my master was working on the details of a new spell designed to lay waste to the wizard's surroundings with deadly efficiency. I strode in and immediately dived for cover, recognising the hand shapes that prefaced fiery ruin. Thengol was so surprised that he halted his spell in mid flow, a squirt of green flame falling incontinently onto the stone floor.

"I've done it, master," I cried as soon as it was safe to pull myself off the floor. "I've killed the Courtesan and completed my Challenge."

"Is this true?"

"Come and see for yourself."

We stole down the stairs and stepped carefully over the crumpled remains of M'Benga before letting ourselves into Sparky's rooms. The corpse was where I'd left it, slumped in a chair, its eyes now shut and an expression of angst on its face.

"Sparky?" called Thengol, lifting one hand and letting it fall, limply to the side. "Are you dead Sparky?" He poked the corpse irreverently in the belly before beginning a sort of victory dance. "I am triumphant," he cried. "The Courtesan is dead. Oh great and faithful apprentice." I coughed sharply. "No longer apprentice but faithful filius. This triumph is also yours, Riff-Raff, now full mage of the covenant." A look of worry spread across his face. "But how do you plan to get away with your evil deed?"

"I have a plan," I began but at that moment the door was flung open and Pedro strode in, a look of alarm on his face.

"Murder! Come quickly, there's been murder done." His eyes took in the scene before him and he turned quickly and ran.

"Oh dear," I said.

The very air in the room seemed heavy and I felt the sightless gaze of the corpse accusing me of my crime. We retired to the guilt free atmosphere of Thengol's rooms and soon there came a hammering on the door. I opened it and saw Adriel and Darius standing in the corridor, their brows heavy with anger and confusion. Behind them stood Pedro, his hand on the hilt of his sword.

"What is this intrusion?" asked Thengol, his voice quavering with ill-concealed guilt.

"You know well," replied Darius blackly. "The Courtesan and his servant lie murdered below and the guilt is on your heads."

"I know nothing of this outrage," replied my master, wringing his hands.

"Thengol, this will not do," Adriel insisted firmly.

"No, master, it will not," I interrupted. "Sparky Phosphortube and M'Benga lie dead at my hand, killed in the fulfilment of my Apprentice's Challenge."

"Seize him," cried Darius to Pedro.

"It's nonsense, he doesn't know what he's saying; the shock has quite turned his mind," fretted Thengol as the swordsman took me firmly by the elbows.

"This is a serious affair and must be answered in High Council," Adriel said as I was led down the stairs and across the courtyard where work had stopped and all the folk of the castle turned to stare. I tripped on the rough flags and stumbled, grazing a shin as Pedro forced me up the stairs to the great door of the old tower. We climbed the stairs in procession, Adriel leading the way, a look of intense concentration on her face. Pedro and I followed, his face a mask of righteous anger, mine reflecting the focus of my mind on the steps below my feet and the blood that trickled down my right leg. Just behind Pedro I could hear the incoherent but joyful shrieking of the ghost and I thought I detected a second voice within the phantasmal screech. It seems that a fragment of Antonio's soul has been drawn into the spirit that once haunted him. Thengol followed the ghost, a mixture of concern and confusion; he had no wish to see me executed and was unsure of his position in the affair. Darius brought up the rear and his expression showed an unbecoming degree of exultation at seeing me brought so low. I knew that I'd receive little mercy from him.

We made our way into the council room and the High mages sat at their usual seats. I stood at the end of the table by the door with Pedro a pace behind me to prevent any retreat.

"Let us get this over with," began Darius briskly. "What punishment is appropriate for such a heinous act?" He paused and the three wizards considered the situation deeply. Into the silence I coughed politely and said,

"It's just a minor point of order, my lords, but shouldn't the Courtesan be sitting at the head of the table?" Darius turned on me angrily,

"The Courtesan is dead, as you know full well." I lowered my eyes and replied diffidently,

"Sparky Phosphortube is dead, as you say, but the Courtesan lives."

"What is this nonsense you speak of? You're talking in riddles in the hope that it will confuse the essence of your case. We have not yet selected a new Courtesan." As Darius ranted I winked at Thengol and indicated that he should address himself to the Law of the Covenant, which lay at his right hand.

"One moment Lord Falconwing," he cried. "It seems that it is not a case of selection of a new Courtesan," and he read, "'On the death of the Courtesan shall Pato assume the title and responsibility of Chief High Mage'. This means that I am Courtesan and I shall sit at the head of the table. Many thanks, my filius."

"Filius?" asked Adriel curiously.

"Yes, for despite his awful crime, Riff-Raff has completed his challenge to my satisfaction and is now a full mage of the covenant." I smiled graciously but Darius could contain himself no longer,

"Enough of this nonsense. We have a murderer in our midst and we must decide on a sentence."

"Surely we should at least establish his guilt thoroughly before we move onto sentencing," suggested Adriel quietly.

"Establish his guilt? He has blood on his hands and a confession on his tongue."

"Well it should be an easy task then shouldn't it Lord Falconwing? Will you present the accusation?"

"If you really think it necessary," and, seeing Adriel raise an eyebrow and nod he continued. "Lord Phosphortube's servant was found stabbed to death outside his rooms an hour ago and inside Riff-Raff and Lord Greydog were discovered standing over the corpse of Sparky himself. The accused had, and still has, blood on his hands and was heard to say that he killed them both. He is clearly guilty and we should move to sentencing."

"Riff-Raff, have you got anything you wish to say?"

"Only to confirm Lord Falconwing's story and to confirm that I killed both Sparky Phosphortube and M'Benga in the completion of my

Apprentice's Challenge and was immediately afterwards made a full mage of the covenant."

"We don't care why you killed them, despicable murderer. You are guilty and must be sentenced to death."

"To death," echoed Adriel.

"Master," I implored, reaching my hand out to the mage at the head of the table but at that moment the door was flung open behind me.

"Nteff," echoed a grunting voice from the portal as we span round to see who had the temerity to interrupt our meeting. "I'be obercome Nteff."

Standing in the doorway was Sparky Phosphortube, or something very like him. His face hung expressionless, his arms dangled by his side and a blank look filled his eyes.

"Sparky, is that you?" asked Thengol nervously.

"Yez," the word was clear enough but spoken in a gruff and slurred voice that was unlike the wizard but yet strangely familiar.

"But you were dead," Thengol stammered. "That is, we thought you were dead."

"I rwas nted," and I suddenly placed the voice. Sparky's body was speaking with the voice of Augustus the corpse. "I rwas nted but my zbell murkt." He then performed a short and rather inept jig, his legs swinging in jubilation until he had to lean against the table to steady himself. I glanced round the table and saw blank looks on all three faces.

"You were dead but you enchanted yourself so that your ghost would animate your own corpse?" asked Adriel.

"Yez. Ve zbell murkt."

"Does this mean that Lord Greydog isn't the Courtesan after all?" asked Darius, the note of jubilation returning to his voice.

"And this animated corpse is instead?" Horror filled Adriel's half-strangled cry and a look of fear crossed Darius' face as the implications of what he had suggested filtered through his brain. "Here, give me that," but Thengol had a firm hold on the Law and was poring over its clauses. Adriel and Darius leaped out of their chairs and huddled round him at the head of the table, all three wizards reading feverishly.

"No," announced Adriel, finally. "There is no provision for animated corpses to be mages of the covenant and even less High mages. Whatever happened afterwards, Sparky was dead by his own admission and Thengol, as Pato, immediately took over as Courtesan." She looked round for confirmation and received it from all present, including the corpse which nodded emphatically. Sparky clearly had enough to worry about with controlling his own body without the responsibilities of being Courtesan. She and Darius returned to their seats and re-focussed their gaze upon me.

"You are to be sentenced to death," reiterated Darius, "in accordance with the law."

"No," said Thengol. "I think that in the circumstances a little mercy is called for."

"What circumstances?" Darius asked turning incredulously to the new Courtesan.

"Well." Thengol paused, searching his thoughts. "He's very young. And Sparky isn't completely dead." The corpse shook its head emphatically.

"Those are details, we must kill the murderer and rid ourselves of this evil taint."

"Lord Darius, I think you forget your position," Thengol cut across him imperiously. "I am Courtesan and I say we show leniency and banish him from the covenant." Darius looked at Adriel and she shrugged and nodded.

"For how long?" he asked.

"For ever. Never to set foot within a league of the covenant or to make any contact, for good or ill, with any member of the covenant on pain of death."

"Very well," Darius growled through gritted teeth.

"Have you anything to say before the sentence is carried out?" Adriel asked me.

I paused and looked at the faces round the room. Darius' hawk like nose was even more pronounced and the predatory glint in his eye was firmly fixed on me. Adriel seemed amused by the whole affair and even somewhat kindly, in the same way as the Comptessa looked kindly on the dancing skeletons when they amused her. Thengol was clearly on a power rush, caring for nothing but his ability to command. Sparky's face was an impassive slab, all expression lost from the dead muscle but his head had tilted to one side as he jerked it round to face me and he seemed somewhat curious. Behind me Pedro stood facing forwards, his hand still on the hilt of his sword, goodness and justice oozing from every pore. To his side I heard the faint whisper of a voice just beyond hearing and in it I registered the sound of vengeance delayed. I turned back to answer Adriel's question.

"Only that I accept the sentence but reject culpability for the crime."

"And who do you think is culpable for your wilful act of murder?" she asked, a smile twitching at the corners of her mouth.

"My master, Thengol Greydog." Thengol's face registered horror, Darius' fury and he half rose from his seat.

"How dare you try to pass guilt onto another for your own actions?"

"You have the Law there, Falconwing," I sneered, angry at his lack of courtesy, "I suggest you look at the section on taking an apprentice." Adriel had already reached over to the parchment and pulled it towards her.

"'The Apprentice shall be taught the secrets of Magic and shall be considered property of his Master who shall take responsibility for all his Actions until he become a full Mage of the Covenant,'" she read. "It seems you have a point young Riff-Raff."

"So where does that leave us?" asked Darius.

"Back where we were!" shouted Thengol, a look of blind fury settling on his face. "Let's forget about mercy, kill him Pedro."

"No!" shouted Sparky, "Thend vor ve judge."

"Actually the corpse is probably right," said Adriel. "We need fresh ears and a clear mind."

"Who is the judge?" asked Darius. Adriel paused, Thengol looked blank and Sparky shrugged clumsily. I waited for inspiration to strike one of them.

"Father Juan has been judge to the Castle of Lovers for the last eighteen years," said Pedro diffidently from behind me.

"Excellent," said Darius although it was clear that Adriel thought differently. "Send for him."

The next half hour was rather difficult as we all tried to avoid each other's eyes and Thengol sent looks of hatred across the table in my direction. Darius was clearly torn, his dislike of me was as nothing compared with his feelings for my master but he felt that he had set out his case rather plainly and was in no position to back out. Only Sparky seemed at ease and used the time to practice standing up and sitting down without falling off his chair. Eventually the emaciated priest arrived at the door, crossed himself and bestowed a blessing on each of us. Adriel flinched as if she had been struck, Sparky shuddered in his seat and Thengol's look of black fury worsened. Adriel explained the dispute as quickly and as clearly as she could and passed the Law of the Covenant across the table to where Father Juan peered at it accusingly.

"You all stand by this sinful and heretical document?" he asked. We all nodded and waited as he read through it.

"I must ask you some questions," he said eventually. "Firstly, Riff-Raff, did you kill Señor Phosphortube?"

"Yes Father," I replied.

"Now Lord Greydog," he continued. "Did you grant Riff-Raff his freedom as a user of magic after he had done so."

"I did, and now regret it," he spat.

"Lord Falconwing, are you satisfied that Sparky Phosphortube was, in fact, dead and is now indulging in the sin of necromancy?"

"Yes," they both nodded.

"Thuktheffful necromanfy," insisted the corpse, nodding vehemently.

"Lady Adriel, was any other business conducted by this council before you summoned me?"

"No," she replied frowning, confused.

"And is it, in fact, the case that this council found Riff-Raff guilty and sentenced him to banishment?"

"Yes," we all agreed.

"Well then, your perverted Law is quite clear. Lord Greydog is responsible for Riff-Raff's crime and is banished by his own decree. Riff-Raff is cleared of all charges and is a full member of the covenant. God's Law is also clear and infinitely more just but as you are all damned by it anyway I suspect you have no interest in hearing how you stand." We all turned to face Thengol whose face turned purple with fury and then ashen as he realised that he must accept the judgement or fight his way out. For a moment his hands flickered towards the familiar fireball pose but Darius and Adriel moved to outflank him and he lowered them to his sides.

"You have one hour to collect your belongings and be gone," said Adriel firmly as he turned to leave the room, his shoulders bent. "See him out Pedro." We watched the two of them walk across the courtyard to his room.

"He could still try to fight his way out?" Darius suggested.

"I don't think so," I replied. "He doesn't have the imagination to plan any kind of attack beyond a series of fireballs that would leave him exhausted and at the mercy of any survivors." We turned back to the window and looked at the covenant imagining the place without Thengol

Greydog's wild ideas, insistent demands and woeful excesses. As he pondered, Darius began to look more cheerful.

"I suppose it could be worse," he said, clapping me on the shoulder.

Eventually we saw the small grey figure leave the new building with a pack on his back and a panther by his side. He turned to look up at the old tower and then the two of them made their way ruefully towards the gatehouse.

"God's work awaits me," said Juan as we turned back to the council room. "I'll not delay it on sinful matters any longer."

"Before you go Father," I asked quickly. "Who is now Courtesan?" He turned to me and I felt his gaze piercing my soul.

"Why, you are Riff-Raff. You are."

"What?" cried Darius and Adriel simultaneously. "How can that be?"

"It's complicated," he replied, "but on Sparky's death Thengol became Courtesan and the post of Pato was vacated. Sparky's subsequent resuscitation has no bearing on the case. The new Courtesan was meant to appoint new high mages but did not, in fact, do so. Therefore when Lord Greydog vacated the position of Courtesan on banishment there was no Pato to take over from him. That being so the Law of the Covenant does not address the succession except in the clause which states that all possessions, titles and responsibilities of a mage devolve to the most senior filius on banishment. Thus Riff-Raff inherits the position of Courtesan in addition to any belongings Thengol has left behind." Shrugging expansively the priest turned to go. "It's your Law," he added.

"This is a nonsense," said Adriel turning to me angrily.

"Ridiculous!" added Darius and they both turned on their heels and stormed out of the room pushing Father Juan to one side as they swept down the corridor. I turned to Sparky,

"Shall I go after them?" I asked.

"Ar duwhoah," he shrugged.

My first task as Courtesan of the Castle of the Lovers was to persuade the High Mages to accept the unthinkable. I went first to Darius.

"What are you doing here?" he asked, rudely. "I hope you don't expect me to go along with the nonsense that priest spouted. He knows nothing of magic or its power. Being a great wizard is more than a title, it's a question of skill and experience and you, young Riff-Raff, have neither."

"I guess you're right," I agreed.

"Well, what are you doing here then?"

"I wondered how you felt about me stepping aside for Lady Adriel to become Courtesan?" Darius looked at me sharply. "She is Lato and a highly experienced wizard," I explained, "even if she is a faerie."

"Well," began Darius.

"I'm sure that the Covenant wouldn't lose too much from a closer association with the faerie world," I continued. "Mongrol seems to have grown used to the chain he wears so I guess the rest of us would manage."

"I'm not sure," Darius began again.

"Of course, she might not be here all the time. Maybe we would all have to spend six months in faerieland and then the faeries would spend six months here."

"I think maybe we shouldn't be too hasty," said Darius.

"Hasty?"

"Let's not rush to any decision," he added. "Let's just leave things how they are and then maybe another option will present itself."

"A very wise decision, Lord Darius," I said, bowing as I left the room. "I shall support your stand on this matter."

Lady Adriel is neither as simple nor as easily manipulated as Falconwing and I prepared an alternative approach as I climbed the stairs to her room.

"You can't be Courtesan, it's ridiculous," she greeted me.

"What alternative do you have Adriel?" I asked. "Do you really want the responsibility yourself? It's a whole political human mess that would drive you insane."

"You manipulated me in this way before," she said, fixing me with a steely gaze.

"Yes, sorry," I grinned. "But I needed to gain Thengol's trust."

"Hmmph."

"Look," I held out a hand, "I won't try to stop you developing your faerie side. I won't make us live in caves. I'll share the covenant resources fairly and if I don't you can make me. I'm not an animated corpse, I'm not a fire wielding maniac. How bad can it be?" She peered at me closely, and I could see her mind turning over the advantages of having an ex-student as Courtesan.

"I can make you share the chaim fairly?"

"I can manipulate politics, but how can I stand against the great Lady Adriel in a magical duel?" At this she laughed, a great belly-shaking guffaw.

"I was right first time, it is ridiculous," she cackled, "but I like it. It amuses me greatly. Very well Riff-Raff, you shall be Courtesan but step carefully my little friend, step very carefully."

Tonight is the covenant feast and I have completed my first reading of the covenant spell. For the first time I felt truly great, wielding untold powers as a crowd of faces surrounded me, supporting me with their thoughts but leaving me standing alone, as the pinnacle of a tower stands above the castle. The moment has now passed and the celebrations have begun. A bonfire has been lit on the cobbles and the people of the Castle of Lovers are dancing, singing and drinking.

I look across and see Romario plucking his lute in a merry jig, his fingers busy but his mind clearly far away; no doubt his creative muse is composing a tragic ballad of lost love and fearful heroism.

Young Dylan is enjoying the music, dancing enthusiastically with a flagon of ale in his hand, great slops spilling over the cobbles as he leaps in the air. As a mark of respect to his father and from a sense of devilry I have appointed him to the vacant position of Kato. Adriel is now Pato and Darius Lato. I have rescinded the Tyranny of the Wizard and we have needed a third High Mage. Darius suggested that Braun take on the role but he is just an apprentice and, besides, I don't like him. If he stays on at the Castle of Lovers after the end of his training I will allow him to sit on the council but until then Dylan is a High Mage though he is no mage at all. He sits and listens carefully, understanding nothing then follows his instincts and the voices of others when he votes. He does surprisingly well and our council meetings have been remarkable for their lack of rancour.

I have invited Sparky to join the Council as an advisor but without a vote and he has been content to sit and listen, occasionally suggesting a barely articulate thought but mostly absorbed by the need to renew his spell by midsummer. His triumphant return from the grave is tempered by this deadline. Until June his spirit is bound to his body but at the summer solstice they will separate and he will be dead indeed unless he can regain his living facility with magic. Tonight, however, he has taken time away from his research to join us in a last celebration. The rudimentary control he has over his body has created quite a spectacle when dancing.

Adriel leans against a wall laughing. This is the first time she has really joined in with our celebrations and she stands apart but clearly entertained by the revelry that surrounds her. She has decided that the two parts of her nature need to be balanced and that she shouldn't dismiss her human side as worthless or irrelevant. I think the politics that finally rid us of Thengol have suggested to her that the Council has a value even if it doesn't quite work on faerie lines.

Braun and Darius are sitting with Mongrol and Pedro and are indulging in a drinking game. From where I stand, it is impossible to discern the rules but the two wizards seem to be losing. Their shapes begin to blur and occasionally I see two drunken Spaniards drinking with a bear and a falcon. Once Darius realised that I was free from my master's tendency to spend chaim like water he has accepted the new situation with good grace and even Braun has developed a certain civility. My new rank within the Castle demands this and one dark night I provided him with a short and painful exhibition of the abilities of a full mage.

Lopez is missing the drinking game because he is attempting to seduce Conchita. She is giggling nervously and looking for an escape as he tries to weave an enticing mesh of words without ever venturing a verb. Soon either he or she will give up and, unless the wine she is drinking is astoundingly strong Lopez will return to drink Mongrol into a position adjacent to the two recumbent magi.

I stand apart from the bustle and happiness around me. My master has left and my closest friends are dead. I shiver as a cool breeze swirls around the courtyard. I feel myself separated from the others; separated by rank and by purpose for this is just the first step in the career of the great Riffrando. The Castle of Lovers has been my home and my world for the last fifteen years but it is small; there is Spain to dominate and beyond that all Christendom, the world. I may be free of my masters but I still have work to do. I hear beside me a low chuckle and I'm no longer lonely. I'll never be alone whilst I have Antonio's ghost. Never alone when I have his voice echoing around my head.

Appendix

The Law of the Covenant of The Castle of The Lovers

"Just as the Year has FOUR *Seasons and the Compass* FOUR *Points; just as all Dead Matter is Governed by* FOUR *Elements and all Living Matter by* FOUR *Humours so shall our Covenant of the Castle of the Lovers have* FOUR *High Mages.*

"These FOUR *Require Names to suit their exalted position. The First High Mage shall be the Courtesan, chief Lover, Chairman and Spokesman of the Covenant. The others shall be the* THREE *Most Senior Mages in the Covenant, excepting the Courtesan. The Most Senior shall be called* PATO, *the* SECOND *Most Senior shall be called* LATO *and the* THIRD *Most Senior shall be called* KATO.

Just as the Royal Throne rests on FOUR *feet, so our Covenant's Power rests on* FOUR *Aspects of our Life: our Wealth, our Authority, our Magickal Power and our Knowledge. Accordingly, each Mage of our Covenant shall spend a* QUARTER *of his time, that is, one Season in Every Year, improving and maintaining these Four Aspects of our Life.*

"On the Winter Solstice, after the casting of the Covenant Spell, the Courtesan shall name the next Year's Treasurer. The Treasurer must keep the Covenant accounts for the year, spending no less than a Season over it, and is Responsible for accounting for all Monies having to do with the Covenant. Also, on the Winter Solstice, also after the casting of the Covenant Spell, shall the Courtesan appoint a JUDGE *who will take responsibility for the Fair Interpretation of Mundane Law and the Dispensation of* JUSTICE. *The Treasurer and the Judge must be Different People.*

"Every Mage except the Treasurer and the Judge must spend ONE *Season in the Year on Covenant duties: either Scribing or Making. Scribing is the scribing for the Covenant Library either of a Book of Magic containing Knowledge of a Magickal Art of a Degree Superior to the Degree of Knowledge of that Art already in the Library, or the scribing of a Book of Spells not already Available in the Library, that is, a Book of Spells containing* NO *Spells already Available, or the scribing of a Book of Mundane Knowledge Superior to any* SIMILAR *book already Available. Making is the manufacture for Covenant Stores either of a Magickal Device or of a Batch of Magical Potions. Any Making which is Judged Worthless by the* FOUR *High Mages, according to Due Process, shall be Discounted.*

"The Wealth and Power of the Covenant of the Castle of the Lovers shall be divided as specified by the Council of the High Mages and by this means shall the CHAIM *of the Covenant and its other riches be assigned to the Mages.*

"All Covenant Decisions shall be Established by a Vote after the Athenian fashion. Each High Mage shall have a number of Votes to Cast, according to his

Station. The Number of Kato's Votes shall be ONE, *the Number of All Shapes, for Kato is the Junior High Mage, full of Potential, his Limits undetermined. The Number of Lato's Votes shall be* TWO, *the Linear Number, for Lato is the Middle High Mage, growing like a young tree, quick and deadly like a Spear. The number of Pato's Votes shall be* THREE, *the Triangular Number, for Pato is the Senior High Mage and therefore a bit like something Triangular. The Number of the* COURTESAN'S *Votes shall be* FOUR, *the Tetrahedral Number, for the* COURTESAN *stands over the other High Mages like the apex of a Tetrahedron stands over its base; his is the solidity of the Mountain and the purifying violence of the Flame. Should any of the High Mages vacate their responsibility for Any Reason, the* COURTESAN *shall appoint more junior Mages to fill the roles in Order of Seniority. However, on the Death, Disappearance or* BANISHMENT *of the* COURTESAN *shall* PATO *assume the title, responsibility and privileges of Chief High Mage for, as the Triangle forms the base of the Tetrahedron, so* PATO *waits below the* COURTESAN.

"However, the COURTESAN *is the Chairman of the High Mages. His Votes are not to be used at all times, but sparingly as his wisdom is Precious. The* COURTESAN'S *Votes are to be counted if the Votes of the other High Mages are Tied, and Otherwise only during the* TYRANNY OF THE WIZARD. *The* COURTESAN *may Declare the* TYRANNY OF THE WIZARD *at any Meeting of the* FOUR *High Mages, and requires only the Assent of* ONE *other High Mage for the* TYRANNY *to be Established. The* COURTESAN'S *Votes are counted throughout the* TYRANNY. *The* TYRANNY OF THE WIZARD *may be ended by a Unanimous Vote from Pato, Lato and Kato only, unless it is ended by the Courtesan by a Fiat.*

"As LOVERS *squabble, so shall there be Times of Discord. In case of Disagreement that cannot be Resolved by Due Process then shall one Mage issue a Proper Challenge to another. The Proper Challenge shall then be Resolved according to* ANCIENT CUSTOM. *At no other time shall one Mage of the Covenant of the Castle of Lovers attack another, nor his Property, his Apprentices or his Wizardry on pain of Banishment.*

"Each Mage shall be free to take an Apprentice as he wishes although no Mage may take more than ONE *Apprentice. The Apprentice shall be taught the secrets of Magic for that is his purpose and shall be considered property of his Master who shall take responsibility for all his Actions until he become a full Mage of the Covenant. After* FIFTEEN *Years, the Apprentice shall be ready; for the* SIXTEENTH *year is the year of fulfilment,* SIXTEEN *being* FOUR *times* FOUR, *the Square of the Covenant number. His Master shall set him a challenge and, should he pass it, he will become a Full Mage of the Covenant, no longer Apprentice but* FILIUS, *son of the magic. Any Apprentice who fails his Master's Challenge shall be*

Slain. On the Death, Disappearance or BANISHMENT *of any High Mage, all Property, Magic, and Power both real and intangible shall descend upon his Most Senior* FILIUS *excepting only those that are addressed elsewhere in the* LAW.

"*For just as the Mages under the Courtesan protect our Covenant from Magickal dangers, so also we need Defence from Mundane attacks. Therefore the Lovers shall have a Protector who shall be known as the* CHAPERONE *and he shall employ such Warriors as be necessary. The Protector shall be known and addressed as* GUARDIAN OF THE LOVERS *in general and when outside the Covenant and as* CHAPERONE *within our walls. The* GUARDIAN *shall be entitled to such Monies and Chaim from the Covenant Stores as shall be deemed appropriate by the High Mages following Due Process.*"